DOUBLE THE PLEASURE

Julie Elizabeth Leto

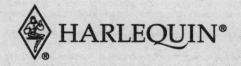

HARLEQUIN®

TORONTO • NEW YORK • LONDON
AMSTERDAM • PARIS • SYDNEY • HAMBURG
STOCKHOLM • ATHENS • TOKYO • MILAN • MADRID
PRAGUE • WARSAW • BUDAPEST • AUCKLAND

For my editor, Brenda Chin, who shows no fear—
and has infinite faith in my talents, even when I don't.

For Krystyna de Duleba,
who brands my books with her innovative artistic vision.

And for Susan Kearney, friend, fellow writer and
critique partner, who has made the journey
so much better.

ISBN 0-373-79053-8

DOUBLE THE PLEASURE

Copyright © 2002 by Julie Leto Klapka.

Printed in U.S.A.

"You are not Zane Masterson!"

Grey took a deep breath, trying to interpret Reina's mood. *Damn.* Just a moment ago he'd been lost in velvet heaven, his mouth merged with hers. For an instant he'd known her. Unbridled. Unrestrained. Until she'd pulled away, his secret revealed. He'd been caught, red-lipped. No woman he'd ever run across would find this situation amusing.

Still, Reina was no ordinary woman.

"Let me guess," Grey ventured. "My brother and I kiss differently?"

Her eyebrows shot up. "I wouldn't know. Why would you ever assume that Zane and I were lovers?"

"You are an incredibly beautiful woman. And there are these vibes going on between us...."

Reina cleared her throat. "Yes, that should have been my first clue that you weren't Zane. As adorable as I find your brother, we've never had the kind of chemistry you and I seem to have. And here I blamed my heightened state of arousal on reading those erotic diaries. Apparently there was more at play."

"Well," Grey muttered, "nothing was at play yet." He shifted closer to her, stroking her bare arm with his finger. "But we were definitely getting there...."

Dear Reader,

Don't you come up with the wildest ideas sometimes when you're chatting with your friends? That's what happened when my pal and critique partner Susan Kearney and I were having one of our daily telephone marathons. We'd wanted to work together on a project for a long time, and finally we had the idea. It started with a cover, then twin heroes who trade places, then a concurrent time line and release dates. We even waited until our editor was in town for a visit and plied her with Cajun food to win her over!

Luckily for us, Harlequin excitedly jumped onto our bandwagon. *Double the Pleasure* is the story of Grey, the older, very private Masterson twin, while Susan's *Double the Thrill* tells the tale of ne'er-do-well Zane. While each story is unique, and very satisfying on its own, I'm certain you'll double your reading pleasure if you get them both this month. And don't forget to drop by my Web site at www.julieleto.com to let me know what you thought of the amorous escapades of the Masterson twins....

Enjoy,

Julie Elizabeth Leto

P.S. Don't forget to check out tryblaze.com!

Books by Julie Elizabeth Leto

Prologue

REINA PRICE licked her lips hoping the action would off-set the tightness in her breasts, the growing shallowness of her breath. The glossy feel of her lipstick, moistened by her tongue, only increased the thrill shimmering through her veins.

"Magnificent."

She traced the lines of the thick, hard shaft with her French-manicured nails, wondering, planning, devising in her mind the best way to work it. Too bad she didn't blow. She'd love to ply her talents on this masterpiece.

Claudio di Amante leaned forward to see which drawing Reina admired with such delight. "Ah, the pride of the collection. Il Gioielliere himself posed for the mold. Fashioned in delicate, blown glass and strengthened with an intricate web of gold latticework. Legend says his mistress breathed into the glass during the fashioning. It was a gift for her use when he was…not available."

Reina shifted in her seat, thankful that her desk blocked her guest's view as she squeezed her legs together to off-set the pulse flaring between her thighs. Il Gioielliere, a sixteenth-century Italian jeweler and predecessor of Casanova, must have been one impressive lover. Judging by the shape and thickness of the penis represented in the gold and glasswork dildo, the man was particularly well endowed. And to add to his natural attributes, he'd created a diverse assortment of sexual implements and toys, many disguised as mere jewelry but each possessing a secret, sensual use. Unfortunately, the original collection had been destroyed, and Claudio di Amante, a stranger who'd walked into her gallery in the New Orleans Arts District with no appointment, now wanted her to refashion the pieces in the next two weeks.

Though Reina had been taught to be proud of her sexual responses and impulses, what this man had brought to her in a worn leather attaché proved more evocative than any of the erotic art she housed in her gallery or the erotic jewelry she'd created in her studio. The drawings alone affected her, raising her body temperature and hampering her ability to breathe.

Accepting Claudio's commission would be both a professional and personal challenge. With her libido so hypersensitive, she'd either have to take a lover or resort to putting her own dildo collection to good use. She didn't have a glass one, though they were all the rage, thanks to *Il Gioielliere's Diaries,* a reprinting of the man's personal memoirs that currently topped the *New York Times* bestseller list. Shamar, the glass artist who displayed her work in Reina's gallery, couldn't keep them in stock.

Claudio di Amante, il Gio's last remaining descendant, sat back into the tall, leather chair, his athletic, middle-aged body molded comfortably into the antique wing chair. Reina tried hard not to stare. Despite his age, he was undeniably handsome, with a glint of a secret dancing in his dark eyes. She supposed he was old enough to be her father but couldn't say for sure since she had no idea how old her father actually was. Still, the man piqued her curiosity on several different levels—starting with why he'd chosen her over other better-known artists to recreate his jewelry collection.

As an only child traveling the world with a famous

mother, Reina had turned to crafting jewelry as a way to ward off boredom. At fifteen, her designs began to reflect the sensual, sexual lifestyle enjoyed by her mother, her friends and, honestly, herself. That's when her brooches, earrings, necklaces and pendants caught the eye of people who knew fashion and weren't afraid to pay for it. Her gallery, opened five years ago when she decided to join her mother and settle down in New Orleans, had only recently received notice with the mainstream press. When a famed haute couture designer chose her pieces to accessorize his spring line last year, Reina finally garnered real recognition for her work.

But she was by no means a household name. She fought to keep her gallery in the black, a battle intensified by two recent robberies that threatened the solvency of her business and the future of her designs. So why had Claudio chosen her? And why now?

The man claimed to be a struggling entrepreneur, but he couldn't hide a natural, elegant style. Dressed in a dark suit with thin lapels and an even darker shirt, Claudio's olive skin provided a startling backdrop for eyes the color of onyx and rare mother-of-pearl. Shots of white along his temples toned down the glossiness of his jet hair, a hue that might have, in his youth, matched her own.

Reina swallowed, wondering when she was going to stop trying to find her father in each and every man over fifty that she met. Claudio di Amante was probably the unlikeliest candidate to date. While handsome, the man didn't have much money, and what he did have, he didn't spend without careful planning—at least that is what Reina had gleaned from their conversation. His modest use of money was enough to take him out of the running for any relationship with Reina's mother.

According to his story, he lived just outside Venice,

quite near her mother's summer home. But when he spoke of his sprawling yet crumbling *palazzo,* Reina knew such a place would never have piqued Pilar's avaricious interests. For twenty difficult years, Claudio had lived hand-to-mouth, watching his beloved family home deteriorate around him. After having his ancestor's diaries stolen and published without his consent or profit, he'd decided the time had come to unearth il Gioielliere's schematics and regain his family's lost wealth. And now, he wanted to turn the treasured drawings and priceless gemstones over to Reina. At the worst possible time. She'd listened to his proposal with real interest, although she didn't think she should even entertain the idea of accepting his commission.

Reina gathered the photocopies of the hand-drawn diagrams and took one last look. Her mouth dried, her fingers itched, her eyes ached to study the drawings in greater depth. But she couldn't accept this design assignment. Not when the jewels he promised to deliver tomorrow wouldn't be safe in her possession.

"I'm so sorry, Signore di Amante," she began.

"Claudio, please. I understand Americans don't much stand on ceremony."

"No, they don't. *We* don't," she amended, still unaccustomed to considering herself American since she'd lived everywhere but in the United States for most of her life. "I learned this lesson over the years."

"But you are American, yes?"

She smiled, aware that a little coy confession went a long way with men like Claudio. "Born in New York City during one of my mother's runs on Broadway. I've only been in the States permanently for five years. I love this country, and New Orleans, but I'm still adjusting. My mother was quite the world traveler during my childhood.''

''Ah, your mother. The great stage actress.''

The hair at Reina's neck bristled. ''You know my mother?''

He chuckled, but the sound was soft, secret, as if there was a great deal he knew but wasn't willing to share. ''Who in Europe doesn't know the great Pilar Price?''

Who anywhere didn't know of Pilar? Reina reminded herself yet again that while theater grew more and more obscure both in the United States and abroad, save a few big Broadway and East End productions, her mother was still a celebrity of international fame—if not for her profession, then for her lifestyle. Paparazzi still stalked the sidewalk in front of her French Quarter home, hoping to catch a glimpse of a senator or governor sneaking out of Pilar's bedroom sometime during the night.

Reina, however, preferred to draw less attention to her love life, such that it was. Her friend, Chantal Dupre, liked to refer to her infrequent dates as ''drive-by lovers,'' which was fine with Reina. Romantic entanglements and messy emotional dramas were her mother's style, not hers. She chose to concentrate on her business and on using her inherited charm and exotic sex appeal to give her an entrepreneurial edge.

What had started as a persona created to match the evocative designs in her jewelry had become her most useful asset, her most effective weapon. Disaffected, bored and well-sexed worked on men and women alike. The women admired her, wanted to emulate her. The men wanted her in bed but doubted their prowess to please her. Either way, Reina called the shots—choosing friends and business associates with care and protecting her privacy...and, more important, her heart.

She shook her head, displacing a curl from the loose twist she'd secured this morning with an ebony clip. She blew the hair aside and, with great regret, stacked the papers together and slid them across her polished desk.

"You have no idea how much I'd like to accept your commission, Claudio. But I can't, not in good conscience. Your jewels would not be safe with me and I don't currently have the funds for added security."

Claudio nodded but didn't touch the designs. "I've heard about the thefts in your gallery. Very unfortunate."

Reina looked askance at the letter on the corner of her desk, the one she'd received last week from her insurance agent canceling her coverage. After two unsolved jewel thefts from the safe in her office, the carrier was no longer willing to insure her business. The timing couldn't have been worse. First, the splash in the fashion world, then the feature in *Elle* magazine, which had highlighted her particular interest in refashioning estate pieces into erotic treasures. Ever since, she'd fielded inquiries from wealthy women and men from around the world about what she could create with a grandmother's old ruby brooch or a collection of unmatched sapphires.

But she couldn't afford the higher premiums of a new carrier or increased security. She'd thought about only keeping jewels in her studio when she had to work on them and then locking them away in a safety-deposit box at night—after all, neither of the robberies had occurred during the day. But Reina couldn't be sure the thief, or thieves, wouldn't become more bold. So, until the cases were solved, she had to turn down all jobs that involved resetting valuable stones.

Including this one.

"Incredibly unfortunate. I can't guarantee the safety of your stones or these plans—" she folded them back into the attaché "—so I must, very regrettably, say no to your offer."

"Can you not hire more guards?"

"I don't have the funds at this time and, frankly, I don't even have an insurance carrier for the studio. Other artists who lease space here from me have purchased individual policies to insure their work. Maybe my situation will change in the future."

Reina had called the police first thing this morning, praying they had found the culprit and made an arrest, but they'd made no headway. Everything pointed to an inside job and she had no idea who could have betrayed her. Her personal assistant, Judi, had been with her since Reina moved to the States five years ago and had become a good friend. All the artists in the gallery had been thoroughly checked out. Everyone had passed lie detector tests, including Reina, though she and the police knew how unreliable the technology could be.

Yet, there'd been no break-in, no damage to the safe or the lock—as if the thief had known the combination, pointing back to a gallery employee or artist.

After the first theft, Reina had changed the combination code and kept the numbers to herself. She'd also spent most of her operating capital installing security cameras and employing a guard—a guard who'd been knocked unconscious during the second robbery. The security tapes had disappeared. With the bulk of her money tied up in investments and, with no insurance, she couldn't afford to put il Gioielliere's jewels at such risk.

"The future is now, Reina," Claudio insisted. "Have you consulted the bestseller lists, lately? *Il Gioielliere's Diaries* is selling millions of copies around the world. Sooner or later, someone will attempt to reproduce the jewelry from the descriptions in the book. There is not the detail I have in the drawings, but we cannot miss the opportunity. Both of us have a lot to gain, and much to lose.''

Shortly after Claudio's arrival, he'd explained to Reina that the original diaries had been stolen from him years ago and published without his knowledge or consent. So someone else, someone the publisher refused to name, was reaping the benefits of the diary's popularity. Extreme popularity. She'd read articles calling *Il Gioielliere's Diaries* the new *Kama Sutra*. The book had already been optioned for a film. Copies were flying off the shelves. Reina had certainly noted an increased interest in glass Shamar's dildos.

Yet none were as delicate or intricate as the one sketched out on Claudio's drawings. Even the peace-loving Shamar would kill to get her talented hands on the tricky design.

''I could use some good publicity again,'' she muttered.

''You could also use the royalties from the tour I have planned, as well as commissions from the sale of reproductions. We can both be rich beyond our wildest dreams.''

''If we're willing to take a great risk.''

''There is no profit without risk. Besides, you don't have to keep the jewels here, where they would be unsafe. Perhaps you have somewhere else where you can work?''

''I have a studio in my home,'' Reina said, thinking aloud. ''I actually do most of my work there and devote my time in the gallery to selling the pieces.''

''You see? I will bring them to your home.''

Reina shook her head. ''I cannot guarantee that my home is any safer than my business.''

Nevertheless, Claudio stood, a confident smile beneath

his thin mustache. "Then find a way to give me that guarantee."

He snatched a memo pad from the corner of her desk, then asked for her address, which she gave.

"I'll meet you at your home tomorrow evening, with the sketches and the jewels. If you have found a way to insure they will be safe, then we, as you Americans say, will have a deal."

She stood when he scooped up his attaché. She offered her hand, and he took it gently, then bent to sweep a chivalrous kiss across her knuckles.

"Until tomorrow, *bella.*"

Once he'd left, Reina slid back into her chair and splayed her hands on the glassy top of her desk, her mouth wide with shock.

What had just happened?

What had she agreed to?

She'd agreed to a deal that could turn her string of bad luck into a business boom. Too bad that, until then, she still had the same problem. Well, two actually. First, she had to burn off the excess sexual energy before she dealt with the collection drawings again. If not, she might end up making some sort of fool out of herself, getting all hot and bothered over pen and ink. Second, she had to find a way to protect the jewels once she took possession tomorrow evening, at her house.

Hmm…sexual energy, protection, her house…

The minute the solution popped into her head, Reina laughed out loud. But she couldn't let a little irony stand in the way of a perfect plan.

She picked up the phone, dialed, and waited for the voice mail greeting to play. Once the beep sounded, she deepened her voice to her most sultry timbre.

"Zane, it's Reina. God, I need you. Call me."

1

GREY MASTERSON SHOOK HIS HEAD, wondering what the hell had possessed him to call his brother. He flipped over the metro section of today's paper and checked the moon's current phase. Not full. Well, so much for that explanation. Perhaps he had simply lost his mind.

"A beautiful woman is stalking you," his brother paraphrased, his voice exactly like Grey's, except for a practiced inflection that said *I'm bored; amuse me.* "And you're complaining? Did I miss something?"

His twin's reaction to the story Grey had just told him made it clear he thought Grey, the editor in chief of New Orleans's second largest newspaper, must have left out something crucial. He'd presented the facts as simply as possible, starting with the publication of a tell-all book by his former girlfriend, B-actress Lane Morrow. Of course, Zane already knew about the book. Everyone in New Orleans knew about the damned book. Everyone in the damned English-speaking world knew about the book.

After four weeks on the bestseller lists, Lane's recount of their once-secret love affair had turned him into a celebrity. Except for the journalists whose paychecks he signed, every reporter with a press card had either called requesting an interview or had staked out his condo, his office—hell, even his regular parking space at the dry cleaner. He'd considered filing a lawsuit against her for revealing the details of their sexual exploits—obviously a blatant attempt for attention—but the thought lasted only ten seconds. She'd written about their hot and heavy encounters precisely to up her celebrity status. She'd revealed his ravenous sexual hungers, then claimed that her leaving him had destroyed his appetites. *As if.* But the public had bought her portrayal of herself as the master seductress and him, the wild man broken by her betrayal.

At first, he'd been too damned mad to contradict her—hoping the hype would die down so he wouldn't add to it by refuting her claims. Her asking price in Hollywood had already soared through the roof. So he'd decided to lay low, stay quiet and find peace in his stressful but ordered world.

Then he'd picked up a stalker, a beautiful one, admittedly, but the last thing he needed was another woman who was obviously seeking him out to sate her craving for attention. Adding that to a rash of problems with production at the newspaper, and Grey had had enough.

He'd called his twin, hoping his ne'er-do-well brother might have some insight into how to rid himself of his stalker. Instead, Zane couldn't even see the problem.

"You don't understand." Grey's intrinsic commanding tone rang through louder than he'd intended, but sometimes his twin needed to remember just who had been born first, even if their parents had mixed them up as babies so that their names were in reversed order. Grey had been the one to accept the legacy of the family business. Grey had been the one to devote his life to ensuring the wealth and prosperity of anyone bearing the Masterson's name.

Zane didn't understand duty and responsibility. He didn't understand stress or pressure or breaking points. He didn't now and never had. How could he? He'd been too busy proving girls weren't the only ones who just wanted to have fun.

"What don't I understand?" Zane asked.

"In addition to being stalked by some lunatic—"

"She's crazy?"

"Well, not certifiable, not according to my investigator—"

"You've had her investigated?"

Grey smirked. Well, of course, he had. Grey didn't consider himself a perfect man, but he did learn from his mistakes. This phone call, for instance, rated on Grey's error scale at number nine, just below his affair with Lane, which unfortunately, garnered a perfect ten. "I wanted to know if she'd escaped from some mental institution before I decided what to do with her."

He should have had Lane investigated before he started dating her. Her permanent record from her school days probably included a long history of being a tattletale.

"Why do you have to do anything?" Zane asked, his tone incredulous.

Grey pictured Zane lounging on his leather couch, kicking his bare feet onto a coffee table that probably cost more than the new computer system he'd had installed at the paper.

"Because she's stalking me, dammit," Grey answered.

"What does she want?"

"I don't know—"

"Why don't you ask her?"

"—and I don't care." Grey marched beyond Zane's interruption. God, he really didn't want to deal with this. Any of it. Lane's betrayal. Her tell-all book and the intrusive backlash. The trouble at the paper. His father's impending disapproval, his mother's disappointed stare. The stalker was almost inconsequential in comparison to the greater questions nagging him. Like what did he really want from life? And why had he waited until he was thirty-two to ask himself that question? "I have other things to worry about than women and their impossible desires."

"Not according to Lane's book."

Grey swallowed a growl. "I'm surprised you actually read a book, brother. And, of all things, that damned piece of—"

"Did you really make love in the back of her limousine while your reporters waited to interview her?"

Yes. And while it had been damned exciting at the time, he now realized the adrenaline rush wasn't worth the price. "That's private."

"No, it's public now, bro. Very, very public. Even I haven't done it in the bathroom stall at Commander's Palace. All these years you've pretended to be so restrained, then I read in this book about—"

"Zane." Grey utilized his harshest tone again, the one he'd been using with more and more frequency lately. He didn't like being a hard-ass. He didn't enjoy inspiring expressions of terror from his employees. Not really. He simply wanted to run the paper with precise efficiency and turn a lofty profit. He wanted his personal life to be private and his lovers to be adventurous but discreet.

For a man with a reputation as one of New Orleans's top power brokers, he didn't get much of what he wanted, did he?

"If you're done having fun at my expense, I could use some of your expertise."

"I have expertise?" Zane asked, his surprise clear even over the phone line. "Can't wait to hear in what."

Grey was almost afraid to ask. "Don't you have a private investigator's license?"

"The instructor was a knockout. The only way I could get close to her was to take her course."

That did it. The reality of Zane's lackadaisical reason for pursuing a license as a P.I. stabbed into Grey's brain like an ice pick. He reached across his desk and retrieved the nearly empty bottle of aspirin.

"Do you remember anything from the class?"

"She had the greatest set of—"

"Anything about the course material?" Grey rubbed his temple at the precise spot where the phantom puncture wound throbbed with very real, very sharp pain.

"I passed the final, didn't I?"

Of course he did. His twin brother relished in the life of the cliché—jack-of-all-trades yet master of none. Well, dammit, this time, he needed Zane to share some of the heat. His twin had enjoyed the fruits of his Masterson trust fund and stock in the privately held newspaper long enough without having to put in even a little work. "I suppose I can count on you, then."

"As good as counting on yourself. We do have the same IQ."

"Yeah, but I actually use mine."

"*You* called *me* for help, remember?"

Grey took a deep breath. All his life, he'd handled his problems—and everyone else's in the family—by himself. Their mother had looked to Grey to supervise Zane when she and their father had gone off on some Western excursion. Dude ranches. Cattle drives. Exploring ancient Navajo artifacts in the Canyon de Chelly. Though both had been born in Louisiana, Grey's parents loved the Old West and were having a grand time retracing the steps of the pioneers. Their father had retired early and handed the reins of the family business over to him, barely out of graduate school. But now some unknown force was threatening the newspaper, the flagship business in a growing media conglomerate that had made the Mastersons one of the wealthiest families in New Orleans.

And the worst part? Deep in his heart, Grey really didn't care.

"Someone's sabotaging the newspaper. For all I know, it could be my stalker. Her name's Toni Maxwell. The newspaper's trouble started around the time of her arrival."

"So post a guard to keep her out."

Duh. He may not have a P.I. license like Zane, but he did own at least a small amount of common sense. "I posted two guards, Zane."

"And?"

"She managed to walk right past them—in a gorilla costume, no less."

"Excuse me?"

"You know, one of those out-of-work stage singers who embarrass people with stupid songs on their birthdays."

Zane's carefree laugh echoed over the phone line. "Very clever."

"Perhaps, but not funny."

"Right. Not funny."

Grey could hear his brother nearly choking in his effort to muffle his amusement.

"So what kind of damage did the singing gorilla do?"

Grey closed his eyes, trying to block out the memory. "For starters, she stripped."

"Naked?"

Thank God, things hadn't gone that far. He could only imagine trying to wring any respect from his staff once he had a naked gorilla woman sitting on his lap.

"The security guards arrived before she took off much."

"Too bad."

Grey ignored his brother. Zane would have undoubtedly enjoyed the whole scenario. There might have been a time when even Grey would have found the situation amusing. Unfortunately, if that time ever existed, it was long, long ago.

"Here's the clincher, brother. While this Toni Maxwell entertained the office staff at my expense, someone poured oil into the ink. We had to reprint the entire run in the main press and hit the stands three hours late."

"And you suspect Toni Maxwell was a plant? A distraction?" A sound of understanding flowed through Zane's voice, causing a brief respite from the stabbing pain in Grey's head.

"Well, she damn sure doesn't work for the local singing telegram outfits."

"You questioned her?"

Grey remained silent. He should have called the police. He knew the woman's name, even knew the name of the boutique she owned in the French Quarter. Hell, his investigator provided her home address, the names of the sisters who lived with her and had even offered to bring in the latest bag of garbage he'd swiped from her curbside. Grey had declined, accepted the information and then called his brother. Zane relished his playboy reputation. Who better to deal with a woman—particularly one intent on stalking him? Grey didn't want to tangle with any more women who either weren't holding a full deck of cards or who possessed some secret agenda.

"You want me to question her?" Zane ventured.

"I don't have the time or the desire."

Grey wondered how much further he should push this,

but decided to go for broke. He couldn't exactly admit to Zane that he wanted more than help with his stalker, but he owed his brother an honest assessment. "Circulation is down. Paper and fuel costs are on the rise. The union is giving my attorneys fits. I'm going to have to fire people who have worked for us for years. And to top it off, I'm handling the fallout from Lane's book. I can't deal with this woman stalking me, too."

"You need a vacation."

Grey shook his head. He needed a vacation, all right. Somewhere in Antarctica might do the trick, but he figured some persistent reporter would follow him there, too, and ask if the ice and snow were his latest remedy for his hot libido.

"Sure, I'll just take off and leave all these problems behind."

"Why not?" Zane asked. "All your troubles will still be waiting for you when you come back."

Now, that wasn't quite the answer he wanted, was it? "Maybe you can go off and relax while the family business is falling apart, but I can't." He took a deep breath. "Never mind, Zane. I'll handle this somehow."

"You always do."

Yeah, right. Grey was considered an expert in solving problems, seeing the big picture, finding a straight arrow path to the truth. But that required energy, enthusiasm. He was fresh out of both.

After a pause, Zane suggested, "Why don't we trade places for a while?"

Trade places? God, it had been years since they'd last pulled that stunt. Still, Grey could easily remember the liberation of Zane's lifestyle. Parties. A little travel. Friends who merely rolled their eyes at you because nothing you did, no matter how wild or outrageous, surprised anyone anymore.

The proposal definitely held appeal. Just the idea of being that carefree, even for a short while, loosened the seemingly permanent clench of muscles in his chest. But he didn't smile, afraid the sound of his mirth might somehow give him away. For the sake of Grey's staunch reputation, he played it straight. If he gave in too easily, Zane might change his mind. His twin loved a challenge as much as he did. Besides, would Grey's controlling nature really let him hand over the reins to his brother?

"Oh sure, and let you run the place into the ground?"

"Hey, hotshot. Sounds as though you're going down fast anyway. This way, if we go belly-up, you can blame me."

Grey continued to question the plan, even though the remembered freedom of switching with Zane held tight to its allure. Days and nights filled with nothing substantial, but loaded with lavish parties, extreme sports and college classes that required minimal study for maximum grades. Hell, had it really been since college? "I don't know if I should let you talk me into this."

"It'll be fun. You'll get to be me. Just think…sleeping in past five a.m., beignets and coffee at Café du Monde nearly every morning, licking powdered sugar off the fingers of—"

"I'll keep my licking to my own fingers, thank you." Grey's fantasy halted. The one downside of being Zane was the women. Since Lane, he'd sworn off the species. At least, until he could find one he could trust. And he wasn't so sure that feminine animal existed.

He switched the phone to his other ear, in time to catch Zane's best argument yet.

"Oh, come on. I'll liven up the newspaper. Besides, I

do have that pesky little degree in journalism, and I've never gotten to use it.''

Grey hadn't forgotten. Zane possessed a natural talent with words that Grey considered a huge waste on a man who had no focus. Yet Zane had no real experience at the *Herald*. Did he really want Zane using his byline on less than professional work? Did he care anymore? ''That's precisely my concern.''

''Think. No more paparazzi chasing you for comments about your sexual exploits. No more whiny lawyers to deal with. No more headaches over paying the bills.''

''You really want to trade?'' Grey couldn't erase the plaintive sound in his voice. He only hoped his brother was too self-absorbed to notice.

''Hell, I can delegate with the best of 'em. You must have some competent employees, so I can't screw up too badly. I'll even buy a pair of reading glasses and wear them. But if you would just take off one day of work and go in for the eye surgery like I did, I wouldn't have to bother.''

Grey slid the gold wire rims off his nose and rubbed the tired bridge. He simply wasn't vain enough to risk possible damage to his eyesight just to get rid of his glasses. At least that's what he told himself. Actually, there was also the little matter of surgery, anesthetic and sharp medical instruments that he didn't much look forward to. ''It won't hurt you to wear clear glasses.''

''Fine. You just need to do one thing for me.''

Grey couldn't imagine. He silently begged God to spare him from keeping Zane's date with some airheaded party girl or maybe filling in for him on some excursion mountain climbing in the Himalayas.

''What?''

''I got a call from a friend of mine, Reina Price—''

Grey perked up. "Reina Price, the jewelry artist?" Though he'd never met the woman, Grey had heard things. Seen her picture. He'd been instantly fascinated. What a time to finally have a chance at a meeting—when he'd sworn off women.

"You know Reina?"

Grey covered the sound of his interest with a gruff cough. "We ran an article on her gallery opening last year. How do *you* know her?"

"We hang out. She leases two buildings from me and needs help with a business problem. If we switch, you'll need to fill in. Might not be easy. She knows me pretty well. I'm supposed to meet with her tomorrow afternoon."

Grey glanced down at his own appointment book. "You'll have to go to the grand reopening of Club Carnal tonight."

"As if I wasn't going already," Zane muttered.

Club Carnal, the hottest see-and-be-seen nightspot in New Orleans, had recently changed owners—the perfect reason for a high-profile party. Zane undoubtedly topped the A list of invitees, because anywhere Zane showed up was considered hip and hot.

"Yes, but as me, you'll need to get there early, interview the new owner and perhaps a few patrons, then get out before things get too wild."

Grey counted the seconds of Zane's pause and winced. He might have just ruined his own chances. Being Grey was never as much fun as being Zane and, for the life of him, he never understood why his brother wanted to switch at all.

"You mean too interesting," Zane countered. "For how long are we switching?"

"For as long as you want."

"And you'll take care of Reina Price?"

"If you take care of Toni Maxwell."

Somehow, Grey knew he'd gotten the better end of the deal.

REINA SLID AWAY from the window and sighed, crossing her arms over her stretchy white lace T-shirt, then sliding her hands down her thighs, over tight black leggings tucked into ankle-high boots. *All dressed up and nowhere to go,* she mused. Actually, she could just go downstairs, into the bubbling pit of sensuality better known as Club Carnal, but what was the point? Only because of her friendship with the new owner, Chantal Dupre, had she showed up at all.

She already knew most of the men writhing in the mass of scented foam, dancing and flirting and drinking with the hippest, hottest babes in the city. None of them interested her. None of them ever had. Her growing ennui wasn't just a key part of her public persona anymore. Reina really was bored. With the club scene. With her predictable personal life.

She grabbed her tiny purse from where she'd laid it on Chantal's desk and marched toward the elevator. Before she could push the button, the doors slid open and her best friend popped out.

"And where do you think you're going?" Chantal demanded.

Reina feigned a look of innocence. "Downstairs to enjoy the bubble bath firsthand?"

Chantal snorted. "Yeah, right. You'll ruin your boots. You're bugging out on me."

Reina huffed, caught. "Chantal, I'm very proud of you for buying the club from your brother and organizing this entire grand reopening and making sure all the right people are in attendance. But I'll go crazy if you make me stay.''

"You used to love club hopping."

"I also used to like cotton candy for breakfast and watching *Beverly Hills, 90210.* People change.''

Chantal chuckled, crossing the long, fourth-floor room her brother had converted into the club's office. "I would have loved to have seen you tell Pilar you wanted cotton candy for breakfast."

"You think she said no? My mother is immeasurably indulgent."

"She's also always been obsessed with the state of her figure—and yours. You got *90210* in Paris?"

"In London. Or maybe it was during the summer in New York. I don't remember. Chantal, may I go, please?"

After tossing a zipped bank bag into a desk drawer, Chantal stared at her friend from the tip of her boots to the top of her head. Reina didn't have to exaggerate the outward signs of her restlessness. If she didn't escape soon, she'd do something totally uncharacteristic. Like scream.

"Oh, all right. It's not like you're actually downstairs filling my coffers with a long drink tab. Where are you going anyway? Hot date?"

"Actually…"

Reina did, in a manner of speaking, have something sinful and sexual planned. Nothing like Chantal imagined, she was sure, but with a little help from the suitcase of toys she stored beneath her bed, she hoped to experience a little release of the tension zinging through her since Claudio allowed her to peek at il Gio's drawings.

"Tell me!" Chantal grabbed her by the wrist and dragged her over to the long leather couch.

"There's nothing to tell. I actually have a date with a hot book."

"Book? Damn girl, you can't tease a recently divorced woman that way. Here you had me thinking you'd finally broken down and taken a lover."

Reina rolled her eyes. "Why do *I* have to take the lover to satisfy your needs? The divorce has been final for three months, Chantal, and I'm sure any one of those studs you have on the guest list would willingly satisfy your libido."

Chantal licked her dark-lined lips, then walked over to the bank of tilted windows that overlooked the club from four stories up. The disco balls and high-tech laser lights glittered starlight colors all around the dark office. The latest techno music pounded through the walls, in time with an accelerated rhythm. Reina watched her friend, tapping her high heels to the beat, look over the mass of sexually charged people dancing and drinking below.

"There are some hunks in attendance," she said, almost absently. "Did you see Zane's twin, Grey?"

"Zane has a twin?" Reina asked, surprised. Zane Masterson was not only the landlord for both her Arts District gallery and her Garden District home, but she also considered him a good friend. They'd dated a few times at the behest of mutual acquaintances, but found more in common for a casual relationship. She considered them to be fairly close, but obviously not close enough for him to admit that his brother and he shared the same genetic makeup.

"Didn't you know?" Chantal asked.

"I knew he had a brother who runs the *Louisiana Daily Herald,* but I had no idea they were twins."

Wait a minute...Grey Masterson, Grey Masterson. Why did the name seem so familiar?

"You should check him out," Chantal suggested.

''He's sort of cute in a serious, suspicious sort of way. He looks just like Zane. Or Zane looks like him. I don't remember which one was born first. Anyway, he just got done interviewing me for his newspaper.''

Reina's memory finally clicked. ''Is this the same Grey Masterson who was featured in the book by that cheesy actress? What was her name? The one who starred in that blockbuster slasher film?''

Chantal nodded. ''Yeah, yeah.'' She giggled. ''I almost forgot. Did you read her book? They boinked like bunnies all over town. Add stamina to the man's appeal.''

Reina shivered. She had nothing against an adventurous love life, but she valued discretion above all else. The idea of having her sexual escapades chronicled in a best-selling book horrified her. She remembered her mother shopping around an exposé of her affairs a few years ago, but, thankfully, no publisher of merit was willing to pay a large advance to a famous but fading stage actress.

''No, thanks. Privacy means too much to me.''

''Well, *he* didn't write the book, the hussy did. Heard he was pretty pissed.''

''I'll bet. Well, speaking of books—'' she grabbed her purse again and this time made it all the way inside the elevator, though she held the door open by pressing the button ''—I have a date with a bestseller myself. Don't be offended if I have more fun with *Il Gioielliere's Diaries* than you have making money.''

Chantal rushed toward her. ''You have a copy? It's been sold out at Book Star for a week. I'm dying to read it!''

Reina frowned, then waved her hands. ''I don't actually have a copy yet, but I'll bet my mother has one.''

''Well, I've got dibs next. From what I hear, that book will put any of those young studs downstairs to shame.''

A shiver of electricity coursed through Reina. She loved anticipation, sometimes even more than sex. Particularly since anticipation had been all she'd permitted herself lately.

"I'll let you know."

She released the button, amused by Chantal's dreamy, envious look as the doors slid closed.

"HAVE A COPY? Love, I have a case." Pilar Price lounged on a velvet chaise, sipping her evening cognac beside a table lit with a dozen beeswax candles. Reina leaned down and kissed her mother, wondering why the woman looked so beautiful, so put together and sensuously arranged at this late hour. Her jet hair, glossy from a fresh application of color, sat artfully arranged atop her head. Swathed in a silky nightgown, she looked no older than Reina, particularly in the candlelight. The woman knew how to set the stage for a seduction. "In the parlor, beneath the Queen Anne table."

"A case?"

"They're very hot property. I ordered them in as gifts. Go along and take yours. But I haven't time to chat, *mi amore*."

At that moment, her mother's maid, Dahlia, charged into the room, scenting the air by pressing the golden bulb of an antique atomizer. "Reinita! You should know better than to show up here at this hour," Dahlia chastised lightly.

Reina smiled as Dahlia swept a quick but genuine kiss across her cheek. "Might run into a paramour, might I?"

Dahlia only clucked her tongue. "Maybe you should find yourself a paramour of your own. Besides, a woman like you shouldn't be charging about the Quarter at this hour."

"Oh, hush, Dahlia," Pilar insisted, waving her hand. "Reina doesn't *charge* anywhere. I taught her much better than that. She only came to borrow a book, which I've told her is a gift to keep."

"Thank you, Mother. I won't overstay my welcome." She hurried into the parlor and retrieved the book from a very large box, shipped, according to the label, directly from the publisher. She clutched the gilded cover to her breast, anxious to get started. She returned to the library where her mother relaxed. "I have an important meeting tomorrow and just need to do my homework."

"Meeting? With whom?"

Pilar attempted to look disinterested by picking at the lace on her sleeve, but Reina knew her mother well enough to recognize deep curiosity. She'd decided earlier this afternoon not to tell her mother about Claudio or his offer.

When she'd told her mother about the thefts at the gallery, Pilar had completely overreacted. She'd railed about danger and demanded Reina move in with her, a command Reina defied, despite two weeks of the silent treatment. Even in her sulking, Pilar had called the chief of police and demanded a full investigation, much to Reina's deep embarrassment. She was thirty years old, for God's sake. She didn't need her mother running to her rescue.

So she opted to keep her new opportunity to herself.

"Zane Masterson."

Reina grinned, congratulating herself for producing a truthful response so quickly. Her mother's lessons in honest duplicity had not fallen on deaf ears.

"Oh," Pilar groaned, rolling her eyes. "You're wasting your time with that one. He's a perennial bachelor, committed to nothing and no one. Or maybe that's why you're dallying with him now, after all these years, so you don't have to risk your heart to love?''

Reina's brow popped up. Her mother wasn't a brainless woman, but she wasn't usually so perceptive about anyone other than herself. Still, Reina had nothing to lose by admitting enough to squelch Pilar's interest. ''Actually, Mother, that's it, precisely.''

Pilar nodded absently, instantly more intrigued by the lay of silk across her thigh. Seduction without love was old hat to Reina's mother.

''Well, then, darling. Have fun.''

With a brief wave, Pilar dismissed Reina, who immediately jumped at the opportunity to escape before Dahlia added her two cents, which usually included something about Reina finding a husband or other such nonsense.

She had no more time for a husband than she did for a lover. Which she didn't need, at least for tonight, so long as she had the book, her toys and her vivid imagination.

2

"YOU'RE LATE."

Grey bristled. Yes, he was late. But he certainly didn't walk into Reina Price's gallery expecting to be snapped at by someone he knew wasn't the owner. He opened his mouth to verbally reduce the petite woman's sneering sauciness to a size more appropriate for her body, but smacked his lips together and grinned instead. Grey Masterson might not suffer such a rude greeting, but Zane Masterson wouldn't give a damn.

"What's new?" he said instead, easing beyond the glass doorway with an unhurried step.

His question stopped her high-heeled march across the gallery. She turned, a perplexed look on her china-doll face. "You're never late. Not unless you're going to a party."

Grey forced his expression to remain nonchalant while he filed the information away for further reference. "Today's no party, then, huh?"

She shook her head before slipping back onto the tall stool behind the reception desk. "I wouldn't know."

Flipping on a headset and then punching a number into the telephone, the young woman dismissed him without another glance. Grey wondered what Zane had done to make the woman so hostile. Probably dumped her. Or worse, turned her down. She was attractive enough, he supposed, but she looked a little naive, despite makeup too thick for her youthful skin and clothes too tight for such a slim but shapeless body. He figured such attire was probably appropriate for an art studio that specialized in erotic creations, but she looked too much like a child playing dress-up for his taste.

Taking a moment to look around the gallery, he tried not to appear as if the pieces displayed on the warm white walls or in glass cases spaced over a black-tiled floor were completely new to him. Grey had no idea how often Zane visited his rental properties but knew Zane had bought this building long before renovation of the Arts District had made the neighborhood hip. New Orleans, a city more inclined to preservation by neglect rather than restoration by design, had embraced the change with its usual laid-back acceptance. So long as they could still throw a party or host a parade on Julia Street, the main thoroughfare, everyone won.

Yet even the leading purveyors of the Quarter's motto *laissez les bons temps rouler*—let the good times roll—had raised shocked eyebrows over the Price Gallery, which featured artists who specialized in sexual art. He glanced at paintings that even he might have considered pornographic if not for the skilled blends of color and original brush strokes. Stopping to admire a glass sculpture of a woman's breast, the nipple erect and tipped with gold, Grey wondered where he would put such a piece if he shelled out the—*good Lord*—ten-thousand-dollar asking price.

Behind him, a buzzer sounded. He watched the snippy receptionist paste on her best smile before she waved in two well-dressed couples. Judging by their clothes, they could easily afford such luxuries. The studio brimmed with interesting, eye-catching pieces. At least a dozen customers milled about, chatting with two artists working along the back wall of the gallery in studio areas that sported neat worktables and a fully operational kiln protected by glass.

The studio was unique, allowing the patrons to see the artists at work. Reina Price had successfully taken the concepts practiced in the square around Jackson Park—artists plying their trade for the world to see—and brought them into a setting made even more intimate by the subject matter. Although he didn't know much about art, he recognized talent when he saw it. Not only in the featured artists, but also in the woman who ran the show. Grey approached a cube-shaped case displaying a delicate flower pin reminiscent of labia and a stimulated clit. Then he spotted the two-thousand-dollar price tag with a small red "sold" label tacked on the top. Yeah, Reina Price knew what she was doing.

He remembered the cultural society's objection during Reina's opening, a prelude to their even more vigorous disapproval when the National Trust Artists' Museum had allowed the Joshua Eastman Gallery of Erotic Art to open. Reina had been considered an interloper, a European-bred upstart riding on the celebrity of her mother, the world-renowned stage actress, Pilar Price. The criticism shifted with the Eastman Gallery, since the Eastman family had lived in New Orleans since before the War Between the States. Evidently, new or old, the grand dames of New Orleans wanted everything overtly sexual and erotic confined to the T-shirt shops on Bourbon Street.

Just a few months ago, Grey had exemplified this code of conduct. For him, sexual preferences and erotic interludes had always gone on behind the closed doors of a bedroom, or a boardroom, or the back seat of a limousine if that's what the situation warranted. But always in private. Now that Lane's book had spent weeks on the bestseller list, he wondered if he'd ever experience such personal privacy again.

One good thing about being Zane was that it became a nonissue. No one expected him to be discreet.

Grey watched for any sign of Reina, suddenly worried about convincing her that he was Zane when she probably knew the real Zane's daily habits better than he did. He'd just learned his brother wasn't known for tardiness. That surprised him. He couldn't remember the last time Zane had showed up on time for a family dinner or meeting of the stockholders. He frowned, surmising Zane only showed up on time for events he deemed important. Grey should have guessed. Zane always had valued his friends, particularly the female ones, over anything else.

Grey had had little time to grill his brother before the switch, so he'd only kept to the most basic information. Not knowing made the game more enjoyable. As usual, Zane had no serious entanglements Grey had to worry about and no other pressing commitments beyond his appointment with Reina. He'd admitted that he'd dated the exotic jewelry designer a few times, but that they were now simply friends and business associates. And while Grey couldn't squelch the curiosity he harbored about Ms. Price, the circumstances suited his oath to stay away from women for a while. He didn't have to pretend to be attracted to Reina, or engage in any of the painfully obvious flirting his brother usually employed, not when their romance was long over.

But when Reina stepped out of her office, Grey wondered if maybe he would have to do some pretending after all.

Before she caught sight of him, she greeted one of the couples who'd entered the gallery after he had. Dressed in slim black silk slacks and a sheer long-sleeved blouse that hugged her flesh, Reina Price was stunning. The dark hue of her clothing, coupled with the ebony gloss of her upswept hair, added an air of mystery to her guarded expression. Her smile exuded natural warmth, but her lips, berry-stained, curved with caution. Her dark, wide eyes, framed by mile-long lashes, enhanced a carefully constructed air of mystery.

Grey slung his hands into the pockets of his slacks, shocked by his instantaneous physical reaction. The pictures they'd printed in his newspaper hadn't done her justice. He hadn't expected her to be so tall, so…stacked. Her stiletto heels and visible satin bra undoubtedly enhanced the effect, but Grey didn't care. He whistled aloud, figuring Zane would never hide his appreciation for such awesome beauty.

She frowned slightly at him, waved over an associate, then excused herself from the customers and approached him with her arms crossed just beneath her breasts, which were even more impressive close up.

"Where have you been, Zane? You said you'd be here by five o'clock." She glanced at a table-size clock prominently displayed in the gallery, shaped like a man's genitals.

"Sorry," Grey said with a shrug. "I got caught up."

She rolled her eyes, arresting Grey's interest with the fathomless, ebony irises and feline shape. "Yeah, I'll bet you did. I hope she was worth it, because now we'll have to leave before I can fill you in. Claudio is meeting me at the house in twenty minutes."

"Claudio?"

Grey noticed that when he said the name, his pronunciation lacked the natural roll of the tongue that gave hers such a deep, musical quality. His Creole-laced accent worked best with French, not Italian.

"Claudio di Amante. I'll explain in the car. Let me grab my bag and talk to Judi for a minute. If we leave in five, we'll arrive at the house just before he does."

Grey bit down his natural inclination to ask more questions and instead stepped toward the door. Even in a rush, Reina moved precisely, her heels clicking gently on the tile floor, her hips swinging with a sweet but controlled shimmy. She walked with a grace that spoke of practice. Did they have cotillions where she came from?

Then he remembered she was a U.S. citizen. Despite his desire to leave his newspaper and staid lifestyle behind, he'd checked up on the woman shortly after putting down the phone with his brother. In the article he'd found in the *Herald*'s archives, his reporter had revealed very little about the woman's background. She was the daughter of Pilar Price, the internationally renowned stage actress. She'd been born in New York City, but raised and schooled mainly in Europe, either by tutors or at exclusive academies. Nothing in the text hinted at hobbies or her social life, which he assumed, since she traveled the same circles as his brother, included the coolest parties with the hottest people.

Well, she definitely qualified as hot.

She emerged from her office with a slim leather briefcase and a black scarf she'd tossed over one shoulder. She stopped at the reception desk and spoke in discreet whispers to the receptionist, whom he now knew was Judi. She joined him and, at the buzz, waited for him to open the door.

That threw him for an instant, before his old-fashioned manners, beaten into the background by one too many liberated women, fought back to the surface.

"Sorry," he muttered, but she waved his apology away.

"Why were you late?"

She walked directly toward Zane's classic red Jaguar, parked just a few spaces up the curb. Apparently, he was driving.

"Nothing's wrong, is it?" she asked.

Grey disengaged the alarm system, then opened the passenger door. He stood back, not only allowing her room to slip into the low-riding car, but also giving himself a clear vantage point to watch her undulate her body into the cramped space. Not surprisingly, she managed the feat with a graceful dip, like a dancer. He slammed the door, wishing she'd been wearing a skirt. A short one.

He grinned. He'd only been Zane for a few short hours, but he was thinking more like him by the minute.

"Nothing earth-shattering," he answered, after buckling his seat belt. "I should have put it off until after I met you. Bad call on my part."

He turned the key and maneuvered the car onto Julia Street, remembering only after he reached the light that he didn't know where he was going.

Wait. Think.

Oh, yeah. He knew. She lived in the house on First Street, the one Zane had inherited from their great-grandmother, who had been born in the bedroom overlooking the garden and died in the kitchen shortly after baking up a batch of her famous praline pecan cookies. Grey smiled. *Grand-mère* Lucretia, who'd passed into the other world at the ripe age of one hundred and four, had been a favorite of the twins. She'd never raised her voice, never forbidden them to explore the entire house, secret passageways and hidden rooms included. Her wartime tales remained with Grey to this day. He would have been jealous that Zane received the house as his inheritance, but he'd gotten the island where her family first settled after emigrating from Canada. He shook his head, thinking of how long it had been since he'd visited the island.

Reina cut into his thoughts. "Claudio insists that I'm the only designer who can do justice to the collection. And the timing couldn't be more crucial. He's counting on me. More than he should."

"Why? You're a brilliant designer."

"A brilliant designer who can't keep her jewels safe. Or rather, his jewels. That's why I called you, Zane. I need your help."

Grey nodded, though he had no idea what she was talking about. Why couldn't she keep the jewels safe? He'd seen security cameras inside the gallery, even noticed a guard. And if this Claudio person wanted Reina to work on a jewelry collection, why was she meeting him at her house rather than at her gallery?

That question seemed natural enough to ask without giving himself away.

"You have my help, Reina, of course. But why aren't we meeting him at the gallery?"

"The gallery still isn't safe, you know that."

Now he did.

He took a chance. "Has something new happened that I don't know about?"

Reina seemed to be a very private person. She wore black. She spoke in a voice that bordered on a whisper. A very cultured, very sexy whisper.

And his brother wasn't one to pry. He didn't doubt Zane and Reina's friendship or their mutually beneficial business relationship, but Grey doubted they were true confidants. As far as he knew, Zane didn't have and didn't want someone to share his innermost secrets with. If he did, he'd choose his twin brother, right?

"After the second break-in two weeks ago, my insurance carrier canceled me. But don't worry about liability," she reassured him. "Each of the artists I'm currently showing has their own policy and I'm not accepting any more commissions that involve valuable pieces. Well, I wasn't. Until Claudio."

Though he doubted Zane cared one flip about liability or insurance, he knew his brother handled his investments with care. Grey managed most of the family accounts and Zane hadn't dipped into his trust fund for years. In fact, Zane could have taken control of the money after his thirtieth birthday, but preferred to let Grey manage the portfolio as he had their entire adult life.

"I'm not worried about the insurance," he said, trying to sound as flip as he figured his brother would about such matters, "but I am worried about you. You shouldn't have to pass up business because the building I'm leasing to you isn't secure."

"Let's not discuss this again, Zane. I can't allow you to pay for any more security at the building. If you'd leased it to that auction house, they'd be responsible for keeping their pieces safe. Just as I am. You already had the alarm system installed before I opened."

"At the gallery," he said, hoping he was correct in his next guess. "But not at the house."

"I saw no need. Before."

Her voice had dipped in volume, and Grey heard the distinct sound of misgiving.

"It's a grand old house," he commented, allowing a break from the tension. "The ten-foot wall and bramble vines kept my great-grandmother safe, even when she lived there all alone."

"That's why I didn't have an alarm system put in. Now, I simply can't afford it. I've spent all my extra money, except what I need to live and keep the gallery open. The rest is tied up in investments until at least the end of the year.''

''You shouldn't have to afford it. It's still my house. It's my responsibility to keep my tenant safe from harm.''

Reina remained silent. Grey shifted a bit in the soft leather seat, wondering if talking about responsibility with such ease was a mistake, since he was supposed to be Zane. He'd often wondered if the word even existed in Zane's vocabulary, but reminded himself that they did, after all, share the same genetic material and had been raised in the same loving household. Except for attending different schools, they'd had nearly indistinguishable influences.

And yet, they remained the most different set of identical twins he'd ever met.

''Zane, you don't know how much I want to deny that.''

''You don't want me to help you? Then why'd you call?''

Reina touched the middle finger of her right hand to the precise center of her forehead, as if the tiny pressure could relieve whatever ailed her.

''I called because no matter how much I don't *want* to ask for your assistance, I can't afford to let Claudio di Amante, his jewelry, or his very generous offer slip away. Crass as it sounds, I need the cash. And, consequently, I need your help.''

Needing money didn't sound crass to him. Probably wouldn't to Zane, either. They'd been raised in wealth, but they had never forgotten that their money had come from the entrepreneurial spirits of their hardworking ancestors.

At a stoplight, Grey turned and faced her, trying not to appear too intense about his offer. ''The least I can do is arrange security for the house. But that may not be enough. All the bells and whistles in the world won't keep someone out if they're determined to get in."

Reina allowed his warning to linger, responding neither verbally nor with any change of her expression. After a moment, she slipped her hand into her briefcase and retrieved her sunglasses, hiding her eyes from his scrutiny. If she was worried, she didn't let on as he drove the car from the gallery to the Garden District.

Some women could be hard to read. Lane had always nibbled her bottom lip when something was bothering her, a problem he could usually solve for her with a spontaneous seduction.

He turned onto St. Charles Street, wondering what Reina Price, the somewhat aloof designer of intimate jewelry, would do if he pulled onto a deserted side street and tempted away her troubles with a long, wet kiss.

"What are you thinking?" she asked.

He hadn't noticed that she'd turned her attention on him.

Clearing his throat, he answered, "You don't want to know, *chère*."

She laughed. "Don't pull that coy crap with me, Zane Masterson."

"Crap? Now you are being crass."

"I've been in the States too long, I suppose."

"Oh, yes…no one curses in Europe. I forgot."

Her chuckle deepened and Grey relished the sound. Deep. Guttural. Honest. Yet mysterious, as if expressing humor wasn't something she did very often.

But she did with Zane.

The rapport she felt for his brother reflected in the way she reclined into the seat, relaxed and trusting, and in the way she spoke to him, with unguarded words and easy confessions. Grey wondered just how intimate a relationship she and Zane had shared in the past. Just how intimate a relationship he had to mimic in his impersonation of his brother.

He shook his head silently. *Tough job, but someone has to do it.*

Zane and Grey had decided to tell no one about the switch. Though Zane assured Grey that Reina could be completely trusted with their secret, Grey reminded Zane that letting anyone in on the situation stole the fun. Grey was, after all, supposed to be on a vacation from being himself, a reward he richly deserved.

"Oh, they curse in Europe," Reina admitted. "But somehow the accents seem to detract from the vulgarity, not to mention the beauty of some of the languages. I used to love to hear my mother lose her temper in Spanish or Italian. Sounded like so much fun."

Grey understood. His great-grandmother, the one who had owned the house Reina now rented, could swear up a storm in Acadian French and it sounded as if she was spouting poetry.

"Do you speak Italian?"

Reina glanced over her glasses. Oops. Maybe Zane already knew the answer to that.

"I mean, do you still speak Italian?"

Reina pushed the shades onto the bridge of her nose. "Mother never spent much time in Italy after I was born, though she had a summer home we'd visit every few years. I get by in restaurants. I know enough Spanish and French. Pilar preferred the stages in London, Madrid, Paris, Prague—though I never could grasp Czech grammar. We did spend a lot of time in New York."

"And now New Orleans."

"Yes, well…your city offered my mother her own theater, her own company of actors and free rein over nearly every aspect of the productions. How could a woman as talented—and as vain—as my mother possibly refuse?''

Grey knew the question was rhetorical, so he concentrated on remembering the way to his great-grandmother's house. He hadn't been there in years, possibly since before he'd learned to drive. Still, the great thing about New Orleans, besides the food, was that little ever changed. After a few uncertain minutes, he made the correct turns and was soon maneuvering the tiny sports car along a narrow alley that ran up to the garage behind the house.

After struggling with a wrought-iron gate he vowed to convert to automatic even before he installed a security camera, Grey helped Reina out of the car behind the house. He nearly instructed her to wait for him before she went inside, but then saw a glossy black limousine advancing along the street in front of the house. The mysterious Claudio di Amante, no doubt.

''He'll go to the front door. I'll meet you inside. Don't want to keep the man waiting.''

The minute Reina disappeared inside through the back door, Grey cursed. He hadn't had time to check the guy out. Taking a chance that his brother wouldn't be at the newspaper on such a gorgeous Saturday evening, he quickly dialed the crime desk while securing the car inside the detached garage.

''Shelby Parker.''

''Shelby, it's Grey. I need a quick favor. What do you have on any robberies over at the Price Gallery on Julia?''

His intrepid, albeit young, crime reporter didn't miss a beat. ''Two robberies, actually.'' He could hear her fingers flying over her keyboard. ''The first one was about two months ago. A collection of antique ruby necklaces taken from a locked safe. Ms. Price was allegedly redesigning new settings for the grand-daughter of a duchess who'd inherited them when the stones were taken.''

''A duchess?''

Shelly snorted. ''No, the grand-daughter. Have you seen Reina Price's designs? She definitely appeals to a younger crowd.''

He recalled the flowering pin he'd seen at the gallery, the one that brought the taste of a woman's arousal to his mouth. He'd experienced the appeal of Reina's work first-hand and doubted it would have affected him any less, no matter his age.

''And the second robbery?'' he asked, needing to keep his mind on the matter at hand.

''Oh, here it is. I didn't cover this one...happened a month ago. Another cache of jewels stolen from the safe—a different, more impenetrable one than the first, supposedly.'' Shelby rattled off the details, which Grey instantly committed to memory. ''The night watchman, hired after the first robbery, was knocked unconscious. Security camera tapes missing. The police suspect—''

''—an inside job.'' Grey had covered the crime beat during his college internship and then as a cub reporter. He'd learned to think like a detective so he could ask the right questions. He never figured he'd have to use his experience to help a friend. Zane's friend. Maybe, some-day, his friend.

''Any suspects?''

''Not according to this. We haven't done any follow-ups. Want me to get on it?''

While he admired Shelby's eager enthusiasm, he didn't need her sticking her nose in Reina's business right now, not with him planning to stay close until he was sure she was safe. He wasn't exactly sure when he'd formulated that part of his scheme, but he figured it was sometime around the moment Reina stepped out of her office in all her sensual loveliness.

"I've got it covered for now, thanks. And listen, if you see me around the office, don't let on that I called you, okay? I'm working on something."

Shelby hissed with expectant curiosity. "Does this have anything to do with the sand in the gas tanks?"

Sand in the gas tanks? Obviously, something new had happened at the newspaper. Grey bit back any questions, determined to allow Zane to deal with the family troubles despite his concern and curiosity. He would just have to find out the details from Zane later. For now he would focus on Reina. "No, it doesn't."

Shelby paused, and Grey could practically hear the sharp mechanisms in his reporter's brain rushing to all sort of outlandish conclusions, conclusions she'd been known to prove on occasion. "Anything I can help you with, boss?"

Grey closed his eyes. The smell of the blossoming night jasmine in Reina's garden brought to mind the exotic scent of her perfume. He let the powerful essence work its magic over his wired nerves, and imagined, for a brief moment, how the fragrance would intensify if he pressed a delicate white petal over Reina's smooth, warm skin.

"No, thanks, Shel," he murmured. "You get back to the grind. I've got this one covered."

3

REINA SLIPPED HER ATTACHÉ beside the worktable in her solarium studio, then surrendered to her strong need to peek one more time at Zane. Zane, the playboy whose charm she'd been immune to since the first moment she met him. Zane, who flirted with her more out of habit than out of seductive intent. Zane, who suddenly seemed to look at her with eyes she'd never seen.

Shielded by the ferns she'd hung near the window, she watched him pace just outside her garage while talking on his cell phone, looking more serious than she'd ever seen him in the entire five years she'd known him.

Not to mention more handsome, more mysterious, more…sexy. Caged, like a powerful animal. Ravenous. Ferocious. Reina closed her eyes and allowed a quick fantasy to rush through her. Duran Duran provided the soundtrack. *Hungry like a wolf.*

"Okay, it's official," she said aloud, shaking her head as she stepped into her guest bathroom to check her makeup and hair before she answered the door to Claudio, whose knock she expected any second. "I am long overdue for a lover."

What else would explain why she was suddenly, powerfully attracted to a man she'd become friends with mainly because they *didn't* want to sleep together? She blamed the diary, which she'd stayed up very late reading. She blamed her long day at the gallery, surrounded by exquisite art, all with sexual content—and the fact that she used her own sensuality to sell the pieces to the public. Subtle sexiness put people off-kilter. They never knew quite how to react or how to respond, so she retained the upper hand. She'd watched her mother employ the same tactics her entire life—only Pilar used it to trap lovers. Reina chose to put her talents toward advancing her business.

And a tiny part of her wanted to see what would happen if she set her sights on Zane.

Lord, she needed a good night's rest. The sizzling content of *Il Gioielliere's Diaries* had made sleep difficult, even after she'd luxuriated in a hot bath and some solo satisfaction. Maybe what she needed was a break from her immersion in all things sensual and sexual.

Maybe she just needed a man.

One who would help her work off her excessive sexual energy without wanting anything in return. One who would understand that she valued her work and her business above all else, and she didn't require love or devotion in order to experience a good orgasm.

She glanced back out the window. God, she really was losing it. Still, she sensed something different about Zane, something subtle. As if he had a secret he couldn't tell her. He was hiding something, but she had no idea what. She briefly entertained the idea that he was reining in his attraction to her, but how could that be? *Not* wanting each other, *not* trying to impress or seduce, had become the foundation of their friendship. Zane, the sought-after bachelor, hardly ever met a woman who didn't want to lure him to her bed. Reina, the aloof seductress, kept men away by presenting herself as more than they could possibly handle. And now, after five years of platonic comfort, had things changed?

The doorbell rang, springing Reina back to the present. She took a deep breath and regained control over her frazzled nerves. She was being ridiculous. She grabbed a tube of her favorite lipstick and swiped on a quick application, willing confidence and control into her expression. Claudio wanted her to reassemble his collection and she wanted the job. If she had to, she'd use every tactic in her sensual arsenal to assure Claudio she could keep the jewels safe. Weird vibes or not, Zane had promised to help her. She believed him, just as she believed that any heightened awareness between her and Zane was just a figment of her oversexed imagination.

REINA HAD CHANGED. Not her clothes, there hadn't been time. Yet, as Grey entered the house through the back door and heard her voice, then turned the corner in time to watch her pour a glass of merlot for her guest in the front parlor, he instantly recognized a subtle yet glaring alteration in her manner.

Her movements were precise but slow—lazy, as if she were a pampered woman with all the time in the world. Her lashes fluttered over her eyes, which were lowered just enough to be construed as seductive, inviting. When she delivered the wine, her delicate fingers brushed coquettishly against her guest's deeply tanned hand. She lingered near him until he took his first sip, then rewarded his appreciative hum with a stunning, pleasured grin.

Reina had turned her sensuality to full blast. Grey nearly whistled aloud, marveling at her power to arouse him when she didn't even know he was there, when he wasn't even the man she sought to seduce.

Her sexiness dimmed only when she turned her attention to the two incredibly large men who flanked the more cultured gentleman—the one he assumed was Claudio di

Amante. Dimmed, but didn't disappear. Grey knew that would be impossible.

"Are you sure you wouldn't like anything, Mr.—"

Grey figured one was probably named Rocco and the other Tony. Big Tony. Or Guido. From the cut of their suits and the steely glare in their eyes, he guessed these wise guys were products of the good old U.S. of A., despite invariably Italian surnames.

"My associates have another engagement after this," the older man answered in a thick Italian accent. "They need, how you say, clear heads?"

Reina grinned, her lips curved coyly. "Of course. They can sit down, can't they?"

Guido and Rocco glanced at each other. The hair along the back of Grey's neck sprang to attention. Just what had Reina gotten herself into? What had Zane gotten *him* into? Had he abandoned troubles at the newspaper to take on a problem with the mob?

One goon took a chair near the window, the other near the parlor door. Grey must have groaned louder than he intended, because he caught Reina's attention. She invited him into the room just as Rocco reached beneath his jacket.

"Claudio di Amante, may I introduce my landlord, Zane Masterson."

Rocco relaxed. Grey swallowed a huff of relief.

"Zane has agreed to help me insure the safety of your collection while it is in my possession," Reina explained.

Grey extended his hand as the man rose from his chair. "Signore di Amante."

"Mr. Masterson."

Claudio shook his hand with a little more roughness than Grey would have expected from a man of such obvious sophistication. His dark eyes, soft with admiration when he looked at Reina, now hardened and stared. Grey couldn't remember the last time he'd been sized up so blatantly, but figured the man had good reason.

Either that or he didn't like his territory intruded upon.

"Reina hasn't had a chance to tell me much about your collection," Grey said, hoping to break the tension, "but I'm assuming it's incredibly valuable."

"Priceless." Di Amante sat, then motioned for Grey to do the same. "I've brought these treasures all the way from my home in Venice, where they've been locked away for several generations. What I have now are loose gems and precious stones and metals that were once the centerpieces of a notorious collection of erotic jewelry created by my ancestor. His name was Gianni di Carlo. In his day, he was known by his profession—a jeweler, *il gioielliere*. Most said only "il Gio" and everyone knew of whom they spoke."

Grey noted the pride in di Amante's voice. The rich history meant a great deal to him, a sentiment Grey could understand, given his legacy from the *Herald*. He lowered himself into a wing chair across from the Italian.

"But the collection was dismantled?"

Claudio's nod was sad. "Il Gio created the collection for his mistress. After she died, he took all the pieces apart and locked them away. But his family knew of the affair, and his daughter, who was sympathetic to the mistress, made sure the remnants remained together, handed down from mother to daughter for centuries. My mother had no daughter and I never married, so the legacy fell to me. And now I want Reina to restore the collection to its original state. The jewels themselves are exquisite in quality. The gold as pure as sixteenth-century processes would allow."

''Sixteenth century?'' Grey asked, not realizing the jewels were antique.

Reina placed a filled goblet in Grey's hand then gracefully arranged herself on an antique settee, her own wine in one hand and enraptured attention on her face. Her eyes glowed with absolute interest. You'd think di Amante was giving her the secret to world peace rather than describing a bunch of old jewelry.

''A legacy from a beloved ancestor. Have you heard of il Gioielliere?'' Claudio waited for Grey to nod. He had indeed heard of the man, thanks to an article his book editor had done on the history of the current bestseller, a diary of some sort. Grey hadn't paid that much attention, except to note that the book had knocked Lane Morrow's tabloid trash out of the number one spot on the *New York Times* list.

''The sentimental value alone makes these jewels irreplaceable,'' Claudio added.

Grey sipped his wine, relaxing into the chair while he watched the man's eyes. Something about Claudio di Amante's expression alerted Grey's journalistic instincts. The man was holding something back. Keeping something important under wraps—and not just from him, but from Reina, as well.

''Why don't your…associates arrange protection for the jewels?'' he asked.

Claudio grinned. ''These gentleman graciously agreed to oversee the transport of the jewels from my possession to Ms. Price's talented hands. I cannot impose on them beyond that, I'm afraid. You can handle the task of protecting Ms. Price…and the jewels, *si?*''

Grey sat up straighter. ''Is there any reason to believe these jewels could place Reina in danger?''

''Absolutely not, unless the thief who has targeted her

business in recent days strikes yet again and employs more desperate measures, like invading her home.''

Grey watched Reina from the corner of his eye, but she didn't say a word. He realized then that Reina hadn't added anything to the conversation so far, hadn't objected—as many women would—to being discussed as if she wasn't there. One glance into her eyes told him she was practicing great restraint, carefully observing their exchange as she casually sipped her wine.

What did she see with those large dark eyes?

"That's why I'm here," Grey reassured him. "I won't let anything happen to either Ms. Price or the jewels. I have a close associate in the security business. I'll have the house wired with state-of-the-art equipment before midnight."

Claudio sipped and stared, his gaze intense, his expression wary. "Do you believe Mr. Masterson can protect you, Reina? I don't wish to be the cause of harm to you."

Reina slid her glass onto a low marble-topped table and brightened her eternally coy smile. "I have absolute confidence in Zane, Claudio. He's been a good friend to me, a reliable one. I haven't made many friends since returning to the States, but the ones I've made—like Zane—I would trust with my life."

Shocked, Grey shook off a chill by sipping more wine. He didn't know what surprised him more—that Reina trusted his brother so implicitly or that she didn't have dozens of friends and admirers clamoring to lay their lives at her feet. He'd known her for less than an hour and he could easily visualize himself doing all he could to keep her from harm's way. Just yesterday, he'd thought himself too exhausted to deal with the combined trouble of a beleaguered newspaper, his trashed reputation and his wacko stalker. But a jewel thief? Maybe the mob? For Reina?

No problem.

Claudio, obviously convinced, nodded to Guido. The large man instantly produced a locked, metallic briefcase Grey hadn't noticed until that very minute. Tapping the side of his watch, Claudio opened a small compartment and slid out a tiny key. He unlocked the case, then, with a glance, dismissed the bodyguards from the room. One went out the front door; the other closed the pocket doors between the parlor and the foyer, likely stationing himself in the hall.

Grey didn't know if the clandestine actions were meant to impress them or if they were truly necessary, but, either way, he understood that his decision to become his brother had taken on a completely new meaning. He'd expected to slip into Zane's carefree lifestyle, go to parties, travel, and medicate his smarting ego with fine food and expensive wine.

Now he was responsible for securing and protecting the frickin' crown jewels of Venice.

So why didn't that bother him? Instead, he felt a surge of adrenaline unlike anything he'd experienced in years, even when tempting fate and discovery during his escapades with Lane.

Claudio opened the case and removed a worn leather portfolio stuffed with papers. Beneath it, cradled in dark sponge, glimmered an assortment of diamonds, sapphires, rubies, emeralds, opals, some elongated lapis lazuli, and a tiny vial filled with freshwater pearls—and a whole bunch of rare gems Grey couldn't begin to identify.

Reina silently gained permission to touch the gems by looking at Claudio with intense longing. Grey shifted in his chair, his sex stirred by the powerful desire shining in her obsidian eyes. He wouldn't mind her throwing that expression his way sometime soon, and not because he was holding some damned diamond.

She didn't reach for the diamond, but instead lifted a fiery orange stone nearly the size of her palm. She carelessly tossed aside the shade of a nearby lamp and held the facets to the bulb. Flames seemed to leap from the stone and dance on the skin.

"My God," Reina said.

"Exquisite, yes?" Claudio asked, easing up behind her. "Look at the facets. Il Gio cut each one himself."

Reina's breath had caught, but slowly, with a sensual hiss, she relaxed her lungs. "And the designs. You've brought them all?"

"Absolutely," Claudio said. "The originals are in the portfolio, though copies do exist in a bank vault in Italy. Still, I'm giving my life to you, Reina. My legacy."

She spun to face Claudio, and Grey watched blatant fear creep into her previously enamored expression. He didn't know all the details, but he didn't have to be an observant journalist to recognize that the value of this collection went well beyond the financial, for both Claudio and Reina.

"You should find another artist," Reina said, her voice rife with regret.

Claudio's smile was kind. "For this collection, there is no other artist."

Grey wondered about Claudio's logic, but filed those questions away for later. "Does anyone know the jewels are here?"

Reina shook her head. "I've told no one."

"No one at the studio?" Grey asked.

"Absolutely not," she insisted. "Judi and the artists whose work I show know that Claudio came to see me yesterday, but when he left, I told them all that I turned down his commission because of the security problems.''

''What about me?'' Grey asked. ''Why do they think I came to the studio today?''

Reina grinned. ''I may have mentioned that the plumbing in the upstairs bathroom had backed up.''

''And you, Claudio?'' For the moment, Grey trusted that no one at Reina's studio was suspicious, but he wondered how much time her lies had bought. ''Your associates out there undoubtedly know what they've brought.''

He shook his head. ''My associates are friends of a friend, a trusted acquaintance who has now repaid an old debt. They have no interest in my business here. I'm confident that as soon as they leave, I will be instantly forgotten.''

Grey nodded, assuming there was more to that story but believing Claudio's confidence. Fencing stolen jewelry was a specialized field of thievery and not every crime organization dabbled in it.

''When will they leave?'' Grey asked.

''As soon as your security is implemented.''

Grey retrieved his cell phone from his pocket. ''Then if you'll excuse me, I'll take care of the details. Reina?''

She'd knelt down on the floor, curling her legs beneath her as she traded the large orange-red stone for a handful of pearls she'd arranged in her palm. She glanced up, claimed to be fine, and then went back to her focused examination.

Her eyes had glittered with raw emotion: awe. Not the kind of awe that sprang from greed—he'd seen that look on lots of women's faces over the years. Her wonder sprang from reverence, the kind only a true artist would feel for their medium.

The kind a lover would express for the body of their mate.

Grey shook away the thought and retreated to the kitchen to call No Chances Protection, a security firm owned and operated by Brandon Chance, an old friend Grey knew he could trust. *Trust.* An interesting concept, Grey mused while he waited for the after-hours switchboard to transfer him to Brandon's cell phone.

So, Reina trusted his seemingly untrustworthy brother with her life. And, apparently, with Claudio's priceless jewels. With any other woman, he might have simply assumed she was a foolish twit blinded by his brother's charm into assigning him more credit than he deserved. With Reina, he couldn't easily dismiss her estimation of Zane's reliability. In the depths of those sensual black eyes, he sensed a wisdom beyond her years, an air of experience only slightly tinged with jade. He had seen the way she'd watched Claudio, had sensed that she'd scrutinized him while Grey had been questioning di Amante about Reina's safety. She took the time to see things, listen to details others didn't bother with.

And now Grey realized he hadn't ever really bothered to know his brother very well. He loved Zane unconditionally, but since they'd spent the better part of their lives trying to prove to the world how different the identical Masterson twins truly were, he'd missed the opportunity to truly become close to his brother. And vice versa.

"Brandon Chance," the voice on the other end announced.

"Brandon, Zane Masterson. How's it going?"

"Zane? I've been expecting a call from your brother. Is this about the newspaper?"

Grey flinched. Maybe, before now, he should have called his old friend Brandon, a former Army hotshot now scoring big in the game of personal protection, but he hadn't felt personally at risk, so he'd put that plan on hold. He had assumed he could handle the mishaps and mysteries plaguing the paper's operation on his own. By the time things got out of control, he'd decided to bring Zane into the mix instead. He'd wanted escape more than anything else. Only a switch with his brother could give him that.

A switch he intended to keep secret from everyone, even an old buddy.

"Newspaper? Nah, that's Grey's territory," he said, reminding himself to mimic Zane's easygoing voice. "I've got a tenant, Garden District, who needs security in her house. Top of the line. Installed tonight."

Grey heard Brandon shift his phone. "Give me the specs and the address. I can be there in an hour."

REINA LEANED HEAVILY against the front door, her forehead hot against the cool stained glass, her heartbeat regulating with arduous slowness. She wasn't sure if Claudio's departure had made her feel better or worse. She had the jewels. Representatives from the local Cosa Nostra remained outside her house, protecting her and the precious gems until Zane and his friend took over. But she was also alone with Zane in the house, yet again experiencing the sharp edge of her heightened libido.

She pushed away from the door, clutching the small, handwritten diary Claudio had swiftly and secretly given her after Zane had left the room.

"This is for you alone," he'd whispered, retrieving a book from a hiding place beneath the sponge that had cradled the stones.

The creased leather-and-gold-leaf pages had felt heavy in her hands. The dire expression in his eyes intensified the weight.

"This belonged to my mother," he explained. "Years ago, when she was a young woman, she found a companion to il Gioielliere's diaries. Hidden in the family home, apparently forgotten. To help her learn English, she translated them herself. What she discovered changed her life.''

Reina had flipped open the first page, lovingly penned in crisp cursive: *Memoirs of Viviana Bazardi.*

Her breath instantly caught and she reverently turned the pages, spying words that increased her curiosity. Words like *passion, insatiable, hungry with desire.* Viviana Bazardi had been the mistress for whom il Gioielliere had created his priceless, sensual collection. The woman millions of readers across the country intimately knew through the words of her once-clandestine lover.

Now Reina held Viviana's most intimate secrets and impressions and wondered how her confessions could change a woman's life. She eagerly flipped to a page in the center.

I learned his length. Memorized his thickness. His heat. If any other man came into my bed, even if I were blindfolded, I would know my Gianni, my Gioielliere, the moment his shaft pressed against my thigh. For an entire year, he denied my yearning to feel him inside me. But tonight, I received my deepest wish and my body still...

''He's gone?''

Reina jumped at Zane's voice but knew better than to try to conceal the book. Instead, she let her hand drop casually to her side. While she indeed trusted Zane with her life, she didn't want to tell him about the diary just yet. Zane would be the type to want to read it with her, and frankly, she didn't think her body could survive the sensual overload. Even now, she was having a hard time concentrating with him standing so near.

"Claudio?" she asked. "Yes, he just left. He knows I'm anxious to get to work."

Zane peered outside, brushing aside her decorative sheers. "The security won't be in place for a few hours, though it looks like Rocco and Guido are still on the job." He turned, leaning casually against the window. "I don't think its wise to have the stones in plain sight when Brandon arrives."

"Don't you trust your friend?"

"Brandon? Definitely. But I'd rather keep all this on the q.t. As I see it, we have two problems to solve. First and foremost, protect the jewels. Second, find out who was behind the robberies at the gallery."

And third, Reina thought, *figure out why I suddenly find you so incredibly alluring, Zane Masterson.*

Reina pressed her lips together, certain she couldn't admit such a strange turn. Not that Zane would be surprised that yet another woman considered him desirable. The minute they appeared together at any party, opening or event, she heard the envious whispers erupting around her. She'd been waylaid in more ladies' rooms than she cared to count, besieged by women begging for confirmation of Zane's sexual appetites. She'd seen him, with a sly wink or a tender touch, turn seemingly confident, self-sufficient women into quivering bowls of jelly. Up until this afternoon, she'd considered herself immune.

She remembered the first time she'd met Zane—or, rather, the first time she'd seen him. At a party, though she couldn't remember the host or the occasion. She'd noticed him the minute he'd walked into the room, late, because he'd caused a stir of excitement unmatched by any other guest—as if everyone, men included, expected to have a great time now that Zane had arrived. Reina, proficient in the art of people watching, had immediately sought a private vantage point. From a perch at the top of a staircase, she'd witnessed his seamless movement around the room, gauged his interest in his companions by the subtle turn of his smile, and learned to read his body language. Hands in pockets? He liked the person he was with. Crossed arms? Bored. Left hand through the hair? Antsy to move along.

By the time he'd finally worked his way to her, she had his number. And Zane, being an apt people watcher himself, had read her knowledge right away. He'd turned down the charm and had become a friend. They'd even dated once or twice, but quickly concluded that what they had gained in friendship, they paid for in sexual chemistry. She admired Zane, trusted him, believed him to be a true catch for any woman who could break down the walls of his playboy nature. But she hadn't once fantasized about him or desired to feel his hand brush against her or longed to taste his mouth in a long, wet kiss.

Until today, that is.

She slipped around him and returned to the parlor, where she replaced the book in the case and latched it shut.

"Why do we have to worry about the gallery?" Reina asked. "I plan to work on this collection from home. Judi can handle the day-to-day operations and I can go in occasionally to take care of anything more complex."

"Don't you think your staff or your artists will get suspicious if you suddenly don't show up every day like you usually do?"

She'd considered that situation last night on her way home from the reopening of Club Carnal, before she'd indulged in the night of self-pleasure she'd hoped would wear the edge off her sexual tension. Maybe she'd done the opposite. Maybe she'd primed her body for intimacy rather than alleviating her needs completely.

"Reina?"

She shook her head, determined to conceal her edginess from Zane and keep to the subject at hand. She had no foolproof solution, but had come up with something that could at least buy her time. "I'll tell them I'm working on a deal to improve the security of the studio. They'll assume I'm looking for an investor."

Zane nodded, visibly impressed. "That should work. For a little while. Hiding from your colleagues may give you time to finish Claudio's collection, but what about afterward? You realize that all of the evidence points to an inside job."

God, Reina didn't want to think about this. Then again, contemplating such betrayal knocked her errant erotic thoughts into submission. "Of course. The police have taken great delight in insisting on that scenario."

"Don't you believe them?"

She sighed. She didn't know what to believe. The facts as presented by the police did indeed point to a perpetrator who had knowledge of details such as the original combination on her safe, the location of the security cameras and the presence of the expensive jewels. Reina often worked with estate pieces, but once the creations were complete, she turned them over to the owners without delay. In both robberies, the stones had been stolen almost immediately after they'd been delivered and before she'd crafted them into one of her signature pieces.

"If I didn't believe them, I wouldn't have asked for your help, Zane. I know I need to root out who has betrayed me. Everyone took lie detector tests, did I tell you?"

Zane shook his head.

"Everyone passed. So either no one at the gallery is guilty, or they are all better liars than I am. Either way, I can't concentrate on investigating further until this collection is reconstructed and delivered back into Claudio's possession. And as soon as your friend has the security system up and running, you won't have to stay here if you don't want to.''

"Who says I don't want to?"

Something in Zane's voice, something sultry—something hot—cautioned Reina not to look at him. She ignored the warning and glanced in his direction, surprised to see such wanting in his gaze when he was looking at her—his friend.

God, no wonder women melted at his feet. One spark of desire in his crystal-blue eyes injected her body with a quick flash of need. Unfulfilled passion stirred inside her, thrumming through her veins, stealing the steady cadence of her breath.

She cleared her throat, hoping to hide herself behind her usual aloof persona, the one she'd never felt the need to use with Zane. Until tonight. "I just assumed you had someone waiting for you at a party…or in some bedroom.''

Mistake. Her gaze darted toward the stairs, where her own boudoir awaited. A flash of a fantasy streaked through her mind. Soft Egyptian cotton entangled around her naked thighs, revealing her bare breasts, which were wet and puckered from Zane's skilled mouth.

"No bedroom awaits me tonight, Reina," he claimed, though his eyes betrayed a quick glance in the same direction as hers, complete with an equal amount of wanting. "Except, of course, yours."

4

HE WATCHED, WAITED FOR her reaction, any reaction. Her lips, wet from a swipe of her tongue moments before, remained still. Eyes wide with strength and confidence hardly blinked. Grey cursed himself for not knowing more about his brother's affairs, though he figured a mainframe computer couldn't keep all his brother's dalliances straight. But had Zane seduced the alluring Reina Price? Had she seduced him? Should he initiate a repeat performance?

Finally Reina grinned. "Save your flirtation, Zane. When are you going to learn that you have no effect on me?"

Her words shouted her indifference, but the claim remained contradicted by the flush on her neck. He'd seen her employ her unattainable seductress persona on Claudio, had wondered about its origin, its purpose. But he certainly hadn't wanted her to draw that cloak around herself when only he was around.

He blocked her escape route, stepping completely into her personal space, and touched one finger to a blotch of red at the base of her throat.

"The lesson will be more convincing when you don't get all flushed at the thought of making love with me."

Her lips curled into a sweet smirk. "Maybe I'm just coming down with something."

"Maybe you just want to come."

Her eyes flashed wider, but if she intended to respond, he saw no indication in her dark irises. She leaned down and grabbed the metal suitcase, swinging it just so he had to jump back or risk damaging his family jewels with jewels both harder and heavier, despite his growing erection.

"I have all I need for that right here in this case. And upstairs in the pink box I keep under my bed. You'll have to find your own means for satisfaction, I'm afraid." She sashayed past, a full-fledged grin on her lips. "Call me when Brandon arrives. Oh, and order dinner. I'm starved."

She disappeared up the stairs, the sound of her light laughter growing fainter until silenced by the slam of a door.

Good Lord, she thought he was teasing.

Desperate to know where things stood between Reina and his brother, Grey pulled out his cell phone, but he stopped before dialing Zane's number. Or rather, his number. Did he want his brother to know that he was toying with the idea of seducing his tenant, a woman who had obviously been friendly enough with his twin to tell him about the mysterious pink box she kept beneath her bed?

What was he thinking, anyway, playing with such a hot fire? Hadn't Grey fulfilled all of his thirst for sexual adventure with Lane, only to have his secrets revealed to anyone and everyone with a basic mastery of the English language and twenty-four ninety-five plus tax?

Apparently not, he decided, judging by the intensity of his hard-on.

Grey hit the menu key on Zane's phone, not surprised to find a long list of restaurant phone numbers programmed in. He found one he liked, ordered a quart of rich chicken-andouille gumbo, a loaf of their signature bread and a cheesecake. He delighted in ordering the dairy confection, mindful of how Lane's lactose-free diet had kept him from indulging. Reina, though slim around the waist and stomach, didn't strike him as a woman afraid to luxuriate in anything sensual, culinary or otherwise.

And once assured she and the jewels would be safe in the house, he intended to find out, in every sense, if his assumption was correct.

Brandon Chance arrived when he promised, cased the house and mapped out an installation plan on a piece of paper in the kitchen. From a large van parked behind Reina's house, he and his partner, his sister-in-law, Samantha, produced a wide range of electronic devices Grey couldn't begin to understand.

He did, however, catch an uneasy vibe between him and his old friend. As soon as Reina came downstairs and assured him she would be fine while he went back to his apartment for a change of clothes, Grey excused himself. Brandon, however, caught him just as he was backing Zane's Jag out of the small garage.

"Okay, Grey. What's this game you're playing?"

He groaned, not bothering to argue with a man who'd known him since they played Little League together in the third grade. "No game, Brandon. Just a break. It's not the first time Zane and I have switched places."

Brandon laughed. "No, I distinctly remember the time you did it in, oh, God, the eighth grade? You conveniently forgot to inform Zane that you had an oral test in history."

"Zane hated history more than I did. He never would have switched that day if I'd told him."

"You flunked because of him."

Grey shrugged. "Yeah, well, it lowered the bar for the rest of the year, didn't it? Sister Catherine thought herself the best teacher in the entire school when she coaxed her poorest student to an A by exam time.''

''Must be nice to have a twin brother to handle all your failures. Is that why he's running the newspaper? So if the problems make the business dive, it'll be Zane's fault?''

Grey didn't want to have this conversation. Besides, Zane could take care of the problems at the newspaper. He had Masterson blood, Masterson genes, a degree in journalism and a high IQ. Not to mention an endless supply of easygoing patience, which Grey, as far as he knew, had never had.

''Since when did you get so insightful?'' Grey asked, not hiding his annoyance.

Brandon grinned like a schoolboy on the last day of class. ''Marriage does that to you, particularly when you wed a woman who makes a living exploring emotions and soothing feelings.''

Grey's eyebrows shot up. The man was whipped. He'd just described his wife as if she were a psychologist, when, in truth, she ran a spa in the French Quarter that specialized in aromatherapy.

''I think you've been sniffing Serena's funny flowers a little more than you should,'' Grey quipped.

''And I think you haven't been sniffing enough flowers, funny or otherwise. Look, if you want a vacation to stop and smell the roses for a while, that's cool. But this business with Reina's break-ins, it's serious. She could get hurt. So could you.''

''You know about that?''

Brandon shoved his hands into the pockets of his jeans. ''Pilar Price is one of Serena's best clients. Yeah, I know about it. I offered to help, but Reina didn't have the cash to pay for my services and refused a line of credit. Pilar even volunteered to bankroll the security, but Reina refused. She really wanted to handle this on her own. The fact that she asked you—"

"Asked Zane," Grey corrected.

"Whatever. The fact that she asked at all means she must be fairly desperate. I don't really know her. She seems like a nice woman, but..."

"You're not going to warn me from hurting her, are you?"

Brandon braced his hands on the car door. "Actually, no, smart ass. Reina has a reputation as a real cool operator. Her mother is a full-fledged femme fatale, with baubles in her strongbox from senators and statesmen. I heard about Lane's book, Grey. I was going to warn *you* from getting hurt."

Grey swore, put the car into reverse and backed down the driveway, careful not to hit Brandon's van even though his fist itched to punch his face. He knew his friend meant well, but since when did he need protection from women?

He tilted his head out the window. "You just worry about the house, Brandon. If someone so much as leans on her back gate, I want to know about it. Otherwise, I'll be back in an hour."

Brandon waved, his smile crooked. "I'll be here. I'll probably be here all night."

Grey threw the car into gear and tore off down the cobbled road, turning in time to wave at Rocco and Guido, parked in a dark sedan at the end of the block. By the time he crossed onto St. Charles Street, he'd beaten his anger back into mere annoyance. He couldn't blame Brandon for offering unsolicited advice. They'd been pals a long time. And he couldn't blame his buddy for mentioning Lane's book. He figured even Brandon had probably read it. Why wouldn't he? Everyone else had. Everyone else in the frickin' free world knew that Grey Masterson, newspaper titan and seemingly serious businessman, possessed a taste for sexual adventures.

Just like every other guy he knew. He also figured that every other guy he knew, with the exception maybe of the newly married and clearly smitten Brandon, wanted to screw Lane Morrow. He'd been the one to do it. Dozens of times.

And he'd paid the price with his privacy, privacy he could only regain by becoming his brother.

He wove through the darkened New Orleans streets on his way to Zane's apartment, wondering what Reina would do if she discovered which Masterson brother she harbored in her home. Despite Brandon's suggestion that she might be as cool a user as her mother, Grey now knew the secret face of a woman with a hardened heart. Reina didn't have that look. But Lane had. Hungry for power, starving for recognition, desperate to see her name in every medium from television to newspapers to magazines and Web sites. She'd betrayed her lover to reach her goal. She'd betrayed herself.

Reina, on the other hand, wore her innate sensuality like a cloak—fashioned in silk and lined with mink. He could see where lesser men would be intimidated by her blatant sexiness, her aristocratic eroticism. He could also see where his brother would build a friendship with someone like her—someone indifferent to his often outlandish but effective charm. Someone who could put him in his place.

He hit the blinker and turned into the parking garage of his brother's exclusive condominium. He didn't know his twin as well as he should, yet he'd agreed to jump into Zane's life and take on his responsibilities. But he'd been desperate and foolishly assumed whatever was on Zane's plate could be handled in a span of five minutes. The upside was he hadn't worried about the newspaper all day, not even after Shelby's comment about sand in gas tanks or Brandon's reference to the problems that could indeed topple the newspaper empire started by his family generations ago. But would Zane be able to handle it?

His twin had clearly earned Reina's trust, something Grey guessed to be no easy feat. Yeah, he could handle the newspaper.

Grey, on the other hand, had a more interesting challenge. He had his experience as a journalist, freedom to roam at will—courtesy of Zane—and an arsenal of sexual knowledge he'd wanted to lock away after Lane's betrayal.

But not anymore.

Grey not only intended to solve the mystery of the robberies at Reina Price's gallery and protect the di Amante collection, he intended to break the code of secrets behind Reina's obsidian eyes—and discover if the sensuality she portrayed on the outside ran as deep as he suspected.

"THAT OUGHT TO DO IT," Brandon announced, carefully maneuvering his large body back through Reina's bedroom window without bumping his head on the frame. He clipped the last wire, camouflaged it with wood-grain caulk, then lowered and locked the window.

"You're done?" Reina closed the magazine she'd been pretending to read and sat back against the European shams on her bed, the stiff metal suitcase hidden behind them. She knew Brandon Chance through her mother, and believed him to be honest and honorable, but she wasn't taking any risks with Claudio's legacy. The fewer people who knew about the presence of the jewels in her house, the better.

"Done in here," Brandon said. "I've got two more bedroom windows to wire and then I'm going to set up the monitors in the guest room across the hall—unless you want them with you?"

Reina skewed her lips, scanning the bedroom she'd carefully decorated for her ultimate comfort and relaxation. At the end of a long day, the walls—her favorite shade of amber silk—wrapped her in warmth. The artwork, erotic pieces she'd collected over the years, soothed her mind with images of desire. Simple. Sensual. Dried flowers and candles scented the air with antiquity. In this room, she escaped into another world. The last thing she wanted to disrupt her fantasy was video monitors and flashing, beeping technology.

"Across the hall is perfect."

Brandon nodded and slipped a screwdriver into his tool belt. "Sam's almost done downstairs and with the back gate. Oh, the delivery guy came with your dinner. I had him put it in the kitchen."

Reina reached across her bed for her purse. "Thank you. What do I—?"

Brandon waved his hand and winked. "I put it on Zane's bill. I'm sorry this is taking so long, but he insisted we be thorough."

Reina tossed her purse aside. "Thorough is good. I appreciate you working so late into the night. Doesn't your wife mind you being out until all hours?"

Brandon swaggered toward the door. "I make it worth her while when I get home." He winked again, then left and closed the door behind him.

She just bet he would. Reina couldn't remember the last time she'd been so besieged by sexy men. First Claudio, then Zane and now Brandon. What woman could possibly resist a handsome hunk laden with hardware, tools he apparently knew how to use? Reina bit back an appreciative sigh. His wife was one lucky woman.

As lucky as Reina was aroused. Well, there was nothing she could do about her aroused state with strangers in the house. And her edgy, sexually charged condition would only worsen, she knew, once she sneaked Viviana's diary back out from where she'd hidden it beneath her comforter. She'd read the first entries while Brandon worked downstairs, amazed at the mistress's blatant honesty and natural use of modern language, then remembered the translation had been colored by the translator, Claudio's mother. Apparently, both women cherished the emotional side of sexuality, rather than just valuing the power of it.

Sex is power. Reina couldn't remember the precise age she'd been when her mother first presented her with that aphorism, but she'd been young. Definitely prior to puberty and long before her first sexual experience. She could still remember how easily she could enthrall the boys who'd visited her all-girl private school for soirees and sporting events. One short, swaying walk would win her a group of admirers. One wink, the hint of a kiss, and she had more invitations to the upcoming ball than any other girl in her dormitory.

The trick was to keep the mystery going and never quite give her latest beau all he was after. Pilar had taught her that trick as well.

Sex had garnered her mother great wealth and influence. Even the promise of sex—a promise never fulfilled—had proved valuable to Pilar. She'd been born in a poor region of Spain, taught herself several languages and honed her acting skills by inventing stories for the tourists. Then she'd run off with the first man who promised her stardom.

According to Pilar, the man hadn't planned on fulfilling his pledge, but in the end, he had. She'd seduced him, enslaved him, twisted him around her finger until he introduced her to a legitimate producer in Madrid. She'd been no more than fifteen. Once he'd given her what she wanted, she'd tossed the man aside. A real Lolita, her mother. Reina had heard this story more times than most children heard tales of princesses asleep in castles or guileless girls breaking into a house full of bears.

Now Reina had a different tale to read. One about true love, true obsession. True submission to the power of a man.

Luckily Reina had already read il Gio's diary and knew the depth of his love for Viviana. She knew him to be a man Viviana could trust, completely, even if he couldn't give her the one gift she wanted most—marriage. Legitimacy. Reina tossed the magazine aside and retrieved the diary, anxious to read more of the story before she started work on the jewels tomorrow.

She'd read less than a line when she heard Zane's voice echo up the staircase. "Reina?"

She swore, then hid the diary.

"I'm here," she called, poking her head through the doorway.

"I know, but dinner's down here."

Zane marched up the staircase, the atmosphere in the cramped hallway altering the minute he came into view. He really was incredibly gorgeous, Reina thought. Deepset, thoughtful blue eyes. Soft, wavy hair, a little shorter than he normally wore it but still begging to be combed by a woman's fingers. And his smile. Always tilted to that one angle that made her wonder exactly what he found so amusing.

Only Zane's smile didn't seem too lopsided tonight. His grin held a tinge of something Reina might best describe as tentative. Wary, even.

A shiver shot up her spine, but she didn't know if the reaction resulted from the difference in Zane's expression or the fact that he'd fully entered her personal space, his shoulder pressed against her doorjamb, his face inches from hers.

"Aren't you hungry?"

He poured a generous ounce of sexual innuendo into his question, snapping Reina back into her protective persona. She licked her lips, then stepped back to blatantly check him out.

"Starved, actually."

He slipped his hand around hers. "Come with me, then."

"I don't want to leave my—" she paused, eyeing Brandon at work across the hall "—treasures unguarded."

Zane lobbed his own appreciative glance down her torso. "No, we can't have that." He nodded toward her bedroom. "If you'll allow me, I can show you how we can alleviate your problem."

Reina bit the inside of her mouth to keep from grinning. This flirtation thing could be a lot of fun, particularly since she knew he was only toying with her because he could. She did know that, right? She used to know that. She and Zane had played attentive lovers at parties on several occasions, mainly to amuse their crowd and keep matchmaking friends from attempting a fix-up. Their feigned sexual attraction had always been a private joke between them.

Right?

Zane pulled her inside and quietly closed the door. He looked around the room, nodding but saying nothing.

"What?" she asked.

He cleared his throat. "I'm just trying to remember what the room looked like before you redecorated."

Reina had to think herself. Redecorating the bedroom had been her first project. "The walls were chintz. Roses, I think."

Zane nodded. "Yes, *Grand-mère* did love florals. Do you remember where the bed was?"

Reina closed her eyes. She knew she'd moved the bed, having immediately thought Zane's great-grandmother had it in a strange place, partially blocking a window. "Over there."

Zane followed Reina's instructions to the window Brandon had just wired, then walked five paces toward the wall. About halfway down, he tapped the wall with his fist. The sound was hard and thick. He adjusted an inch and knocked again. This time, the sound echoed.

Instantly, with a mechanical grunt, a panel of the wall slipped aside.

"Wha—?"

Zane grinned. "Apparently, I never told you about some of the special features of this old house."

Reina scurried to the opening, stepping back when a ripe, musty smell assailed her. She grabbed a large lit scented candle and thrust it into the narrow opening. The flame flickered, but remained steady as fresh air seeped inside. The room, a closet really, barely had enough space for anyone to stand fully upright.

"Extra storage space?" she asked.

Zane took the candle. "Not quite."

He leaned into the darkness and tapped the inner wall.

Another panel slid aside. Stale air crept out, tickling her nostrils so that she nearly sneezed.

"Another room?" Reina guessed, grabbing a tissue from the box on her dresser.

"There are several," Zane told her. "Most of them are on the bottom floor, but this floor and the attic each have one and a passageway leading to the others. *Grand-mère* claimed they were used by the Underground Railroad to hide escaped slaves until they could be smuggled out on Yankee ships. My brother and I used to play one wicked game of hide-and-seek in this house."

"Who else knows about these rooms?" Reina retrieved the candle from him and ventured inside. In Europe, she'd always been fascinated by the castles and ancient architecture and, as a child, had been notorious for slipping away from the docent to explore on her own. New Orleans, with all its dark and devious history, held a similar appeal. She hadn't had much time to delve into the city's many mysteries since she'd moved to the area, and never would have guessed she had something so interesting in her own house.

"My brother, of course. My father, probably, though I'd bet he's long forgotten. His mother didn't get on well with *Grand-mère*. He didn't spend a lot of time here in his youth."

She stepped across something sticky and silky, and swiped the web away. "You think it's safe to hide the jewels here?"

"I think it's safe enough for you to work in here. You can't tell now, but during the day, this particular room has good light from a skylight hidden by the eaves."

"It'll be hot," she said.

"Isn't it always when you're working?" Zane chuckled and Reina wished she hadn't chosen that exact phrasing.

"I can rig a cooling unit. There's an old one in the garage that might still work."

Reina thrust her hand into the darkness, allowing the candle to throw uncertain light on the interior room, empty except for a few old crates and decades worth of dust. She'd have some serious cleaning to do before she could set up shop, but if Zane helped, she could begin work on the collection by tomorrow afternoon. She nodded, silently agreeing that the room would work. She hadn't liked the idea of having to lock up the jewels each time she left her studio, maybe just to run to the bathroom or to grab something to drink. Now, with Zane in the house, the secret room, and Brandon's security system protecting the perimeter, she felt confident she could work without fear.

She eased back out of the tight space, startled when Zane blocked her retreat into her bedroom. The candlelight flickered as she pulled up short just a few inches from Zane's chest.

"Perfect, don't you agree?" he asked.

She glanced over her shoulder into the darkness. "Should have enough space, and if the light is what you promise..."

"I always fulfill my promises."

Reina gulped in the musty air, the taste bitter and dry. What was up with Zane, anyway? He was pouring it on a little thick, even for him. Or maybe he always flirted like this and, under normal circumstances, she rebuffed him without a second thought. That was, to some extent, a game they played—though usually not in private. Alone, Reina and Zane established a safe zone, a reserve where each of them could exist without having to worry about what the other might be thinking, might be wanting. Still, with Reina growing increasingly bored with the endless party scene, she couldn't remember the last time they'd been together. And something in their established dynamic had definitely changed.

"You don't usually make promises, Zane."

For a moment, his expression faltered. His ultimate Zane cockiness dropped away and a flash of uncertainty sped through his eyes before he blew out the candle, dousing them in darkness. He folded his large body out of the secret passage and back into her bedroom.

"No promises. A fine way to keep from ever disappointing anyone."

He took her hand and helped her out, but released her fingers the minute she stepped clear. Reina noted his silence, wondering how he could support his theory about making no promises when he had so many broken hearts littering the path of his love life.

She shook her head. "Is that your secret?"

"I don't have any secrets," he said, his gaze focused somewhere, anywhere, other than directly on hers. "Not any good ones, anyway."

Reina retrieved the metal briefcase, which he slid into the passage before knocking the wall and closing the panel. She waited right next to him, demanding his attention by not moving out of his personal space, just as he'd done to her a moment ago. "I don't know. These secret rooms are pretty handy."

"I'm nothing if not handy."

Reina blew out a contemplative whistle, but didn't say another word until she'd crossed the room and opened the door into the hall. She spared a glance at the lump in her comforter, the hiding place of Viviana's diary, then at the space beneath her bed where she stored her collection of sex toys and pleasure aids. She couldn't remember the last time she'd used any of the ones intended for couples, nor could she remember ever doubting that satisfying herself would relieve her sexual anxiety.

After reading il Gio's diary last night, she'd indulged in an hour's worth of self-induced pleasure, starting with a long hot bath and ending with a rather intense orgasm. But now, with the combined thrill of embarking on a new project and confronting Zane's suddenly potent masculine charm, she was convinced that some steamy water and even a dildo weren't going to put a dent in squelching her libido tonight.

No, for that, she'd need a flesh-and-blood man.

Zane seemed interested, even if he never had before. And he wouldn't want anything she wouldn't willingly give—like commitment, promises and glimpses into the secrets of her heart. In fact, if ever a man existed who could share sexual gratification with her and still retain their special friendship, Zane was that man.

"Handy, huh? We'll just see about that over the next few days, won't we?"

5

WITH A BONE-CRUNCHING STRETCH, Grey glanced at the clock on the stand beside his untouched bed. Three in the morning. Brandon had left less than twenty minutes ago, task completed. The house on First Street was now the most secure in the entire Garden District. So that Reina could go to bed, Grey had been completely trained on the operation of the security system, and had promised to show Reina in the morning how to work it.

Only she wasn't asleep. A thin gleam of light reached out from beneath her door. Every so often, amid the settling sounds of the old house and the light hum of the video monitors, he heard the distinct whisper of her body shifting on the sheets, the twang of her bedsprings, the creak of the headboard that had been in that bedroom for over one hundred years.

Not only was she not sleeping, she was restless.

And, heaven help him, so was he.

Combing his hand through his hair, still damp from his shower, he secured the drawstring on his pajama pants and shrugged into his T-shirt. Maybe she couldn't sleep because she was worried about the jewels. He was honor-bound, of course, to alleviate her fears, right? Maybe the dinner he ordered hadn't agreed with her...but he doubted that.

They'd lingered over their meal, enjoying the food and each other's company. He'd entertained her by recounting his and Zane's childhood adventures in the old house, having already learned that Zane hadn't told her much himself. Grey had been very careful not to assign all the blame for their subsequent punishments on his brother, since he was supposed to be him. As a result, he'd gained an interesting perspective.

Maybe Zane really hadn't been to blame for all their mischief. Grey wondered precisely when it had become so easy to categorize his brother as "the bad twin," but figured the habit formed so early in their childhood, neither one of them could have done anything but live up to the expectations set by the adults around them.

But now? Now Grey knew he was every bit as risk loving and adventure-seeking as his brother. He just preferred his exploits to remain private. As they could now, here, in Reina's house. In her bedroom.

He rapped on her door. "Reina?"

"Come in," she answered, her voice lethargic, sultry.

Turning the knob, he took a deep breath, expecting to find her curled beneath her covers. Instead, she sat propped against a collection of pillows, her face scrubbed free of makeup, her hair loosely clipped atop her head and her body swathed in long, silky black pajamas.

"Can't sleep?" he asked.

Her smile barely curved her lips, but lit her eyes nonetheless. "Oh, I could sleep, I think. I haven't tried yet. Brandon left?"

He nodded. "We're safe and sound."

When she turned toward the table beside her bed, she slipped a small book beneath the covers. "Brandy?" she asked, indicating the decanter and snifter beneath her lamp.

"Sure."

He accepted the glass, then glanced around the room

for somewhere to sit. While an overstuffed chaise and a striped wing chair were available, he preferred something closer. He slid onto the edge of her bed and propped himself against one of the tall posts, grinning when she didn't seem to mind.

"What are you reading?" he asked.

She pursed her lips, forcing Grey to realize that the pout he'd been admiring all day wasn't a result of her carefully applied lipstick. Her bottom lip possessed a natural curve that immediately drew his attention, instantaneously sparking his desire to kiss her.

"A diary."

Grey sipped his brandy. The liquor, incredibly smooth and undoubtedly expensive, warmed and relaxed him. "The one by the jeweler?"

She hesitated, swiping her tongue over her teeth, then reached across the pillows to fill another glass for herself. "Not exactly." Swirling the bronze liquid, she inhaled, watching him from over the rim.

He smiled. "Reina has a secret."

"Unlike Zane, Reina has a lot of secrets," she answered.

"Tell me one."

She took a drink, then stretched her leg from beneath her. Grey supposed that, by design, her nightwear would be considered tame. Long pants, long sleeves, satin buttons. Styled like men's pajamas but, on her, decidedly feminine. Her ample breasts curved enticingly beneath the silk, and the black color couldn't disguise the points of her nipples any more than it could hide the sleek shape of her thighs.

"Just one?"

"For starters," he replied.

Her gaze darted aside and she squirmed a bit. Grey

sensed a tension in her body, in her motions, that seemed totally out of character. He already knew Reina dropped her guard with his brother, altering the aloof seductress persona she presented to men like Claudio and customers in her gallery to a more natural sensuality—one she couldn't rein in so readily. Still, if he didn't know better, he'd guess his presence—Zane's presence—now made her uncomfortable.

And aroused. Or was he just indulging in a little wishful thinking?

She slipped her glass onto the table and retrieved the diary from under the covers.

"This was written by the jeweler's mistress."

She handed him the book. The leather cover had hardly a nick or crease. The pages were yellowed and the ink slightly faded, but even his untrained eye determined the diary hadn't been written in the sixteenth century. "It doesn't look that old."

"It's not. This is a translation of her diary, probably written, I don't know, fifty, sixty years ago. Claudio's mother did it, supposedly to improve her English. I've been reading for a few hours. The woman did a very good job."

He flipped through the pages, wishing he had his glasses. He'd used them several times tonight, when Reina wasn't around. But Zane had had surgery to correct his farsightedness, so Grey couldn't very well retrieve his glasses now, could he?

"Read some to me."

She snatched the book from his hands. "I don't think so."

"Why not?"

"It's very…revealing."

He took another sip of brandy. "I can see that." Even

without his glasses and with the light relatively dim, he saw the flush of pink across her skin. "You mean *erotic,* don't you?"

She only nodded. "Have you read *Il Gioielliere's Diaries?*"

He shook his head.

"Well, everyone's been calling the man's recount of his trysts with his mistress the new *Kama Sutra.* He kept copious notes on the best ways to pleasure his woman, not to mention several interesting ways to pleasure a man. But, Viviana's recollections..." She held up the book. "Truly incendiary."

He now understood Reina's physical antsiness. She *was* aroused. Unfortunately, not by him. At least, not yet.

"Read me something."

She licked her lips again. Her quick glance at the memoir betrayed her temptation.

"You sure?"

She meant more than she said. Had Zane been the one to end their former relationship? Had Zane been the one to insist they keep their interactions platonic? That wasn't unlikely. Stupid, but not unlikely. If the relationship he'd had with Reina had gotten too deep, too serious, Zane would have found a way to end things. Actually, so far as Grey knew, Zane had never had one interaction with a woman that could actually be called a *relationship.* Grey had relationships. Zane had flings.

And tonight, and for at least the next couple of days, he was Zane. "Absolutely," he said.

After only a second more of hesitation, Reina retrieved the book and flipped through until she found the page she sought.

"This is the first time he came to her. The man had style. Patience and style." She moistened her lips with a slow, stiff tongue, then settled back into the cushions before she began to read.

"Il Gio visited me today. He brought money for my necklace, and he was generous, paying more than the bauble was worth. He also brought me a gift—a very long, thin gold chain with beautiful soft links and a heavy charm on the end shaped like a lock. I thought he was only being kind, maybe even sorry that I had to sell my fine jewels to pay my taxes, but he claimed the metal would help keep me cool during the summer night. He said I should wind the chains around my neck and keep the lock near my heart.

"The light of a secret danced in his eyes. I couldn't resist him. I dressed lightly for bed, only a camisole and his chain. I kept the doors to my balcony open, wishing for a breeze. None came. But he did.

"I don't know when I awoke or when I realized he stood beside me. I didn't open my eyes. But I knew it was him. He whispered my name. Insisted he was not really there, only an apparition conjured from my own desires.

"The sheets were tangled around my thighs. He tugged them free. I wore nothing beneath my camisole. I knew the moon was high. He could see me. All of me. Without touching me, he removed the laces. He whispered to me. How beautiful I was. How much he wanted me. But like a priceless diamond, he couldn't yet afford me. If I would, if I agreed, he would buy my love with pleasure.

"Pleasure? I laughed. I admitted to him that I'd read stories, heard tales, but I didn't know the pleasure of love firsthand. He told me my pleasure would

*be his greatest creation, if only I promised to keep
my eyes closed. I did. I could still see his image in
my mind, his dark skin and bright blue eyes...''*

Reina faltered, cleared her throat, and reached across to
the table for another sip of brandy. A moment elapsed
before Grey realized that the description of the man she
read about fit him as well.

"So," Grey asked, breaking the silence. "How did they
know each other?"

Reina smiled. "She was a young widow, considered
incredibly beautiful, but because her husband left her with
no dowry and a load of debt, no man would marry her.
She had no family. She sold il Gio her jewelry just to
keep a roof over her head."

"Why didn't he marry her, I mean...if he was so interested?"

"He was already married."

"But he didn't love his wife?"

Reina shook her head. "An arranged marriage to a cold
woman. According to *his* diary, when he tried to awaken
his wife's sexual appetites, she ran off to a nunnery and
prayed for his soul for over a year. She returned and forbade him to ever enter her bedroom again, unless he
wanted more children. They already had three sons."

"So, apparently, they'd already had sex."

She pulled a copy of il Gio's bestselling diary off her
night table and tossed it toward him. "It's all in the first
few chapters. Yes, he'd made love to his wife, but the
experience was hardly memorable. Some people just
aren't compatible, I guess. From what I've read, she encouraged him to take a mistress. At first."

Grey flipped through the pages, but then put the book
down. Not only could he not read very much without his

glasses, he'd rather Reina narrated, if for no other reason than to hear her voice. Soft and sultry, the timbre possessed a natural music, highlighted with hints of a European accent. Rounded vowels and clipped consonants. And even though they were alone in the house, she spoke in a whisper just as she had during dinner, as if she wanted him to have to lean forward, scoot closer, to hear everything she said.

"Things changed?"

"His mistress became his obsession. His business suffered for a little while, since all his creations were for Viviana and were not for sale. But soon, there were rumors about his jewels, their potential uses for pleasure. Men traveled from all over Italy to buy his wares. He became very rich. But he never sold anything he'd created for Viviana. Not even a copy."

Grey nodded toward the discarded, translated diary. "And his obsession never faltered?"

She put the brandy aside and took up the book again, their brief pause of conversation resurrecting her enthusiasm. "Not according to Viviana. This first night started a cat-and-mouse game of seduction and satisfaction that lasted twenty years."

Grey whistled. He couldn't imagine an affair lasting that long. A marriage, sure. His own parents were nearing forty years together. Though Grey doubted they experimented with sex toys—he actually didn't want to go anywhere near that possibility—the passion between Elizabeth and Nathan Masterson seemed as fresh today as it had been when Grey and Zane were teenagers. The boys had found their parents' cuddles and kisses embarrassing at the time, but being raised in a house where affection overflowed probably explained why Zane and Grey both had a healthy predilection for sex from such early ages.

"Read more," Grey asked.

"It's late."

He groaned at her flimsy excuse. "So what? We've been to parties together that lasted all night and into the next day. I want to know how this guy seduced her. That first night. How far did he go?"

With a wiggle of his brows, Grey challenged Reina, certain his brother would have been just as curious as he was, though Grey realized he had ulterior motives. He wanted her to read more because Viviana's confessions stirred Reina's desires. He had seen the telltale blush of wanting on her skin. He'd witnessed the soft, dreamy look in her obsidian eyes. He wanted to inspire those reactions himself, and he figured reading a little more of the confessional might help in that direction.

She retrieved the book and found her place.

"As he instructed, I'd worn the lock near my heart, wrapping the chain twice around my throat. It was so long! I couldn't imagine why someone would want a chain that reached nearly to the knees. But with light fingers, he showed me. He lifted the heavy gold piece, then stretched the cool metal chain to its full length, pulling the soft links over my bare skin. He dipped the lock between my legs, so that any tiny movement slapped the weight against my labia."

Grey nodded, impressed. The devil had placed a weight on his paramour's sensitive outer lips, and he could imagine the chain dipped over the tender ridge, close to her clit. He closed his eyes, imagining Reina draped similarly across her bed, undressed, with him standing over her, wielding the glimmering gold over her flesh.

"The chain tightened around my throat, but with only enough pressure to remind me to be still. I would not choke, but if I turned my head too quickly, the thin gold would break. He manipulated the chain, brushing the cool metal over my nipples, twirling the links around my breasts. Around and around. Pulling tighter. The sensations made me squirm and the lock between my legs slapped against me. Wild thoughts flew through my mind. I wanted to feel the gold inside me. I wanted the pressure. The weight. I would have felt ashamed, except he forbade me to feel so. Women were made to be pleasured, he claimed. And from the moment he kissed me, deeply, his tongue tangling with mine, I believed him."

Reina closed the book.

"That's it?" Grey asked, disappointed. He also realized he'd let his eyes close again, enraptured by the sound of her voice painting such an erotic picture.

"Have you ever made love to a virgin?" she asked.

Grey chuckled, wondering how she jumped from one topic to another. "Viviana wasn't a virgin, was she?"

"Technically? No, but she'd never known pleasure, never had an orgasm, until il Gio. He took such care with her. Such patience. Have you ever been a woman's first?"

Grey thought, fully aware that he was scrunching his eyebrows together in an expression that was decidedly more Grey than Zane. But he honestly couldn't remember being any woman's first lover, which now that he thought about it, said something about the types of women he found attractive.

As for Zane? Frankly, virgins weren't his brother's style any more than they were his. They both gravitated toward more sophisticated, experienced women, women with no reason to fear the unknown, no excuse to shy away from sexual satisfaction.

Types like Reina…unless…

He attempted to erase any hint of true curiosity from his face. *Look bored, look bored.* "Why do you ask?"

Her sigh possessed a wealth of regret. "I sometimes can barely remember my first time. I was so young." She waved her hand at him before retrieving her brandy and draining the snifter in one long sip. "But I've told you about that."

Grey silently cursed. He couldn't very well pretend he'd forgotten something so momentous and personal in order to coax her into retelling the tale, no matter how much he wanted to hear about it. She was young. How young? Sixteen? Younger? Who had been her first lover? For some reason, he suspected an older man, but the thought bothered him so much he pushed it aside. He wondered if she, like Viviana, had a diary he could peek into. If she did, he'd be the one to find it. He knew every crack and crevice in this old house.

But he wouldn't look. That would be an invasion of privacy. The sting of Lane's revelations, some exaggerated but most true, was still fresh. While he could care less what Lane told her fans about her sexual exploits, he didn't consider himself a public figure who deserved to have his sexual preferences written about for all to read—especially recorded in such a derisive way. He'd thought he was simply sharing some carnal adventures with a woman he admired. And he had admired Lane, from the first time they had met during a junket for her latest film until the first time she refused his call. Then, the affair had simply been over. No regrets, no second-guessing.

Until the book had hit the stands. Until he'd figured out that he'd been her means to an end—more publicity.

Grey preferred his own affairs to be private, even if he did make a living poking around in the lives of others and publishing accounts of their foibles in black and white. But his paper didn't dwell on scandal or rely on innuendo. If someone committed a crime, he reported it. If they were mixed up in bribery or had questionable relationships that hindered their ability to perform whatever duty they were elected or hired to do, he took them to task.

But Reina was no politician or billionaire CEO. She was just a woman trying to make a name for herself with her art. He wondered how any man survived in the presence of a woman with such a strong sexual energy for more than an hour without going mad.

Luckily for him, he had honed his interviewing skills long ago. If he asked the right questions, he could get the answers he wanted without letting on that he hadn't been the Masterson brother to whom she'd once confessed her intimate secret. "Do you ever see him anymore, your first lover?"

"Martine?" A sweet smile curled her mouth. "He still lives in St. Tropez. I saw him, oh, five years ago. He's married, has three girls. Still runs the old hotel with his father and brother." She laughed. "I wonder if Paolo ever realized how he made my first time so special?"

Why didn't it surprise him that she retained a friendly relationship with the man who'd taken her virginity? But wait…Paolo?

"Paolo? I thought Martine was your first lover?"

"He was. But Paolo, who was only a year older than Martine—that would have made him seventeen—he had just made a fool of himself with his first lover, a French college student on holiday. He'd come before the woman had her clothes off and she complained to anyone willing to listen. He was, to say the least, humiliated. Martine was determined not to make the same mistake. He took all summer to seduce me.''

The melancholy in her voice, accompanied by a glassy nostalgia in her gaze, tugged at Grey. Made him jealous of a boy barely sixteen, who'd taken his time awakening his lover, if for no other reason than to insure he didn't embarrass himself. He'd probably read books. Watched movies. Guys like him torked Grey off. He should have had to flounder and blunder like the rest of the teenage boys in the world.

''No fumbling around, huh?''

Reina blinked her eyes, as if clearing the memory away so she could answer. ''Martine? So gentle, so fascinated by my reactions, almost as if he was taking notes. I'm sure he must have fumbled, but how would I have known? I was only fourteen.''

Grey tossed back his brandy, attempting to hide his surprise.

''What?'' she asked immediately, sensing his shock. ''I told you that before. In fact, if I remember correctly we made a contest of it and I won the first month's rent on this house.''

She crawled closer to him on the bed, attempting to look through the glass he tried to hide behind. He finished the brandy quickly and diverted her scrutiny by handing her his snifter. ''I know. Never fails to throw me.''

She put the glass on the bed stand and slid back onto the comforter, an inch or so closer to him than she had been before. ''You weren't much older, or did you exaggerate before?''

The challenge in her eyes, in the way she leaned forward on both hands, her pajama top billowing out and allowing him a shadowed view of her breasts, stole Grey's ability to think.

He swallowed, but his mouth had become very dry. Thirsty. For a sip of her. For a taste of the brandy he could smell lingering on her heated breath.

''I was fifteen.'' Not a lie. For him or Zane. They'd both lost their virginity with the same woman, a twenty-year-old neighbor who'd made it a challenge to seduce both twins, though neither knew at the time, nor cared when it was all over.

She nodded, obviously remembering as she sidled closer, her perfume reminding him of hot cinnamon. ''Both of us young, both seduced, both enjoying the experience thoroughly.'' Her breasts heaved with her heavy sigh. ''No wonder we're both such sexual creatures.''

Her gaze captured his, her pupils and irises blending into fathomless centers. When she licked her lips enticingly, Grey stopped fighting his instincts. Even Zane wouldn't be able to resist kissing such a sensuous woman, no matter their past.

He launched forward, their mouths colliding. Whether from shock or from desire—he had no idea which and didn't give a damn—he found her lips open. Her heat drew him, ensnared him, even as their tongues curled and clashed. Like the brandy flavoring her kiss, Reina imbued him with the kind of heady heat a man should sip and savor.

Only she escaped. A rush of cold met his mouth the instant she broke the kiss. She dashed off the bed, spun for a second, and then took two strides back.

''You're not Zane!''

6

GREY'S SENSES OVERLOADED, blocking his ability to read Reina's expression. *Damn.* Just a moment ago, he'd been lost in velvet heaven, his mouth merged with hers. Even as his desire surged, he'd kept his hands to himself and focused only on her taste, her scent. For an instant, he knew her. Unbridled. Unrestrained. The real Reina Price, the woman beneath the sexy clothes and thoroughbred air.

Then she'd pulled away, his secret revealed. He took a deep breath, trying to interpret the look on her face. Shock? Definitely. Horror? No, not exactly. Anger? Yes, at first, but the indignation quickly drained from her eyes, replaced with her cool, practiced indifference.

"You…are…not…Zane…Masterson."

She ended her staccato explanation by rolling her lips inward, as if she was trying to suppress any emotion brought on by this revelation. For an instant, Grey thought a flash of humor lit her eyes, but he figured he'd imagined it. He'd been caught. Red-lipped. No woman he'd ever run across would find such a lie amusing.

Still…Reina was no ordinary woman.

"Let me guess, we kiss differently?" he ventured.

Her eyebrows shot up, then just as quickly relaxed. She'd showed him her surprise rather than her apathy, if only for a second. "Frankly, I wouldn't know."

"Excuse me?"

She shrugged, returning to the bed as if the lie and the

kiss were nothing of consequence. Fortunately, he knew better.

"Your brother and I have never kissed."

Grey took a moment to catalogue that information. "You've never slept with my brother?"

Reina grinned, obviously amused by his inability to swallow the reality she handed him. "Zane and I always have been and always will be strictly friends. If he told you otherwise, Grey—" she emphasized his name, probably just because she could "—he was lying. Or exaggerating. He has been known to do that."

She rolled her eyes, apparently remembering some instance when his twin's penchant for blowing things out of proportion had caused some stir, one that apparently she hadn't minded. No wonder his brother liked this woman so much. She seemed totally unaffected by his playboy charisma. She was probably a damned good influence on Zane's inflated ego.

Grey held up his hands. "Honestly, he didn't tell me anything. He said you two were just good friends, but I assumed…"

"That we'd once been lovers?"

"You are an incredibly beautiful woman. And these vibes have been going on between us."

She cleared her throat, then refilled her brandy glass. "Yes, that should have been my first clue that you weren't Zane. As adorable as I find him, we've never had the kind of chemistry you and I seem to have. And here I blamed my heightened state of arousal on reading the diaries and on Claudio's collection. Apparently, there was more at play."

"Well," Grey muttered, "nothing was really at play just yet. But we were getting there."

Grey expected her to try to deny his claim, particularly

now that he'd lied to her, but she reclined against her pillows, her brandy snifter poised between her palms.

"I prefer to know the identity of the men I kiss," she said after several pensive sips. Then without warning, she slid across the mattress, nearly to the place where she'd been when he kissed her. Close enough for him to smell her exotic scent again. Close enough to inhale the brandy on her lips.

Grey almost moved back, as if the sheer force of her confidence had the power to push him aside. Instead, he scooted forward. She was an incredibly fascinating woman. Like a mystery he had to solve, an investigation he had to break before the deadline on the morning edition.

"Sorry for the switch," he said, his fingers inching across the comforter, his hand inexplicably drawn to the silky softness of her pajamas.

She paused, her gaze expectant but patient. He couldn't think of anything else but the possibility of resuming their kiss.

"You don't really think that's enough of an explanation, do you?" she asked after a quick sip of brandy. "Or do I need to call Zane if I want the whole truth?"

"Haven't you heard? I'm considered the honest, hardworking Masterson twin."

"Oh, I've heard. From Zane. I think he appreciates your efforts to be his complete and total opposite. Keeps anyone from ever handing him more responsibility than he wants. Maybe I should call him, just to make sure he's surviving. I'm assuming he's busy being you right now?" She glanced at her bedside clock. "Hmm. What would Grey Masterson, notorious New Orleans newspaper editor and lover, be doing so late on a Saturday night? Ordinarily, of course."

Grey scrunched his brow. "The real Grey Masterson would probably still be working at the newspaper, getting an early jump on the Monday edition. But my brother called a few hours ago and I basically told him to do whatever he pleased without asking where he was or whom he was with. That's why I'm here, Reina. I'm tired of being me all the time."

"So are a lot of people. Tired of being themselves, that is. Too bad we don't all have twins we can switch places with. I think the two of you are rather lucky."

He watched her eyes, and though they still possessed that heavy-lidded quality that made him wonder if anything could truly excite her, he wanted to believe her easy acceptance. "You aren't angry that I didn't tell you who I was? That Zane didn't tell you?"

Her lips twisted a bit while she considered his question. "I'll live. Tell me, what if Zane doesn't portray you the way you want to be portrayed?"

"Zane can't make me look like any more of a fool than Lane Morrow did. The woman has the whole world thinking that she not only tamed my wicked ways, but she broke my heart and left me to wallow in my despair, unable to date, unable to connect with another woman."

"Have you tried to prove her wrong?"

"Why should I?" He snapped, then paused. Reina didn't need to hear his troubles. He'd become his brother primarily to escape having to think about Lane or the tabloids or his newspaper or anything else associated with his life. Even now that she knew his secret, he had no intention of slipping back into his old ways. He'd wanted to be Zane so he could have some fun. Even her problems with the robberies at her gallery wouldn't keep him from that pursuit.

"I'm sure Zane will take care of proving Lane wrong.

He has a natural propensity for finding and seducing beautiful women. I even left him one to start with.''

Grey told Reina about his stalker, about the troubles at the newspaper. And about the ulcer he'd been self-medicating with bottles of antacids, though he hadn't planned on filling in so many details. But he did owe her the truth, particularly since he still needed her help to continue his ruse.

He also confessed that when he'd called Zane for help with Toni Maxwell, he'd secretly hoped Zane would suggest they switch places. Just as Zane had predicted, Reina found the entire situation slightly amusing and rather ingenious. She probably would've found it downright funny if he'd told her who he was before he kissed her.

She was indeed a unique woman. Like both him and his twin, maybe even more so, Reina had been assigned a role to play at an early age. The daughter of a celebrity, she'd been under public scrutiny from birth. He'd already noted the way she morphed from an aloof seductress in public to a comfortable-in-her-skin sensual woman in private. He only wondered if there were more layers he could peel away, more facets he could discover.

"So Zane is running a newspaper?" Reina didn't bother to hide her cynicism from her expression or her voice.

"It's his turn. He owns nearly as much stock as I do. And he does have a journalism degree. Did he ever tell you that?"

"No, but I have a degree in art history," she countered. "Doesn't mean I'm qualified to run the Louvre."

"Zane'll do fine."

She eyed him skeptically, but he had a strong feeling she wasn't doubting Zane's ability as much as she was questioning Grey's perfunctory confidence in his brother.

She was insightful, this woman. Fact was, Grey had come to realize he didn't care that much if Zane saved the paper or not. He simply wanted out.

"Your brother is incredibly resourceful and shamefully overeducated," she said. "I'm equally sure he'll do fine. But I am still surprised he didn't tell me about this switch. I would have played along—he knows that."

Grey nodded. Zane had told him as much, but Grey hadn't wanted Reina in on the secret. Never, in all the times he'd switched places with his brother, had anyone outside the two of them been aware of the switch. In the past, they'd suspected having co-conspirators would somehow spoil their fun. This time, however, Grey simply hadn't wanted to be himself—at all or with anyone. He considered the desire childish now, but hadn't he been entitled to a little selfishness?

"I had no idea he had a friend he could trust so implicitly. Apparently, I was wrong. I mean, you weren't even lovers, but you shared the secret of your first sexual experiences."

Reina grinned slyly. "And now you know my secret, too, don't you?"

Grey sat up straighter. "Did Zane get more details? 'Cause personally, I'd love some. I need them, if you think about it. If I'm going to present an accurate portrayal of my brother, I should know everything he knows. Particularly about you."

His attempt at humor didn't fall as flat as he expected. One corner of those luscious lips of hers raised ever so slightly upward.

"You'd like that, wouldn't you? But first things first, Grey Masterson. Now that you're not who I thought, what should I do with you?"

REINA COULDN'T DENY the ache of exhaustion tightening the muscles around her eyes, but she absolutely couldn't attempt sleep until she had the answers to several burning questions. At least she knew why she'd suddenly been attacked by a raging case of lust for Zane, a man she'd been immune to for years. This sexy charmer wasn't Zane. He was Grey. According to Zane, Grey was the serious twin. She wondered. According to Lane Morrow—whom Reina wouldn't trust with the name of her dog groomer, and she didn't own a dog—he was a militantly private man with a taste for kinky sex. According to Chantal, who'd read the book from cover to cover, the B-movie bitch had delighted in intimating that Grey's appetite exceeded even her feminine prowess, and yet, when they'd parted, he pined for her and hadn't dated since. Reina had no idea if this was true, but she had a strong suspicion that if it was, it wouldn't be for long.

She'd believed him to be Zane when he'd come into her room tonight. That's why she'd let down her guard, why she'd decided to consider pursuing the potent chemistry suddenly brewing between them. But she hadn't planned on the power of the kiss, hadn't planned on the instantaneous explosion of awareness that cleared the smoke from the screen of his deception. No matter how much she loved Zane as a friend, no matter how much she trusted him to forge a sexual relationship with her—one with parameters they could both tolerate—he never would have kissed her without first laying down the ground rules. They'd both lose too much if things didn't work out.

But with Grey, what did she have to lose? The man obviously enjoyed sex as much as she did. He probably wasn't looking for anything serious, and after the debacle with Lane Morrow, he'd value discretion. And God, but the man did things to her libido that threatened to drive her insane. She wanted him.

And Reina had been taught to always go after what she wanted.

He took away her brandy, placed it on the floor and then scooted back into her personal space. His blue eyes gleamed with a potent mixture of promise and possibility.

"I have several interesting suggestions about what you could do with me, Ms. Price, if you'd like to hear them."

A flutter deep within her stole her breath. When was the last time a man had such an immediate, powerful effect on her? She'd seen his face a thousand times before, and yet she was fascinated by the nuances of his expressions, the subtle, perhaps even imagined, differences between Grey, the stranger, and Zane, her friend.

This is Grey, she reminded herself. Before today, she'd never seen him. Never spoken to him. Knew him only through his brother and by his reputation. Tonight, though, they'd shared a kiss. Brief, but intense. Searing with enough raw and honest lust to show her the truth.

What would another kiss show her?

"I'd rather *experience* what you have in mind," she answered. "Some men can be all talk."

His sly grin burgeoned into a full-fledged smile. "I can say the same for most women."

Touché. Lane Morrow had undoubtedly done her share of talking, although only after she'd done her share of doing. Well, Reina wasn't about to be lumped into any classification that included a wench like Lane Morrow. She inched her face closer to his, her gaze drawn to his perfectly shaped lips, her tongue desperate to taste him again.

"I'm not most women," she whispered, allowing a teasing swipe of mouth against his.

"Prove it."

His challenge shot a surge of adrenaline through her and she rode the electric wave until her mouth pressed against his, her tongue eager to duel, her breath ragged with need. Grey met her with equal force and, before she knew it, she'd thrust her hands into his hair, clutching him as a sudden release of her pent-up lust sent her into an unfamiliar, uncharted spiral. She couldn't think, couldn't reason. Confusion must have shone in her eyes the minute he pulled away. She quickly tempered her expression.

"Wow," he said.

She tossed her hair aside. "Just a kiss," she claimed, trying to convince him—convince herself—that nothing special, nothing unique or different had just transpired. Even if she did, for a brief liberating moment, feel completely out of control.

He narrowed his gaze. "You don't really believe that, do you?"

She moistened her lips, unwilling to admit that the simple joining of lips had rocked her to her core. "What do you want, Grey? Tell me."

"That's obvious. I want you, Reina. I have from the minute I walked into your gallery."

She tried to steady her breathing, tried to stop the rapid rise and fall of her breasts so that his gaze would remain only on hers. Not because she didn't want him to admire her breasts. She did. She wanted him to admire them unclothed and with more than just his eyes. She ached to feel his hands on her, his mouth on her. Shaking her head, she tried to clear the dizziness. Reina never shied from exploring her sexual side, or from sleeping with a man she desired. But never had she wanted a man so much that she wasn't willing to wait, didn't aim to draw out the seduction, stoke their desire until the flames became unbearable.

But the fire licking her skin from the inside out was already an unqualified conflagration. How could she feel any hotter? Any deeper in need?

She grabbed the lapels of her pajamas and tore them open, popping buttons, laughing at the tinkle as they dropped to the floor. Pulling her arms languidly from the sleeves, she dropped the shirt to the floor, then leveled her gaze at him as his stare dropped to her bare breasts, her aroused nipples.

"What are you waiting for, then?"

Hunger widened his clear blue eyes to china saucers. That all too familiar swell of feminine power rushed through her blood, intensifying her pulse at each sensitive point—her throat, her wrists, her breasts. Moisture trickled between her legs. A kiss had her ready. He could strip her completely bare and thrust into her right here, right now—her body was prepared.

He inched his hands onto her waist, his touch explorative and yet possessive. She closed her eyes, prepared to feel him completely. When his palms stopped along her rib cage, she blinked and caught her carnal reflection in his eyes.

"You're waiting again," she pointed out.

"You don't know me."

"I know enough."

"I don't know what you want from me."

She allowed a tiny grin, then tugged his shirt over his head in one quick movement. Splaying her hands over his broad chest, losing her long fingers into the soft curled hair there, she pressed her palm against him until she could count the rapid beats of his heart. "I want sex,

Grey. Amazing sex. Earth-shattering, you-ought-to-write-a-book-about-it sex.''

She glanced at Viviana's diary, barely visible beneath the increasingly disordered comforter. She wished she'd taken up the habit of committing her liaisons to pen and ink because, right now, with Grey's hands inching up her rib cage, his roughened fingertips teasing the sensitive swell of her breasts, she couldn't remember any other lover with whom she'd shared such an instant, overwhelming connection.

''I don't write books about sex,'' he said. ''And I don't like reading them. Unless they're a couple of centuries old.''

In the heat of her desire, she'd forgotten about Lane Morrow.

''Can't blame you,'' she answered, swiping her tongue across her dry lips, then doing the same to him, just in case he thought a little reluctance and one bad experience with an unscrupulous woman was going to change her mind about making love to him. ''Discretion is a powerful turn-on for me, Grey. Or should I say *Zane?* I can play whatever game you want.''

Grey growled, dragged her up and kissed her long and hard, his tongue even more insistent, his teeth knocking with hers, nipping at her lips.

''I like games, Reina. But while in your bed, I'm Grey. And I am going to make love to you.''

She tossed her head back, yanked the clip and let her hair fall across her back. ''You're still all talk. Isn't there anything better you can do with that mouth of yours?''

FIRE. THE WORD POPPED into Grey's mind in big, bold letters the moment he caught sight of Reina's eyes.

Flames licked the obsidian centers, flashing with the purest heat he'd ever seen—completely purged of any fear or reluctance. He needed to burn with her.

And he would, just as soon as he demonstrated all the delicious things he knew how to do with his mouth, and other parts of his body, to bring her the pleasure she craved.

"Wait here." He dashed off the bed, escaping so quickly he barely heard her frustrated sigh. After a quick stop in the guest room to retrieve a condom from his overnight bag, he ran down the stairs. He wondered if he wasn't insane, leaving Reina alone for so long. But she deserved better than fast and furious. He didn't know if this would be their only liaison, and he wanted to make it count.

He trusted her to be discreet. He trusted her to value creative lovemaking. And as he turned the corner into the old sunroom she had converted into her studio, he trusted her to have what he needed to make their first time unforgettable.

When he returned to the bedroom, he found the lamplight replaced by the glimmering glow of a dozen candles. She'd doffed the bottom half of her pajamas and now reclined on the bed, the comforter folded beneath her feet, in unabashed nudity. He kicked off his pants, then tossed the condom on the side table. His hand, clutching a spool of gold chain he'd pilfered from her worktable, remained hidden behind his back.

"What have you got there?" she asked.

"A surprise. Close your eyes."

She smiled. "I'm not Viviana, Grey. I've known pleasure."

He chuckled, unwilling to let Reina's alleged experience dampen his intentions. Grey may have been humiliated by Lane's book, but his embarrassment didn't stem from her reports of his prowess as a lover, at least not the parts that were true. Yes, he was an insatiable, demanding bedmate. Yes, his desire could be stoked by something as simple as sharing a delectable dessert or riding around in the back of a limousine during a rainstorm. But he'd never failed to insure his lady experienced an orgasm. Even Lane admitted that in black and white. So no matter how accomplished Reina claimed to be in the pleasure department, she'd never had an orgasm courtesy of Grey Masterson.

"Have you? Really?"

He revealed the spool of glittering gold chain, unraveled a few inches, then dangled the slightly sharp end over her stomach, beneath her breasts, and across one taut nipple. She gasped at the sensation, then closed her eyes as he'd instructed.

7

FOR A BRIEF, SCINTILLATING moment, Reina's mind shot back to St. Tropez. The balmy breezes. The thrill of the forbidden. The adventure of being young, carefree and careless of consequences—the long-lost treasure of not knowing exactly what would happen next or how it would make her feel. Yet the minute Grey dragged the sharp edge of the chain gently across her neck, her consciousness locked into the present with the man who desired her, who knew his way around a woman's body, and who had promised to pleasure her beyond her own vast experiences.

Still, the electric hum of innocent anticipation remained.

Amazing.

"Lift your head a little," he instructed.

She complied, knowing he intended to wrap her in the gold just as il Gio had done to Viviana, knowing the chain he'd stolen from her studio was heartier, thicker than what the mistress had described, but trusting Grey nonetheless. The metal chilled her skin. As he manipulated the gold around her breasts, her nipples puckered, the press of each individual link arousing her as if he had a thousand fingers to ply on her skin.

"Your breasts are amazing." He circled her right breast once, then curled the chain across to do the same to the other. "No tan lines. So round, so sensitive. Can you feel how your nipples reach out to me?"

She sighed in response, well aware that he didn't need her to answer his question. He wanted to stimulate her with his words as well as his actions, making her totally conscious of each and every response in her body. She concentrated on increasing tautness as he wound the chain back and forth, shaping an increasingly smaller figure eight from one breast to the other, working the gold closer and closer to the sensitive points. Then, anticipating a jolt of sensation when the cool links finally met her aching tips, she inhaled sharply. But, instead, he redirected the chain down her belly, leaving her nipples free to pout for his touch.

"Lift your hips, *chère.*"

She folded her knees up, cognizant of how he allowed only the chain to scrape her skin. His body, his hands, remained a billow of heat directing the gold down her torso, between her legs, pressing aside one lip of flesh before he twined the chain beneath her thigh and back around her hip.

"This is like wrapping a present," he whispered, "and opening the gift at the same time."

She kept her hips off the mattress while he plied his magic weave around her stomach, then down again to tug the other lip open. When he finally instructed her to slowly relax, she did so with care, hissing with intense pleasure as the chain tightened ever so slightly against her sensitive skin. She had to keep her knees raised, her legs spread, to insure that the links didn't move from their delicious position.

She'd never felt so exposed, vulnerable and cherished all at the same time. Her nipples ached for his tongue, her center trickled with another wave of hot moisture. Her mind reeled from the countless possibilities of what he'd do next, particularly after she felt the grasp of the chain around her throat.

"Can I open my eyes?" she asked.

"Not yet."

She heard him pad away, toward her dresser. He returned, laid something flat and heavy beside her, then left and returned again.

"Now?"

"Not quite. One thing first, to complete the picture. I'm going to touch your mouth, add some of that color you wore earlier, that, for the record, drives me wild."

He smoothed the sponge tip of her crimson gloss over her lips slowly, like an artist putting the final touches on his masterpiece. The tiny detail surprised her, heightened her curiosity about him, about what he intended to do with her next.

"I never would have pegged you as a visual man," she said, listening as he closed the cylinder of gloss. "You make your way with words."

"But I am a man, and we're an inherently visual species. And what I'm seeing right now is most stimulating."

"Too bad I can't see for myself."

The mattress purled as he lifted the flat, heavy object he'd laid beside her. "But you can, Reina. Turn your face toward me. Open your eyes."

Her lashes fluttered, her eyes taking an instant to adjust in the dim light. When the image focused, she saw herself, reflected in the gilded hand mirror she'd bought in a French Quarter antique shop. First he allowed her to see only her face—eyes wide with desire, lips glimmering with dark scarlet gloss. She glanced up at him, standing beside the bed in breathtaking, naked glory, but he admonished her to keep her eyes on the mirror.

He stepped aside, turning the mirror so she could see how he'd twined the gold around her breasts, tight enough to cause soft indentations in her skin, to make her nipples higher, her breasts taller. He then leaned the mirror over her, following the single linked path down her belly, then reflecting back the full picture of her desire.

"Have you ever seen yourself so aroused, so erotically arranged?"

She would have shook her head, her tongue thick, but she was afraid the movement would dislodge the intricate web of gold.

"No," she said with a rasp.

"Reminds me of that piece in your gallery, the seashell with the pearl."

She swallowed deeply, knowing precisely the design he meant, a piece she'd created not too long ago from a shell she'd found during a trip to the Caribbean. The deep pink hue of the inner shell, the slightly teardrop shape of the natural pearl. She'd fashioned the ocean treasures as an allusion to female arousal, but she'd never expected to be so accurate.

He dropped the mirror on the bed, but the image remained imprinted in her mind. He'd only just begun to orchestrate her pleasure, and she couldn't imagine wanting a man inside her more than how she wanted Grey.

Apparently in no hurry, he strolled around to the other side of the bed. With her promise to keep her eyes closed forgotten, she feasted on the sight of him—his torso lean and muscled, his erection long, taut and ever so slightly curved. A second wave of anticipation surged through her. She'd made love to enough men to know which shape suited her, and he would be perfect. With the chains holding her open to his perusal, the sensations of blood rushing to her center intensified.

She held her breath and remained incredibly still.

He slid beside her on the bed and retrieved the dangling end of the chain that he'd dropped at her throat. He flicked the gold across her skin, tugging just enough so that her breath caught when the links tightened around her neck.

"You shouldn't move too much," he warned. "You'll undo all my handiwork."

"I won't." She relaxed into the pillow and closed her eyes. "But you shouldn't waste all this handiwork, either."

His sapphire irises gleamed with reflections of candlelight and gold. "Unlikely, Reina. Very unlikely."

He took her hand, free of the gold chain, and lifted her fingers to his mouth, kissing each one softly, then blazing a path down her arm, across her shoulder. When he met the chain, he licked a trail, following the links down to her breast, swirling his stiff tongue along the edges, spiraling from one side to the other until he'd moistened all her flesh there with his mouth, until her nipples strained for his attention. With slow precision, he traced around her wide areola, then, finally, slipped her hard nipple into his mouth.

The sensation rocked her. She arched her back, pressing her flesh farther into his mouth until the chain reminded her to relax. By the time he attended her other breast, the warring instincts to remain still and thrash with pleasure lulled her into an erotic stillness she'd never known before.

His mouth descended, following the line of gold. Grey shifted his body around her raised knees and poised his mouth where she wanted him most. But how could she not move when his tongue thrust inside her?

"Grey," she managed by way of warning.

He answered her uncertainty with a wicked grin, then

after a pause, he stretched upward, bracing his nude and glorious body over her in rigid parallel. The muscles in his shoulders bulged at the strain, but he loosened the chain around her neck.

He paused, stared straight down into her eyes. "I don't want you constrained, afraid to move, when I taste you."

She searched his eyes, nearly losing her sanity in the intense blueness. How could a man appear so nefarious yet so selfless at the same time? "Kiss me first."

He pursed his lips, considering, then shook his head. "Oh, no. When I kiss those ruby-red lips again, I'll be inside you. One kiss might distract me, keep me from pleasuring you the way I promised. Are you willing to wait a few moments more?"

With his mouth, he retraced his downward course, following the path still damp on her skin, plucking each nipple with his teeth before slipping his arms beneath her knees. He captured her gaze with his head poised inches from the dark curls of her mons. But instead of his tongue, he slipped a finger beneath the chain and jerked, pulling the links tight against her swollen flesh.

"So sweet," he murmured, then lapped at her, gently at first, then with increasing intensity until Reina nearly flew out of her skin.

She grabbed his head, moving him, directing him, remembering somewhere in the back of her mind that this man didn't know her, hadn't been taught her likes and dislikes, her preferences or predilections. He pulled back and censured her with an indignant look.

"Relax, Reina. You asked me if I could do anything better with my mouth than talk. I'm about to show you. Trust me."

She swallowed her reply, closed her eyes and tried to do as he asked. Trust him? Not since Martine had she allowed a lover to explore her body without direction, without him knowing precisely what she wanted him to do to her and when. How could she trust him? If he didn't please her, if he didn't make the spontaneous decision to sleep with him worth her while, what would the affair mean? How would she justify the decadence?

And yet, as the skillful twirls of his tongue caused a renewed wave of captivating sensations to roll over her body, how could she not trust him?

Her faith was instantly rewarded. He used his mouth, he used the chains, he used his fingers until she reached the precipice of delight and willingly jumped without hesitation. She cried out his name, urged and demanded, until her insides exploded in pulsing waves. In the psychedelic world of the downward slide, he unwound the gold chain from around her, donned his condom, then lay down on the bed beside her.

She followed her instincts and curled into his hot, hard body. She'd been sated, but the effects wouldn't last. An insatiable thrum echoed through her. Until he was inside her, until she experienced the full breadth of this man, she'd never be completely satisfied.

"So you *are* talented with your mouth," she murmured. "How about showing me your other aptitudes? Or, better yet, giving me a chance to show you mine."

He chuckled, having no idea how rare her offer was. Reina nearly couldn't believe she'd said anything so... ribald, so forward and lusty. She'd made love dozens of times with dozens of men—men she chose carefully, knowing from the first kiss precisely how much of herself she'd be willing to share, in bed and out. But Grey roused a rare side of her—the natural side, the impulsive side, the part of her that desperately wanted to show a lover all she was, all she could give…if only she could discover the secret to opening her heart.

Yet when he finally kissed her, his mouth possessing hers entirely, the taste of her sex flavoring his tongue, all doubts evaporated, all expectations floated away in a rush of hot need. He'd showed her the intense pleasure of surrendering control to a lover, but old habits were hard to break. She pushed him onto his back and straddled him. Before her mind could fully register the concentrated bliss of his hard tip pressed to her pulsing lips, she eased him inside her and straightened her spine.

Instantaneous delight jolted her. Beneath her—his hands clamped on her hips—he grinned.

"Shaped just right for you, aren't I?"

She couldn't answer, fearing that the movement of just speaking would toss her into another orgasmic wave before she'd had a moment to catch her breath. But Grey took the upper hand and shifted beneath her. She shook her head, trying to deny the electric storm sizzling deep inside her, but he merely lifted his body higher, deeper. He slid his hand between them and with one finger, unlocked the last of her control. From that moment on, time passed in a mindless flurry, ending when both of them came long and hard and loud.

GREY HAD NO IDEA how long Reina lay over him, her body still joined with his, her breathing alternating between labored and nonexistent, as if she held her breath every so often in an attempt to calm the rapid pants. He knew she didn't like to lose control. Hated surrendering control even more. Still, he'd managed to take the reins long enough to show her just how incredible yielding to a lover could be. He hardly knew her, but the truth of what this woman needed seemed just as clear to him as black-inked words on a crisp white page. What puzzled him was why he felt so compelled to fulfill her need.

When he heard her exhausted sigh, he rolled her over, withdrew from her warm and luscious body. He blew out the candles, then pulled the tangled comforter over them, ignoring the signals she sent that told him she'd prefer he go to his own bed. Too late. He'd already tasted the manna of overriding Reina Price's desires. So long as he was able to replace them with something better, something that she possibly didn't even know she wanted, she'd have to do something less subtle than rolling a few inches away and hugging the covers tightly to change his mind about her.

She'd been made love to before. She'd admitted that truth with great pride and no shame. Good. But he'd bet the entire advertising revenue of the newspaper that she hadn't allowed a man freedom with her body since that young stud on the French beach.

But she'd let him. Somehow, he'd won a level of trust from her that he doubted any other of her lovers had ever achieved. He couldn't help the pitch of pride rolling through him, or the mystery her choice presented him with. Why him? Why now?

Her tired sigh broke his thoughts. He doused the lamp and pulled her into his arms.

For a long moment, silence ruled. But Grey knew from her quick breathing that she hadn't fallen asleep.

"You don't have to do this," she finally said.

"Do what?"

"Hold me until I fall asleep. Pretend we're sharing some tender emotional moment. I'm not one of those women."

Her bold statement shouldn't have surprised him, but did.

"What kind of woman is that?"

"The kind that assigns something deeper to sexual satisfaction. You're an incredible lover, Grey, but I won't be falling in love with you."

He didn't know whether to be insulted, relieved or impressed. Reina Price loved presenting herself as cosmopolitan and cavalier about love and lovers, but he wondered how deeply the attitude truly ran. After all, he presented a similar face to the world, when he knew, deep down, that he wanted a soul mate as much as any man who'd finally acknowledged his loneliness.

"You're so sure about that?" he asked.

"Of course. I don't intend to fall in love with anyone."

"Ever?"

Her shoulder tucked beneath his, he felt her shrug. "Oh, I never say never. Maybe someday, when I finally figure out what I want from a marriage. It's not as if I'm overly familiar with the institution."

"Your mother never married?"

He knew Pilar Price was notorious for her affairs, but didn't know any of the details. Even before his debacle with Lane, he left the entertainment section to the editors who seemed more inclined to follow the latest gossip.

"No. She told me once she'd proposed to a man a long time ago, but he turned her down, so she's done the same to every man who had the courage to ask her since."

"And you want to be like your mother?"

That sent her sitting upright. "Bite your tongue! I love my mother, but she's the last woman on earth I want to emulate."

He remained lying beside her, but cradled his hands behind his head. "Then why are you?"

"Why am I what?"

"Emulating her? You have this exotic, mysterious persona. You take lovers, but don't want to fall in love. What part of this doesn't sound like Pilar?''

Moonlight spilled in a silver stream through her window, lighting her face just enough so he could see the indignant purse of her lips.

''The part where I take lovers to satisfy my sexual needs, not my financial ones. The part where I control my own career, my own art, not where I flit from Svengali to Svengali until I've amassed enough fame to call my own shots. The part where…''

As her volume rose, so did Grey's remorse. He certainly hadn't meant to make her angry. In a quick movement masked by the darkness, he tugged her back into his arms. She struggled, but stopped once he said, ''I'm sorry.''

''For what?''

''For speaking about topics I obviously know nothing about. I'm a newspaperman. I should know better.''

She remained quiet, but her cheek quivered against his chest.

''Am I forgiven?''

''You aren't the first man to make such an assumption about me, Grey,'' she admitted, a familiar sound of practiced boredom lacing her whisper. ''I doubt you'll be the last.''

Grey cursed, but before he could come up with a way to turn the conversation to something less charged, she'd fallen asleep. Exhaustion muddled his brain. He yawned, and the sensation of her warm body lax against his lulled him to close his eyes. Yet, as the scent of jasmine and expensive French perfume teased his nostrils, he couldn't help entertaining a few questions. Did he want to prove her wrong about him somehow, or should he remain focused on the plan he'd formulated back at the gallery that afternoon, about having a quick discreet affair with Reina and nothing more? For all he knew, his stupid choice of postcoital conversation had taken the decision from him.

"Then again," he murmured, his tone smug as her hand slipped sleepily over his cock, "maybe not."

8

REINA SHOVED HER FISTS onto her hips and surveyed her handiwork, ignoring the grimy feel of the dust clinging to her skin, hair and clothes. Once she showered, the last speck of centuries-old dust and dirt in the hidden room would be gone for good. An air filter hummed in the corner of the room. The wood floors gleamed like polished amber. The vacuum cleaner, cord wrapped around the handle and the bag changed for the second time, sat propped between the inner panel and the outer room until she could return it to the hall closet. She glanced at her watch. For a relatively inexperienced housekeeper, she'd managed to clean the room by eleven o'clock, only two hours after waking from the most restful sleep she'd enjoyed in years.

Yet the minute her brain had attempted to figure out the reasons for her deep, invigorating rest, she'd sprung into action, not wanting to think about Grey Masterson or his inventive lovemaking. Instead, she'd dug out last season's workout wear, twisted her hair into a haphazard ponytail and tried to remember where the woman who cleaned her house twice a week kept the dust rags and brooms.

"Wow, for a debutante, you sure know your way around a can of Pledge," Grey said, squeezing past the vacuum cleaner with a cup of coffee in his hand.

She wiped her hands on her nylon shorts before accepting the china. "I was *never* a debutante," she countered, inhaling an invigorating whiff of coffee and chicory before taking a cautious sip. A little too much sugar and milk for her taste, but she appreciated the sentiment. "And what's a can of Pledge?"

His grin told her he didn't buy her ignorance of cleaning products for a minute. So she watched a little television every now and again. So she often worked out creative blocks by grabbing a rag and helping polish the silverware her mother had given her—remnants of an affair with a British financier. Big deal.

"Oh, I forgot," he said. "You're a lady of leisure."

She couldn't contain a derisive snort. "Oh, yes. A lady of leisure with work to do. How soon until I can start working on the collection?"

He slung his hands into the pockets of his jeans, the denim cut loose but still highlighting his sinfully muscled legs. Of course, it didn't help that Reina couldn't dim the clear, crisp picture of Grey stalking her around her bed last night in pure naked magnificence. She took a longer sip of coffee, wincing when her tongue sizzled from too much heat.

"I can move your worktable and the air conditioner up here as soon as we're done, and you'll be good to go by this afternoon."

"Done? With what? The room is spotless."

Reina took a deep breath, and willed herself to be patient. She wanted to work now. Engross herself in the jewels and designs. Anything to keep her mind off the probing look in Grey's devilish blue eyes.

He nodded. "Wasn't talking about that. Have to show you how the security system works. Also, I've been over the police reports from your robberies and have some questions."

"Can't the questions wait?"

"If I wait, how am I going to occupy my time all day while you work?" He stepped toward her, his eyes glinting with wicked intentions. Though not as lopsided as Zane's grin, Grey's smile managed to charm her just the same.

"You could go out," she suggested.

"And leave you and the collection alone and unprotected all day?"

"We have the security system," she reminded him.

"Yes, but what'll you do if someone tries to break in and you're here all alone?" He closed the distance between them with two long strides and Reina fought her instinct to back away. Damn, but the man had breached her defenses. She struggled to regain her composure, praying he wouldn't notice how she shook. "I suppose you could seduce the hapless devil into leaving you alone—" he touched her chin with a crooked finger and she met his stare boldly "—but what if your thief is a woman? You'll be defenseless."

She rolled her eyes, but didn't bother attempting to argue with his cool, accurate assessment. Her sexuality was indeed a tool, reminding her for the second time in two days that she was more like her mother than she had ever planned to become.

"We have no evidence that someone will try to break in." She rooted her feet, determined to stand her ground. Still, her lips thrummed, sparked with awareness when his knuckle skimmed across them.

"As far as I can see from those police reports, we have no proof that they won't, either, since we have no idea who 'they' are. Of course, I might change my mind after you answer some questions. The sooner I catch your thief, the sooner you get your house back to yourself, if that's what you're worried about.''

"I don't mind you staying here," she lied, counteracting her instinct to shift from foot to foot by swallowing the last of her coffee. Her action broke the magnetic force humming between them, so she immediately turned and set the cup on a windowsill, then began collecting the wayward cloths and paper towels she'd left scattered around the room. "I appreciate your help protecting the collection. I just thought you might want some time to really be Zane, like you wanted. Get out there and enjoy life. That is why you switched places with him, isn't it?''

Grey's expression resembled a scowl, but since Reina strongly suspected that a genuine Grey Masterson scowl was most likely a look she wouldn't have any doubt about, she figured his deep furrowed brow and tightly drawn lips meant something more than anger. She wasn't certain she wanted to know precisely what, though she suspected he was simply considering all angles of her assumption before formulating his response. She'd already learned that Grey's intelligence and creativity were tools he used carefully, just as she used her sexuality. And with equal skill.

In fact, the man wielded his sexuality rather adeptly as well. She was going to have to match him wit for wit to come out of this affair unscathed.

Finally his stoic look disappeared, replaced by a relaxed expression that would have made Zane proud. "I'm enjoying myself right here. Aren't you?''

"The sex was great, if that's what you mean.''

His shrug was noncommittal. "The sex could continue to be great, if that's what you want.''

He took the collection of rags from her, slapped them into a bucket and dropped them at her feet. His cologne, powered by the base essence of ginger, teased her nostrils and threw her mind right back into the bed in the other room. She'd slept in the man's arms all night. She couldn't remember the last lover she'd allowed to remain in her private sanctuary until dawn. Only Grey hadn't stayed until dawn, had he? The minute his warmth and his scent had disappeared from her bed, she'd woken to watch him slip back into his room. Still exhausted, she'd rolled over and drifted back to sleep, comforted by the fact that Grey enchanted her dreams with his puzzling, potent warmth.

How she could ever have mistaken this man for his brother was a mystery she might never solve. Zane's aftershave, while equally pricey, leaned toward citrus essentials, the results sporty and crisp. Grey, on the other hand, enhanced his natural male musk with more striking extracts. Asian spices. Earthy oils. Mixtures she couldn't easily dissect, just like the man who wore them.

Despite her vast experience with the male species, Reina couldn't figure Grey out. He wanted freedom so desperately he'd switched places with his brother and abandoned his beloved business. And yet instead of losing himself in Zane's favorite parties and spontaneous excursions to exotic places, Grey remained with her, trapped in the house, intent on solving the robberies at her gallery. And most perplexing of all, though he'd been publicly burned and humiliated by a woman who had outed his unique sexual preferences, he didn't shy away from diving straight into an affair with her.

She wasn't certain that expending the energy to figure out what exactly made the man tick would be either wise or worth her time. What if she liked what she discovered and wanted more of him?

Or worse, what if she didn't like what lingered beneath

his mystifying charm, but lost her heart to him in the process of discovering the truth?

She destroyed that disturbing scenario by asking the obvious. "What woman doesn't want great sex?"

Grey's laughter echoed across the empty room. "Believe me, I could come up with a significant list in a relatively short span of time."

Reina found that very hard to believe. Except for Judi, her assistant, who'd had too many tragic relationships in her short lifetime, all the women Reina knew constantly prowled for capable lovers. Her best friend, Chantal. Her mother. Heck, even her mother's maid, Dahlia, kept her eyes peeled. Reina would be an idiot to dismiss Grey so soon just because she entertained some silly suspicion that he was the type of man she could fall in love with.

"Well, I won't be on that list, I can assure you." With nothing more to do in the secret room, she crossed through the tiny closet into her bedroom, dragging the vacuum behind her.

"I didn't think you would be."

Reina took one look at her bed, the bed they'd shared, and turned to face him. If she wanted to accomplish anything with the collection today she had to get the man out of her bedroom.

"So, why don't we look over the security system and those police reports?" she suggested, knowing Grey had spread his paperwork across her dining room table downstairs.

"Would you like to shower first? Change? I'll reheat some of the gumbo from last night and we can eat and talk."

Reina smoothed her hands down her shorts. *Oh, great.* The man was considerate, too. How the heck was she going to fight this one? "Sounds like a plan. Can you take this?'' She rolled the vacuum over to the door, making it clear she wasn't removing one stitch of clothing until he was out of the room. "It goes in the closet at the end of the hall."

Grey's eyes flashed with understanding. "Of course." He grabbed the handle and rolled away. He turned just as she was pushing the door closed behind him. "You don't have to lock that, you know. I won't come in unless I'm invited."

She won her battle against scowling and managed a half-amused smile. "Of course, you won't. You seem to be the perfect gentleman, Mr. Masterson."

He leaned slightly forward, the movement arresting her heartbeat, and she realized that she secretly feared— hoped—he might break his word. "Depends on your definition of 'perfect' and 'gentleman.'''

After a quick visual sweep of her, his eyes glowing with unchained lust and admiration, he let out a whistle and disappeared down the hallway. Reina shut the door soundlessly, then leaned against the cool wood and released a sigh. She knew exactly how she'd define both words. Question was, would Grey Masterson fit her classifications as truly as she suspected, or was he, once again, just playing a role?

Heaven help her, but she couldn't wait to find out.

GREY WATCHED the caller ID flash on the phone beside Reina's worktable. He'd already dismantled the lighting and magnification instruments and was working on the wide, flat surface when the phone trilled. In the old house, he could hear the water from Reina's shower trickling through the pipes. According to the LCD display, the caller was her mother. He wondered how Pilar would react to Zane answering her daughter's phone. In the what-the-hell spirit of his twin, he picked up the receiver and greeted the caller.

"Zane Masterson, what are you doing answering my daughter's phone?"

From her tone, Grey couldn't decide if Pilar was angry, annoyed or simply surprised.

"Saying hello. How'd you know it was me?"

She sighed as if bored. "Where's Reina?"

"In the shower."

"Alone? You must be losing your touch."

Grey paused. Okay, he wasn't touching this one, but damned if Pilar's comment didn't imply that she knew Zane a bit more intimately than as her daughter's landlord and friend. Of course, his brother's reputation was almost as widely known and accepted as Pilar's. Though Zane's tastes normally ran toward younger women, not older ones.

He answered her bait with a loud sniffing noise. "You don't really believe that, do you?"

Pilar hummed her skepticism but changed the subject. "Why isn't Reina at the gallery? I've never known her to miss a day, not even for someone as charming as you."

"Oh, come on. No one is as charming as me."

"May I speak with her, please?"

He heard the water stop and glanced toward the stairwell. He had the perfect excuse to dash up the stairs and deliver the cordless receiver. The thought of catching Reina in the act of drying off, maybe even helping her, urged him to step out of the workshop. But doing so with her mother on the phone was a little too kinky, even for him.

"Is there something I can help you with?"

"I'm calling to remind her about the reception at the Eastman Gallery tonight. Seven o'clock."

Grey forced himself to remember. He was certain the newspaper would be covering the gathering, but as a patron of the museum, he knew he would have received a personal invitation. He'd looked over his calendar carefully before switching places with Zane and he didn't remember seeing a notation. Of course, the get-together could be a private affair, one he'd know nothing about.

"The Eastman Gallery? I've been meaning to check that out."

"By all means, come along. I'm sure Reina would be delighted to have an escort. These events can be tiring."

"Then why go?"

Pilar laughed, the sound so practiced and perfected—at once feminine and sexy—Grey pulled the receiver away from his ear, marveling at the level of manipulation Reina's mother had achieved. If not for his experiences with Lane, he might not have been so acutely aware of counterfeit responses. He might have fallen hook, line and sinker for Pilar's seductive ploy.

"Why, indeed? Yes, you *must* come. You'll be a refreshing change."

She disconnected the call, leaving Grey without a valid excuse for interrupting Reina's shower. He returned to the solarium workshop and completed his dismantling of her equipment, stacking the pieces beside the stairs. He'd just set the gumbo in the microwave when Reina entered the kitchen, her hair twined into a damp braid, her face scrubbed free of smudges and dusted with a light powder, her lips gleaming with that burgundy gloss he'd admitted last night drove him wild.

Tease.

"Your mother called."

"You answered?" Her eyes widened to the size of quarters.

"Why not? Zane wouldn't stand on ceremony."

She nodded, apparently in agreement. "Did she want me to call her?"

"She didn't say. She wanted to remind you about the reception at the Eastman Gallery tonight."

Reina paused, her mind lost in thought, then disappeared into her workshop, returning with her purse. She pulled out her calendar and scanned the page designated for today.

She snapped the leather-bound book shut. "I could have sworn I told her I wasn't going."

The microwave dinged. He took out the bowls of gumbo and set them on the table. "Maybe she forgot."

"My mother never forgets anything associated with her social life. It's more likely she's counting on me forgetting that I said no."

He grabbed the rolls he'd tossed into the oven, still wrapped in the tin foil from last night, then poured iced tea into tall glasses. She eyed his kitchen acumen, obviously impressed. He went for broke and held out her chair.

She slid into the seat, finally laughing when he snapped a napkin across her lap. "Don't tell me you used to be a waiter."

Grey sat beside her. "I inherited the family business very young and never worked anywhere else, I'm afraid. However, the old saying goes that the way to a man's heart is through his stomach, but I have long suspected that the reverse is true. Women love a man who knows his way around a kitchen. Takes the pressure off."

Reina picked up her spoon. "I think you're probably right, but, for the record, I can cook."

He raised his eyebrows. "Studied in France?"

"Of course," she answered. "You don't think my mother taught me, do you? She'll hire a caterer to boil water for her tea. I like cooking, but I'm hardly ever home. I can't remember the last time I whipped something up in this kitchen.''

Grey cleared his throat, biting back the naughty suggestion on the tip of his tongue. He'd long considered the kitchen one of the sexiest rooms in a house and he relished an opportunity to show Reina the proper way to prepare a feast for the senses.

''We can fix that, you know.''

She nodded, but he wasn't sure if there was a twinkle in her eye because they were thinking along the same lines or because the reheated gumbo tasted even better today than it had last night.

''So, do you cook or do you just order in and wow a woman with your presentation and reheating skills?''

Grey's mind flashed with an image of a cooking session from the recent past that he didn't want to think about with Reina so near. He'd always considered it bad form to recall making love to another woman in the presence of a new lover, particularly one so much more genuine than the last.

Something must have showed on his face, because she put down her spoon and watched him with sad eyes.

''Thinking about Lane Morrow, aren't you?''

He scooped a large spoonful of gumbo into his mouth, shaking his head.

''Yes, you are.'' She sipped her tea, as if his denial meant nothing.

''I don't want to talk about her. She's ancient history.''

''Women like her are so pathetic,'' Reina continued, ignoring him. ''Shameful, really.''

He didn't know why he had a sudden desire to defend Lane, particularly since he agreed with Reina's cool assessment. But still, admitting Lane was a heartless, self-serving bitch more concerned with her own celebrity than whose trust she betrayed said as much about him—the man who fell for her—as it did about Lane.

He polished off a roll first. "She's been an actress her entire life, with an insatiable need to be the center of attention at all times. I shouldn't be surprised she used me to get herself booked on every talk show in the free world."

"Maybe not surprised," Reina said, tearing off a serving of bread, "but that doesn't mean you don't have the right to be angry."

"Oh, I was angry, believe me."

"Was?"

Grey had already lied to Reina once, when he'd pretended to be his brother. He certainly owed her the truth from this point forward, even if it did include information he'd rather not admit. "I can't waste any more of my time on anger. That's one of the reasons I switched places with Zane. I figured that if I spent a little time away from the media limelight, I'd have a chance to put the whole fiasco out of my mind."

She sipped her iced tea. "All the more reason for you to get out of the house today. There's a very hip, very CNBC concert at the park today. You should go."

"CNBC? Like the news organization?"

She clucked her tongue. "CNBC as in see-and-be-seen. Better brush up on your lingo before you venture out as Zane again."

He smirked, impressed by her determination. "All the more reason for me to stick around. I promise you won't even know I'm here. Besides, if you want me to be Zane again, I could pretend to be him at that soiree at the Eastman tonight."

"Zane wouldn't be caught dead at a fund-raiser for an

artists' colony struggling to survive in the mountains of Spain,'' she reported, her distaste for the event apparent.

"Then why are you going?"

"I'm not. Mother asked me to appear on her behalf and I told her weeks ago I wasn't interested. Seems she once had an affair with the Impressionist who runs the place and she has no desire to see him. But, of course, she still supports his cause. She's in the art scene herself now with the theater troupe. I don't think she wants to offend anyone who might turn their wallets her way.''

"You'd better call her then. She seemed certain you'd be going.''

Reina shook her head and dipped some bread into the gumbo. "I am not up for that argument. She'll know I didn't go when my name doesn't show up in the social column of your paper tomorrow.''

"Speaking of the paper,'' he said, unable to squelch his curiosity about how today's edition had turned out.

"Oh, I forgot. It's probably still out on the porch.''

Grey waved for her to stay seated, scooping out and swallowing the last of his cajun soup. "You eat. I want to go over the security system and those robberies so I can finish setting up your secret workshop and you can start on the collection.''

She rewarded his enthusiasm with a suspicious smile and a facetious tone. "I didn't know you cared about my ambitions so deeply.''

He stole a chunk of bread off the roll in her hand. "I don't. But I've already seen how the jewelry turns you on and, frankly, I'm all set to help you relieve a little more sexual tension.''

"Bastard,'' she said, her accusation softened by the electric glint in her eyes, visible only for a moment before she turned her nose to the air and proceeded to ignore him.

"You have no idea," Grey answered.

He found the paper rolled up in plastic on the front porch, but he shut the door and hesitated before taking the newsprint out of the wrapper. Here it was. The first full edition his brother had put to bed without any input from him. How bad could it be? Zane did have a way with words, and, despite his devil-may-care personality, he possessed a true respect and love for the family legacy.

Grey took the paper out, scanning the front page as he strolled back into the kitchen. From the corner of his eye, he saw Reina rise from the table to bring her bowl to the sink. The headlines were all in order, no misspellings or naughty double entendres. The articles all contained the requisite facts in the first two paragraphs of text.

All except one, that is.

One new column in a special, shaded box highlighted by his picture and byline.

Grey skimmed the content, sat down and allowed the laughter bubbling inside him to burst to the surface.

"What?"

In the midst of his mirth, he noticed Reina didn't even attempt her usual aloofness.

"Read my special report." He tapped the gray box. "Looks like I'm having a really hot affair with a sexy, mysterious woman. And everyone in New Orleans now knows all the sordid details."

9

REINA SNATCHED A DISH TOWEL and wiped her hands, more fascinated by the sound of Grey's unfettered laughter than by whatever Zane had apparently written in the paper. But was it about her? She found that highly unlikely. Zane wouldn't betray her privacy, not even to help his brother. And if he did, he had to know she'd have him drawn and quartered.

Apparently surmising that Reina's breeding wouldn't allow her to race across the kitchen to snatch up the paper and react like some crazed, paranoid maniac, Grey slid the paper across the table. She picked up the newsprint, relieved to read that Grey—or rather Zane—had written a front-page editorial about his affair with a sexy boutique owner, identified only as T.M.

"T.M. Could that be Toni Maxwell? Your stalker?" Reina asked.

Grey wiped a tear from his eye. "Yes, ma'am. I'd joked with Zane about him seducing her to find out what she was up to. I should have known he couldn't resist such an opportunity."

Reina blinked several times, reading the article from start to finish and hearing the natural inflection of Zane's voice as she scanned the words. According to the article, "Grey" had met Toni Maxwell at the grand reopening of Club Carnal, then again at a political dinner at Muriel's. The attraction had been instantaneous, powerful. The two planned to spend significant time together over the next few days and "Grey" intended to chronicle his affair for his readers, down to the sordid details.

Sales at the *Louisiana Daily Herald* were undoubtedly about to go through the roof.

"Sounds like Zane's having more fun as Grey than you are as Zane," she concluded, tossing the paper back onto the table, feeling sorry for this Toni Maxwell woman, even if she did bring the notoriety onto herself by chasing after the real Grey.

Grey snatched her hand before she could retreat. His fingers wrapped around hers roughly and, when she glanced into his eyes to see what had prompted his possession, she gasped at the intensity there. The flash of fire lighting his blue irises quickly cooled to a steady burn, enhancing the heat when he lifted her knuckles to his lips and brushed soft kisses over her skin.

Stares locked, he reeled her closer, bending her wrist so he could swirl his tongue in her palm. The act, so simple, stirred her insides as if he'd taken an intimate taste of her. Her nipples tightened against her satin bra. Her pulse pounded. When he drew a wet path along the life-line on her palm to her wrist, the muscles in her legs quivered.

She had no idea how he did it—how this unpretentious, intelligent, but emotionally wounded man so easily slipped past her defenses. Hadn't her mother taught her anything? Hadn't her own experiences prepared her to battle the effects of such overwhelming male confidence?

When he nibbled on the sensitive inner skin of her wrist, she knew the answer was no. When he spoke again, his voice a raspy timbre of desire, she added an exclamation point to his answer.

"Not possible," he claimed. "If he's enjoying himself

more than I am, right at this very moment, it's only because he's dead and somehow charmed his way into heaven.''

Reina dislodged the thickness in her throat with a quick swallow. ''You don't mind Zane leading the entire city to believe that you're having some torrid affair? And providing details?''

''It's brilliant,'' he claimed, placing a trio of upward moving kisses along her arm. ''The tabloids have had a field day exploiting that I haven't dated since Lane, solidifying her claims that she broke my heart. If Zane plays his dalliance with Miss Maxwell right, my reputation can only improve.''

''What about your privacy?''

He scooted his chair away from the table and pulled her closer. ''I have my privacy. Right here. With you.''

Before he could mesmerize her further with his bedroom voice and slick tongue, Reina grabbed the nearest chair and moved into it, pulling the stack of files he'd left on the table closer to them. With considerable effort, she shook off the anticipation of feeling his mouth on her belly, exposed by the midriff-baring blouse she'd chosen to wear after her shower. She'd dressed for comfort, she reminded herself. Because she had work to do and so did he. They would play later.

Oh, would they play.

''What are those questions you wanted to ask me about the robberies?''

After a quick look of disappointment, Grey pulled a legal pad from beneath the files, then winked at her. ''Can't stand the heat in the kitchen, huh?''

''I can stand your heat just fine,'' she claimed, then leaned forward enticingly, aware that her T-shirt enhanced her already ample breasts, giving him a dose of his own sexy medicine. "But I don't like to be rushed. If we work now, we'll have something delicious to look forward to later. Don't forget what the collection does to me."

"Screw the collection. *I* want to be the reason you're so hot and bothered."

She leaned back into the chair, saying nothing. She certainly wasn't about to admit that she hadn't so much as glanced at il Gio's designs or Viviana's diary since waking up this morning, and yet her flesh simmered with sensual anticipation—for him and only him.

"You'll get your chance, if you ask the right questions."

GREY GLANCED DOWN at his notes, willing himself to concentrate. Reina's scent lingered in the kitchen, milling with the warm spices from the gumbo and the sharp tang of chicory and coffee beans still simmering in the pot. He grabbed the legal pad and manila file folders and retreated to the solarium, now empty except for the wicker furniture set he remembered from his childhood. He glanced at his watch. It was nearly three o'clock.

After interviewing Reina and instructing her on the security system, he'd completed the reconstruction of her workshop upstairs and now had settled down with his notes, his cell phone and his laptop computer. Time to be Grey again. Time to break the story. Time to solve the mystery, even if solving the break-ins could prematurely end an affair Grey couldn't believe had only started the day before.

He was falling, and falling fast. How could he not? Reina was practically the poster girl for his perfect woman. Sexy. Adventurous. Educated. Private. Too private, he realized. Cloaked in sexuality, Reina possessed barriers around her heart that rivaled the Great Wall of

China in thickness, height and depth. She didn't hide her attraction to him, but he had no clue what she wanted from life, from a man, or partner, beyond sex. The women he'd dated always seemed so anxious to bare their hearts to him. Even Lane had, though what she'd confessed during their pillow talk all ended up being big fat lies.

Funny how that didn't sting so much anymore.

He knew if Reina ever opened up to him, she'd tell him nothing but the truth. The trick would be breaching that erotic defense system of hers, a powerful array built on the fact that she didn't fear anything about sex. The possibilities of making love with her quickly torpedoed any wayward thoughts about using traditional means to get her to open up about her emotions, her desires. But Grey figured that with his equal sexual prowess, he'd develop a system to battle her resistance.

Because like any good newspaperman, he had to know the truth. And like any good Masterson man, he wasn't about to retreat without a fight.

The thought led him back to the notes he'd scribbled during their interview. Just as the police had concluded, Grey felt certain that whoever had stolen the jewels from Reina's safe must have either worked with her at the gallery or had an accomplice who did. According to their interview, none of the artists who had left the gallery over the past five years harbored any ill feelings. She hadn't fired any employee, not even a deliveryman, since she opened. The ones who'd quit had done so to relocate to another city or for a better-paying job. She'd written all of them glowing recommendations.

During the first robbery, the thief had unlocked the safe, seemingly with the combination, and had left no fingerprints. At the time, several employees and artists had known the code. But after the break-in, Reina had replaced the safe with a newer model and kept the numerical sequence to herself.

She'd told no one, assured him that she hadn't written it down. And still, the second robbery also resulted in no damage to the safe or the locking mechanisms. She claimed no one could have guessed the code, either. She'd chosen a combination of numbers personal to her, numbers she felt certain no one else could figure out, or unless they knew her incredibly well.

He'd left the question at that, figuring there wasn't anyone in her employ who could have penetrated that intense privacy of hers. Probably no one in her entire life.

Except…

He dashed up the stairs, entering her bedroom through the open door. She'd closed the secret panel to the large interior room and had hung a few blouses in the smaller bypass to enhance the illusion that it was just a closet. He knocked lightly, in the succession of raps they'd agreed would mean he was the one asking for access.

"Come in," she called.

He opened the panel but didn't enter. She had the sheets of schematics spread across her worktable. A small blowtorch sizzled beside her and a collection of gold nuggets and chains were lined on a soft cloth. She'd tucked her safety glasses in the scooped neckline of her T-shirt. She looked busy and he didn't want to interrupt for too long, not when he anticipated what they'd accomplish once she was done for the day.

"Just a quick question. That second combination, the one you said no one could possibly guess—what numbers did you choose?"

Reina hardly hesitated. "Twenty-five, sixteen, seven."

"What do they mean?"

"Pardon me?"

"You picked the numbers because they're related somehow, right? What was it? Your combination in high school?"

"Give me some credit, Grey. I wouldn't pick something so obvious after being ripped off the first time. The combination is the ages I was each time my mother bought a house in the United States. I was seven when she purchased the cottage in Virginia, where we lived during the summer while she was on Broadway. I was sixteen when she bought the beach house in Malibu. We lived there during a theater run and movie shoot. I turned twenty-five just before she bought the house here in New Orleans."

Damn, but the woman did have a complicated mind, didn't she?

"So your mother might have been able to figure out your combination?"

Reina laughed aloud. "Pilar? My mother can't remember her own telephone number. Or the real year she was born."

"What about her maid?"

This time, Reina paused. "Dahlia might remember the years we lived in the States, but how would she guess I'd form those into a combination for a safe? How would anyone guess that? Besides, I only used numbers associated with homes we purchased. We lived here several times in hotels."

"Still…" It was a long shot at best, but he had nothing else to go on.

"Let's say Dahlia is either psychic or possesses a brilliant criminal mind. Why would she steal from me?"

Grey shook his head. He didn't have answers to either of those questions, but he did now have a lead to follow, sketchy as it was.

"You trust this woman?"

"Dahlia? She was the one constant in my childhood. My mother hired her shortly after I was born. She's more than just a maid. She's Pilar's right hand. She raised me."

"So you told her things, confided in her."

Reina's mouth dropped open slightly and Grey ached at the expression of horror that briefly crossed her face. But she shook the disbelief away and waved her hand at him. "Dahlia has no reason to steal. My mother pays her very well, and she has no real expenses. My mother buys her clothes, takes her to exotic places. Not to mention that Pilar has left Dahlia a considerable portion of her estate in her will. If she betrayed me like that, my mother would cut her loose without a backward glance. She'd lose everything. The jewels that were taken weren't equal in value to what she stands to gain financially from my family."

Reina's argument made sense, but Grey decided to investigate further. He'd already decided to run extensive background checks on every artist and employee involved with Reina's gallery. He'd just add Dahlia to the list.

"You're right," he said, attempting to reassure her. She probably didn't need the distraction of considering that a longtime family friend had possibly betrayed her. "I'm just grasping for straws. I'll let you get back to work."

With a quick coolness Grey knew now to be finely honed, she dismissed him and his suspicions and returned to her work. He closed the panel and bounded down the stairs, hooked his cell phone to his computer and dialed into his favorite search engine for background checks, requesting the basics first—social security numbers, last known addresses, employment records, credit reports. Using Reina's ground line, he ordered a case of cognac for an old college buddy who worked for Interpol, arranging to have it delivered immediately to his flat in London. Most of Reina's associates had European connections. He'd need Richard's resources. He winced when quoted the price, but figured even such a steep charge would be worth the investment. Particularly when he solved Reina's mystery and won her undying gratitude.

But until then, he'd have to find more basic ways to get under her skin. Starting tonight.

REINA GLANCED UP at the hidden skylight, aware that the last few rays of the sun had fallen beneath the horizon at least two hours ago. She hadn't brought a watch into the workshop, but guessed she'd been working steadily for at least five hours. To show for it, she'd reconstructed the mold for one of il Gio's rings, an exquisite sapphire that, according to his diary, he would wear to town to secretly inform Viviana that he intended to sneak into her bedroom that night but that he'd be in disguise.

She'd also laid out her plans for the restoration of a single crescent moon earring, centered with a pearl, which the jeweler would also wear for Viviana. This piece, highlighted by a long, removable chain and clasp that would attach to his penis, his scrotum, his nipple—anywhere Viviana chose—was worn beneath his clothes whenever he attended a social event with his wife, an intimate reminder of to whom he truly belonged.

The final creation had been relatively simple to reconstruct, but still had taken Reina the bulk of the afternoon. The design was intricate and had piqued her curiosity on so many levels that she'd consulted not only il Gio's designs and published diaries, but also scoured Viviana's memoirs for her personal reference. Though Reina had experimented with various sexual aids and toys, she'd never tried anything like this one, even if they were popular today.

However, she remained completely certain that none of the sex toys available on Bourbon Street matched il Gio's in both functionality and beauty. Fashioned in pure gold. Weighted by rubies she'd reset in the original carved ivory pendants. Softened by kid leather. That part had almost kept her from completing her project since the fabric il Gio saved had withered long ago. Then she'd remembered the gloves she'd bought last winter in Aspen, and after a desperate search in her cedar chest, she'd been back in business.

Despite the ache pressing between her shoulder blades and the crick in her neck no self-delivered massage could break, Reina couldn't suppress her need to try on this particular design.

But she wasn't wasting such decadence on herself, not unless Grey was there to help her experience the full effect.

She found him in the kitchen, cooking.

The aromas of piquant andouille sausage, garlic, onion and green pepper assailed her nostrils and made her stomach growl. "You weren't kidding about that way to a woman's heart thing, were you?" she asked, heading straight toward him and his sizzling skillet.

He leaned across and retrieved a bowl of beaten eggs. "I don't kid about important stuff." With a practiced flair, he poured the egg into the pan in a long, golden stream. "Have a seat. I was going to bring this up to you."

"Culinary and considerate, too," she murmured, briefly turning her gaze to him.

"My brother isn't the only jack-of-all-trades in our family. Are you done for the day?"

Reina paused. Technically, the answer should be yes.

Despite her use of her magnifying system, her eyes ached. And her fingers were stiff. Under normal circumstances, she would have treated her work-induced strain with a shot of bourbon and a long bath. But beneath her bra, her breasts strained for the pleasure il Gio's chains, clamps and jewels might give. Her pulse pounded with a potent mix of curiosity, lust and excitement.

And deep down, in a part of Reina's heart she rarely heard from, she acknowledged that she would never have entertained the notion of testing the piece she'd reconstructed if Grey hadn't become her lover.

"Not quite. One of the pieces I fashioned today is a little complicated. I was hoping to get your…opinion."

Grey's gaze, previously focused on flipping the omelettes, caught hers. "Let's skip dinner."

"You'll need your strength," she said, attempting to erase the sound of triumph in her voice.

Rounded with surprise at first, his eyes narrowed, then he grabbed two plates and served. "We'll eat fast."

Reina laughed, pouring the red wine he'd set out with equal speed. Though they both did indeed wolf down the delectable omelettes and large goblets of cabernet in record time, she doubted the giddiness she felt as they dashed up the stairs hand in hand had anything to do with alcohol. The capricious wave pushing her into her bedroom, allowing her to ignore the ringing phone without a second thought, was stirred by her need for Grey.

A need for sexual pleasure? Yes, she acknowledged as he disappeared into his guest bedroom, no doubt to set the security system and retrieve a condom. But she knew it was also more than that, more than she'd ever previously been willing to admit to herself. After reading Viviana's account of using this particular piece for the first time, Reina now knew what she wanted from Grey.

And she intended to get it.

He appeared in the doorway just as she whipped her T-shirt over her head.

"Mind if I watch?" he asked.

"Actually—" she popped the top button of her jeans "—no."

He crossed his arms over his broad chest and leaned a muscled shoulder on the doorjamb. The pose stole her breath, reminding her of his size, his power.

"Where do you want me, then?"

She kicked off her sandals. "On the bed, of course. You might want to get undressed first, but get beneath the covers."

"I'm not ashamed of being naked," he reminded her.

"You have no reason to be. But to do this experiment correctly, we need to take our time."

He strode across the room, dispensing with his shirt and jeans in quick flashes of fabric. "Whatever you say, chère. You're the boss."

She lifted her brows, surprised at his assumption that she wanted to be in charge. Then again, she shouldn't be shocked, should she? Only last night, she'd struggled with handing over the control of their lovemaking to him. If not for his skilled mouth and hands—and her unexplained need to trust him—she would have balked at allowing him to set the pace and call all the shots. But the result had been more pleasure, more freedom, than she ever dreamed a man could give her, particularly when wrapped in chains.

Speaking of which...

She lifted il Gio's creation from off the dresser, wondering if he'd have any idea what it was from this distance.

"Oh, I don't want to be the boss tonight, Grey."

He'd climbed beneath the covers and was propping pillows against the headboard when her claim caught his attention. He turned and narrowed his gaze, his perplexed look sending a naughty thrill across her skin.

"What is that?"

"The piece I'd like to try out."

Skepticism in his eyes warred with the expectant grin on his lips. "What does it do?"

She turned, retrieved Viviana's diary and tossed it to him from across the room. "Open the book to the page with the red ribbon. Read it aloud. We'll find out together."

10

GREY WAS NO FOOL. He did as he was told. Despite the instantaneous yank of his cock to sharp attention, he caught the book and turned to the right page. In the meantime, she sashayed across the room, dimming the overhead light and clicking on the lamp beside her bed.

"Something to read by," she said.

He silently nodded, but still had trouble focusing on the handwritten words on the page. *Ah, hell.* He'd forgotten his glasses. But where?

With sensual grace, Reina dipped down on her knees, retrieving the wire frames from the pocket of his discarded shirt. She stood, stretched her leg over his lap and crawled atop, placing the glasses on his nose herself.

She rocked her hips, snuggling her panties against his bulge beneath the sheet. He couldn't feel if she was wet, but the look in her eyes alone told him she was ready. Knowing all he could do right now was wait caused him to groan with a strangled combination of passion and impatience.

"Power turns you on, doesn't it?" she surmised.

He noticed that while he was engaging the security system from the control panel in the guest room, she'd painted her lips with the red gloss he loved on her. Realizing she'd added the detail for him, his mouth dried.

"Power turns everyone on."

"Some women like to be submissive." She adjusted his glasses with a light, erotic touch.

"And others just toy with the concept," Grey guessed, wondering exactly what she had planned and how far she'd be willing to go. "You can't be submissive, Reina. It's not in your nature."

Her eyes betrayed a hint of surprise. "You don't know me that well."

"Sweetheart, a man only has to be in your presence for ten seconds to know you're the type who wants to be in charge."

She answered with a delicious shimmy of a shrug. "I wasn't in charge last night."

Oh, now he got it. "And you liked that, didn't you? More than you expected. Maybe so much more that you'd like to try again? Raise the stakes?"

"You have to ask?"

His chest filled with pride. He'd given Reina Price, the seasoned seductress, a fresh thrill, a novel sexual experience. Now she wanted more—and the gold and chain contraption she'd showed him had something to do with her new fetish.

Grey was game, of course. But he wasn't about to lose this opportunity, either. Reina wanted something special. He'd give it to her, but he needed his quid pro quo.

"On one condition."

Her eyes flashed with surprise. "Always the negotiator?"

He answered her insight with a shrewd grin. "Wouldn't you be disappointed if I wasn't?"

She slipped her hands around his neck. "What do you want?"

"Answers."

"About the robberies?"

Her indignant look nearly caused him to laugh. Instead, he licked his lips, then did the same to hers. "What robberies?"

She nodded in understanding. "You don't mean answers, you mean confessions."

"Such an intelligent woman. And sinfully sexy." He nibbled her shoulders and neck, groaning as the flavors of her skin whet his palate for much, much more.

"I'm a very private person, Grey."

He tugged aside the thin strap of her bra and placed a kiss along her collarbone. "Your…responses…will be completely off the record."

He didn't bother to hide the wicked glint in his eyes and was impressed when she matched his iniquitous expression with one of her own. "And the whole of New Orleans thinks Zane is the wicked twin."

"Suckers, aren't they?"

He traced the scoop of her bra with his tongue, pausing above her nipples to dip deeper and swipe the sensitive nubs. As if he'd jolted her with pure electricity, she shot back and climbed off the bed.

"Don't get ahead of yourself. You'll regret it. We both will. Okay, I'll accept your terms. You give me what I want, and I'll give you what you want. That's what our affair has been about from the start, hasn't it?"

Grey held his tongue, acknowledging his agreement with a small nod. She was right, of course. Up to this moment, their affair had simply been about sating their mutual desires and nothing more. When he'd taken over Zane's life, he'd thought that's all he wanted. Hedonism at its finest. Pleasure and play without having to hide, without having to fear the repercussions. Zane's persona was both accepted and ignored by the public, since they expected nothing less than scandal and sin. *Oh, it's just*

Zane, having another meaningless, naughty liaison instead of *Good God! Grey Masterson likes to have sex in limousines!*

If only they knew. If only Lane had had the insight to realize that it hadn't been the limousine that turned him on, but the mask of privacy the tinted windows and moving car had provided, one with eyeholes to the world, openings from his isolation. He'd always hated having to rein in his emotions, control his reactions and urges simply because he was the "good" twin, the "responsible" one, the one everyone counted on to keep the business afloat and respect the family name and reputation.

But Reina? She understood. With her, he had the best of both worlds. Unlike any other woman he'd ever met, she guarded her privacy like a fierce Amazon protecting her queen. She wrapped herself in a cloak of jaded sexual power, daring men to try and amuse her, knowing they'd invariably fail. She counted on her air of mystery to keep everyone, including him, at arm's length. Last night, he'd proved his inventiveness. And arm's length wasn't good enough for him anymore.

He'd been inside her once and the sensations had awakened more than just his libido. He'd be inside her again, but, this time, they'd transcend the physical.

All he had to do was figure out how that contraption worked and make sure he used it right.

REINA EASED OFF Grey's lap and returned to the dresser. What did he want from her? What kind of confessions? What sort of answers? She wondered if he realized the depth of what he'd asked for, and suspected he did. The man possessed a wealth of insight into who she was, possibly because they had so much in common. But she couldn't think about that now, could she? She'd wanted this liaison tonight to be about pleasure, about risks, about trying something she'd never tried before, but she'd foolishly expected the evening's experiences to be limited to the physical, the sexual. She should have guessed Grey would find a way to raise the bar.

She faced the mirror, twisting her arms behind her to remove her bra. Lifting the chain by the tiny clasps she'd softened with cutouts from her gloves, she closed her eyes and concentrated on the moment, the here and now.

She watched Grey read silently in the mirror's reflection.

"What has Viviana to say about this contraption?" she asked.

He glanced up. "Haven't you read it?"

"I skimmed. I didn't want to ruin the surprise."

He laughed and turned back a page. "Come here," he demanded.

Good start, Reina concluded. She spooled the chain into an old velvet-lined case that used to hold the pearl necklace someone had given her years ago. She'd tossed the single strand into her lingerie drawer without a second thought, knowing the design she'd struggled to recreate all afternoon deserved a better home than a foam-lined metal attaché. After kicking off her panties, she joined Grey on the bed, the flat, rectangular box set between them.

Grey's eyebrows seemed to stay in a permanent position of surprise.

"Wow," he said, his gaze darting back and forth across the page. "Your Italian jeweler put a lot of forethought into his seduction, didn't he?"

Reina took the opportunity to stretch her back. She'd been working all day, and, besides, the movement lured Grey's attention to her breasts.

"According to the diary, they didn't make love completely until nearly a year after he started his seduction."

Grey frowned. "Too late for us."

She shrugged one shoulder. "I don't want to be Viviana, Grey. I just want a taste of what she experienced."

"Was she as strong willed as you are?"

She pointed at the diary. "What do you think?"

Grey read aloud.

"My hands quiver as I write this. My heart pounds like the hoofbeats of a thousand horses. I've even taken to writing not in my bedroom as usual, but in a small space hidden in the corner of my house, a tiny candle at my feet. If anyone were to discover my secret...!"

"You can feel her battling between the thrill and the forbidden, can't you?" Reina asked.

Grey nodded and continued.

"Last night, il Gio's seduction tested all that I am. I am frightened by what I have discovered. What is a woman who would do anything for pleasure? And yet, I cannot feel shame. I do not. Not when my lover, even when he demands, holds my heart in tender hands—hands that have brought me so much delight, I wonder what more he can give me."

Grey glanced up at Reina, and his expression, at once unfathomable and serious, injected an ounce of doubt into her plan. She felt certain he'd play the game she'd laid out, not for him, but for her. Did Grey hold her heart with tender hands? she wondered all of a sudden. And if he did, how had he gotten hold of it in the first place?

*"He sent me the satin box yesterday morning. I did
not know what the jewelry was. I suspected a necklace, but had already learned that il Gio's creations
served two purposes—beauty on the outside, decadence within. The chain had three ends…"*

As Grey read, Reina scooted back on the bed and removed the chain from the box, laying it out between them
as Viviana described it.

*"The clasps twisted in place like baubles for the
ears, two large and padded with soft leather, the
third smaller and tighter from a spring."*

Grey closed the book.

"Don't you want Viviana to tell us how to use it?"

He lifted one of the large screw-on clasps. "I'm not a
sixteenth-century woman, Reina. Neither are you. We
both know what this is for."

He reached out, poising the clasp at her nipple, but he
was too far away to reach. "I'll have to come closer."

He crawled on his hands and knees, stalking her across
the bed like a tiger on the hunt. In the dim light, his blue
eyes sparkled with unadulterated lust and single-minded
pursuit. The chain, still clutched in his fist, caught a glint
from the lamplight.

She pulled her knees beneath her, bringing her breasts
to the level of his eyes.

He clucked his tongue and shook his head. "You're
not erect enough for a snug fit. I'll have to fix that."

A surge of excitement trilled through her, anticipation
born from both the rough sound in his voice and knowing
he'd soon take her in his mouth. He licked his lips hun-
grily. Her breath caught.

"Give me your breast," he ordered.

Her pulse quickened, but she did as he asked, lifting her breast to his mouth so he didn't have to move. He rewarded her compliance instantly, suckling her until she was tight and hard and wet.

He finished with a soft, reverent kiss—his gaze locked with hers—causing a burning sensation behind her eyes.

"Now the other."

Once he had her hard and ready, he knelt across from her and released the chain. The gold dangled down his bare body, brushing against his thick erection and powerful thighs. Reina watched him fumble with the clamp, her anxiousness building to such a pitch she had to fist her hands to keep from grabbing the nipple clamps and putting them on herself. With any other man, she wouldn't have curbed her impatience. With any other man, she wouldn't have possessed any patience at all, much less worked up the courage to use it.

But with Grey, she did.

What was happening to her?

The mechanism she'd reconstructed only a few hours ago from pieces hidden away for over three hundred years seemed too small for his huge hands. But, not surprisingly, his fingers soon proved nimble. In seconds, he had the soft inner pads of kid leather pressed to either side of her nipple.

"You'll have to tell me when it's too tight," he said, then began to twist the screw that controlled the fit.

Reina didn't know which sensation rocked her more— the slow, increasing squeeze on her sensitive skin or the fire from the intensity in his eyes.

She glanced down, afraid of what she saw in his stare. Too much concern for her comfort, too much care for more than just her body.

"Look at me," he said.

He turned the screw.

She gasped and met his eyes.

"Tight enough?"

She swallowed. "No."

He flicked the pad of his thumb over the protruding nipple. The feeling was such a mishmash of pleasure and pain, she could only whimper in response. "You're sure? I don't intend to hurt you."

She nodded. "Just a little..."

He slowly turned the screw, stopping when she gasped. He found the other clasp and turned his attention to applying the same forbidden pleasure to her left breast. When he had the clamps in place, he dragged his hands down the Y-shaped chains. The exquisite, teardrop ruby she'd set at the joining point, as detailed by il Gio's designs, skimmed just above her navel. From there, a single chain dangled farther, a smaller clasp designed with a tiny spring at the end.

He lifted the last piece. "I suppose this is supposed to attach, where? On your lips? Your clit?"

She nodded, unsure if she possessed the ability to speak while the clamps provided a constant, exquisite pressure on her nipples.

"Ah, lover's choice. But when il Gio first used this on Viviana, he didn't intend to make love to her, did he?"

She shook her head, pressing her lips tightly together, reveling in the slick feel of her glossy lipstick. The one he loved. The one she'd worn just for him.

He dropped the last clasp and scooted nearer. His erection swatted the chain aside and caused a slight tug on her nipples. She gasped, but he seemed to ignore the sound.

"He probably just toyed with her, didn't he? But she

didn't know what she'd miss if he gave her an orgasm without being inside her, did she? Not yet. But you know, Reina, don't you? You know.''

Yes, she knew! She didn't want the empty pleasure of an orgasm without intercourse. She could manage that herself. She wanted only what Grey seemed to be able to give her—fulfillment. Completeness. Pleasure that touched her deep, deep inside.

She managed a nod.

"Tell me.''

"I want you.''

"Oh, that I know. But at this point, you'd want any man, wouldn't you?''

He tugged the chain again, this time toward him, stretching her nipples the most infinitesimal, exquisite amount.

"No,'' she confessed. "Only you.''

"Why?''

She shook her head, unwilling to call to action the clarity of mind to formulate an answer. To think so hard meant she'd have to ignore the sensations coursing through her, from the tight clamps on her breasts to the increasing moisture between her legs.

"Tell me, Reina. We had an agreement, remember?''

She spied the roguish glint in his eyes and spat a vulgar curse.

"Why?'' he repeated.

She swallowed deeply, willing her mouth to work. "You excite me.''

"You're a fairly excitable woman, so primed.'' He dropped the chain and splayed his hands across her backside. The possessive spread of his fingers, the pressure as he clasped and kneaded her buttocks, reminded her of all the other erogenous zones on her body, all the ones she'd ignored while her breasts experienced the breathtaking torture of the clamps. "You're so aware of your every want and need. And you're willing to do whatever it takes to find satisfaction, aren't you?"

He dipped his fingers low, spreading her so that a kiss of cool air sparked a quick but potent thrill. Like a match to kerosene, a fire caught at the base of her wetness and traveled straight inside.

She fought a whimper and straightened her spine. She couldn't tell if he meant his assessment to be a compliment or a backhanded criticism, but she didn't care. She was who she was and she couldn't change. Wouldn't change. Not for any man. Not even him.

"Yes, so what?"

"Are you willing to let down your defenses? Tell me a secret, Reina. You said last night you had a lot of them. Tell me one I'd never guess."

Before she could answer, before she could decide whether she even intended to answer, he dipped his head and flicked her nipples with his tongue. A shock wave shot through her and she had to grab his shoulders to keep from falling. Her flesh, numb from the constant pressure, sought the sensations of his mouth like dry soil needing water. Lots and lots of water.

He blazed a path from breast to breast, then traced his tongue to her neck, where he marked her with wondrous nips and bites. Just enough to stir her passions to a fever pitch, just enough to leave tiny evidence of his loving on her skin.

When he straightened to make love to her ear, he moved the last few inches closer so that his erection slipped between her thighs. He was so hard, so curved. Memories of how perfectly he had fit inside her the night before flooded her brain, erasing whatever response she almost had to whatever question he'd asked a moment before.

He pulled back, leaving her skin moist from his kisses. "Well? I'm waiting."

She swallowed, willed herself to breathe, tried to find the answer to his inscrutable question somewhere in his eyes.

"I don't know what you want from me, Grey."

"Don't you? I want a glimpse inside your heart. I want to know what you really want from a man, besides an orgasm."

She felt herself shaking her head even before she realized how she couldn't answer the question. Not because she didn't want to share the intimacy he wanted, but because she didn't know the answer—truly, completely, honestly—she didn't know.

"I don't want anything from you."

He arched an eyebrow. "You don't think you do, but you do. Dig deeper, Reina. Tell me what you want. I promise, I'll do everything I can to give it to you."

His persistence piqued her ire, but the feel of him so close, pulsing with need that matched her own, toned her anger to clear indignation. "Grey, I swear. I don't want anything except you, inside me, taking me outside myself, for an instant."

She turned her gaze aside, and in the moment it took for her to recover from her loss of control, he sat, donned a condom, then began removing the clamps around her nipples.

The sweet gentleness of his touch renewed the trickle of hot fire down the back of her throat. The minute the golden torture device dropped on the comforter, a searing heat burned her breasts. Before she could even wince in response, he used his mouth and hands to soothe her skin, renew her desire.

"I'll give you more than an instant, Reina," he said, moving his legs between hers and positioning her above his erection.

"Give what you want to give, Grey. I won't ask…"

Her voice died away as the truth struggled closer to the surface, but he burst the elusive conclusion by grabbing her hips and easing inside her.

"You don't have to ask. Not with me. I know what you want from me, *chère,* because I want the same from you."

He rolled them over, carefully, dislodging their connection so briefly Reina hardly remembered the loss when he penetrated her to the hilt. He took her wrists, poised them over her head and spoke firmly.

"Don't move."

He eased back until only the tip of his penis remained cupped inside her.

"Feel me," he said, thrusting slowly, fully, filling her until she arched her back to take more. "Yeah, that's it."

He transferred both her wrists to one hand, then lifted her knees with the other so her shins pressed against the taut muscles in his chest. The pose allowed him to drive deeper, farther. When he gently unfolded her legs and crossed her ankles over his left shoulder, she thought he'd somehow found his way beyond the last barrier that kept them two separate beings.

In this position, she couldn't touch him, couldn't pleasure him, couldn't do anything but lose herself in the complete and unhindered satisfaction of her deepest desires. Yet she heard the escalation of his excitement, the deepening of his voice, the raggedness of his breath that told her he didn't need her to do anything more but feel him inside her to glean his ultimate gratification.

The slow build of pressure burst into a wave of sensations she couldn't fight. Not that he wanted her to. "That's it," he repeated as her moans grew louder and his sex drove deeper.

They came together, tight and tense and long. When she shouted his name, he continued to thrust, continued to push her so high her eyes flashed open in amazed wonder.

She didn't remember anything after that until he snuggled beside her beneath the comforter, his hand curled protectively across her belly. She waited for his breathing to regulate, for her to hear the sounds of his sleep.

But she didn't hear them. Long minutes ticked by as she watched the digital clock tucked unobtrusively behind a cloisonné tile she'd bought on Royal Street last summer. She tried to remember that shopping spree, who she'd been with, what else she'd bought, where she'd stopped for lunch. The details flitted by, never rooting, never allowing her the reprieve she desperately wanted, a short respite from the realization that Grey Masterson meant something to her. Something important. Something that, even if he left tomorrow, would forever alter the woman she was and the goals she'd set for her life.

"Reina?"

A mechanical beeping sounded from across the hall before she replied.

They both shot up in the bed. Reina clutched the sheet to her breasts. "What's that?" she asked, guessing the security system had been tripped but not wanting to accept that possibility.

"The alarm. Stay here," he ordered, dashing over her on the bed and grabbing his pants in the process.

This time, however, Reina had no intention of allowing Grey to be the boss.

11

GREY SCRAMBLED INTO HIS JEANS, not bothering with the zipper or button. He heard the rustle of the sheet as Reina dragged it around her and followed close at his heels. Damn if she chose now to revert to her normal mode of doing whatever the hell she pleased. He tapped a code in the control panel and immediately silenced the beeping.

"Why aren't alarms going off? The loud ones?" Reina asked, her voice breathless, and clearly annoyed.

"Do you want to scare your thief away, or catch him in the act?"

Reina remained silent, and his blood surged. He didn't doubt she was an adventurer at heart, but risking the collection was something he didn't think she'd do under any circumstances, even if it meant catching her thief. Of course, except for the contraption they'd just put to incredible use, the bulk of il Gio's jewels were stored safely behind the hidden walls of the secret workshop. And they had no way of knowing if whoever had just crossed onto Reina's property was the same person responsible for the robberies. For all he knew, her mother had stopped by to find out why she hadn't attended that fund-raiser tonight.

He read the panel of lights and flipped on the video monitors.

"Whoever it is hasn't come up the walk," he said, waiting for someone to come into view on the monitor poised over the front porch. "But that beep was on the front gate."

"The front gate? Doesn't sound like a robber," she said, the smirk clear in her voice. "Sounds like a visitor."

Grey glanced at the time display on the computer. It was after ten o'clock. "At this hour?"

"In New Orleans? Absolutely. Can you see who it is?"

Grey waited, but he saw nothing. The view of the gate, now closed tight, remained empty. He flipped to the back door. Nothing. With clouds blocking out the moon and the porch lights focused on the doors and windows, he couldn't see if anyone lurked along the thick rows of ferns or behind the barrel-trunked live oaks or massive magnolias.

"Someone could be in the yard, waiting."

Behind him, she yawned. "Maybe an animal tripped the alarm. A cat or a squirrel," she reasoned.

Grey shook his head and waited. "I don't think so. I have a strange feeling…"

He picked up the phone and dialed the number Brandon had written on a card and taped to the side of the main monitor. He gave the address and the pass codes to the operator that answered, then instructed them to ignore any alarm set off at their address for the next hour.

"Why did you do that?"

Without taking his eyes off the screens, he fastened his jeans and slipped on a T-shirt. From the bottom of his bag, he pulled out a gun, checked the safety, then tucked it into his pocket.

"I don't want to scare anyone away." He grabbed his cell phone and tossed it to her. She caught it but nearly lost the sheet she'd twisted over her body like a toga. Grey entertained a quick but potent vision of her as Athena, the beautiful goddess of wisdom and war. They hadn't discussed the details of handling a potential break-in at the house, but he knew she possessed enough intelligence and resourcefulness to accept any challenge he threw her way.

She used the phone to point at his gun. "I didn't know newspaper editors came armed and dangerous," she said, her voice devoid of any inflection that would have told him whether or not she approved or disapproved. The woman's ability to veil her emotions was starting to grate on his nerves.

"Newspaper editors sometimes have to go into undesirable neighborhoods. And, as the phrase goes, 'My momma didn't raise no fool.' Don't worry, I know how to use it."

Reina rolled her eyes with adorable impatience. "Why don't I doubt that? However, if I'm going to confront a potential prowler, even if it's just to assault him with your cell phone, I'd rather do so dressed."

She spun toward her bedroom, and Grey swallowed a chuckle then cautioned her in a whispered voice. "Fine, but don't turn on any lights. I'd rather whoever it is think we're not home."

As he leaned forward on the desk, his eyes darting back and forth between the three small monitors, he wondered why he hadn't asked Brandon to set them up with sound capabilities as well. Brandon had offered, but Grey had refused, claiming the advanced home security technology amounted to overkill. Still, right now, he'd like to know if he could hear any rustling beyond the sound of Reina dropping her sheet in the other room. The quiet slide of her closet door. The grate of hangers. The open and closing of a drawer. His gaze flashed toward the doorway to her bedroom, but she'd followed his instructions and hadn't turned on the light.

What does a woman of style choose to wear to greet a potential burglar?

The more time that passed without anyone approaching the front or back doors, the more Grey guessed either the gate alarm had been a false alert or they did indeed have a prowler on their hands. Twice, he thought he spied movement just outside the range of the grainy black-and-white monitors. He considered going outside and doing a sweep of the grounds, but wouldn't follow through until Reina joined him.

And she did rather quickly, dressed to the nines in a slim black cat suit covered with a long, sheer jacket and soft-heeled boots. She slipped behind him and watched the monitor from behind him.

"If all the female cops in New Orleans dressed like you, criminals would turn themselves in willingly," he quipped.

She clucked her tongue at him. "My fatigues are at the tailor. This is the best I could do."

Grey swallowed the thick lump of desire in his throat. "Your best is, as always, amazing."

She slapped him on the shoulder and pointed toward the monitor again. "Anything?"

"Just a few suspicious shadows. But a visitor would have knocked by now, don't you think?"

"You'd think," she answered.

"The collection is safe?"

"Completely locked up. What do we do now?"

Grey pulled out the chair tucked beneath the desk, sat down on it, then pulled her onto his lap. "We wait. Another five minutes. Then, if we don't see anyone, I'll go downstairs and investigate."

She twisted on his lap, undoubtedly attempting to find a comfortable position, but stirring his need for her instead. She smelled like sex, warm and musky, tinged with that subtle spice that anchored her favorite perfume.

The second time she moved, he groaned. "You need to stop that," he warned.

"Sorry," she said, but the humor in her tone told him she didn't mean her apology in the least. "I need my own chair."

"Torture though it is, my lap will have to do." He shifted this time, so that his growing erection pressed against the curve of her buttocks.

"You are an insatiable man, aren't you?"

"Just as insatiable as you are. Even if you do shy away from certain things," he taunted.

She twisted around so quickly her hair whipped across his face. "I don't shy away from anything."

He needed to watch the monitors, but spared her a quick, doubtful glance first. "Really? Then why won't you ask me for anything?"

"Why does it bother men so much when a woman doesn't need them?"

He answered her question by yanking her fully against his hard sex. "Oh, you need me, *chère.*"

"I meant for anything other than sex. That is your complaint, isn't it? An unfounded one, considering that I'm currently depending on you to help me keep the collection safe."

"Something you asked for only out of sheer desperation and only because you thought I was my brother, with whom you admittedly share no sexual chemistry."

"Zane is a good friend. I'm going to kill him next time I see him," she muttered through clenched teeth, "but I can always depend on him."

"And you've never met any other man you could depend on?"

She turned her eyes back to the monitors. "No."

Grey narrowed his gaze, watching her expression, cast in the shadows of the bluish silver light from the small screens. There was so much she wasn't telling him, so much she probably wasn't even allowing herself to think.

Too bad for her that Grey didn't let go of a mystery, or an interesting story, so easily.

"What about your father? Couldn't you depend on him?"

He knew it was a loaded question. Though she apparently had a close relationship with her mother, she'd never once mentioned the man who'd given her the other half of her genes.

"I never knew him."

"You never met?"

"I don't even know his name."

"You never asked your mother?"

Her laugh lacked any hint of amusement. "I asked, she refused to answer. I don't even think Dahlia knows— mother hired her when she was already pregnant with me."

"That doesn't bother you? Not knowing your father?"

"Of course it bothers me." When she turned this time, he instantly recognized signs of deep sadness. Her eyes seemed a little more glossy. Her jaw quivered, as if she clamped her mouth shut with a bit too much pressure. She inhaled deeply before finally speaking. "For many years—hell, even now—whenever I meet a debonair man around my mother's age, I wonder if he could be the one. Doesn't matter if he looks like me or not, since I look like my mother."

"You have no clues? Nothing to go on?"

She shook her head. "When I was young, I used to snoop around in my mother's things, hunting for something that could send me in the right direction. I even read her diary, which, quite frankly, made Viviana's confessions seem like recipes for yellow cake. Whoever my father was, he had nothing to offer my mother, or she would have kept him around a little longer, if nothing else.''

Grey nodded, wondering if the conclusion his intellect told him to draw would be a fair one. ''So you don't commit to men because you fear they'll abandon you, like your father?''

She laughed. ''My, my, Dr. Masterson, such an astute diagnosis and I haven't even inspected your therapy license.''

''Maybe I should start editing the advice column.''

''Maybe you should tune into something other than Oprah every so often.''

He chuckled, and so did she. Sharing the humor defused the tension in her body and she relaxed, leaning back a bit against his shoulder.

After a long silence, she said something he didn't expect. ''I'm not so complicated, Grey. My whole life, I've watched my mother bleed men dry. Of their money and of their love. Chances are, she did the same thing to my father. I love her deeply, but I don't want to be like her.''

Grey pressed his lips together, his heart thrumming, his mind reeling, certain that confession had cost Reina more than the worth of the entire collection of gems and gold stored in the next room. This was what he'd wanted from her during their lovemaking—a glimpse into her heart.

Only he wouldn't have guessed he'd find something so sad.

''I hate to point this out again,'' he said, knowing he treaded dangerous waters, but equally certain she could handle the undertow, ''but you're a great deal like your mother in many ways. You look like her, you have the same innate sensuality…"

"Innate? Darling," she said, sounding so much like Pilar Price, he shivered, "there is nothing innate about my sensuality." She turned, kicked her legs over the arm of the chair and smoothed her hand over the stubble-rough skin on his cheek. "The Price women have honed their tempting powers from years of practice."

Grey frowned. For the first time since he'd met her, he recognized the difference between the sexuality she turned on at will, like during her meeting with Claudio the evening before, and the charm she'd exhibited with him, even when she'd thought he was Zane. *Particularly* when she thought he was Zane. He sent a mental thank-you to his brother for never attempting a seduction of this amazing woman, for being her friend, for allowing a trust to exist that Grey, as her lover, now had the opportunity to take to a new level.

A higher level, one he himself had never climbed, despite years of searching for the right woman. Grey finally had the chance to fall in love—with a woman who could truly appreciate the emotion, since she'd certainly never allowed herself to experience it before.

Just like him.

"Powerful stuff, that Price sensuality," he said.

A bored glaze descended over her eyes just before she turned lazily back toward the monitors. "Yes, I suppose it is."

He opened his mouth to speak but was interrupted when she stood, her finger pressed against the center screen. "Grey, look!"

Grey shot up, sending the chair rolling back until it crashed silently against the bed. A figure, small in stature and dressed in dark colors from a ball cap to a dark jacket and jeans, walked furtively onto the back porch. After glancing both left and right, then leaning back to check the driveway one last time, the person stepped completely forward and pulled a key chain out of her pocket.

"Oh, my God," Reina whispered, her voice hoarse with shock. "That's Judi."

REINA PRESSED HER HAND to her mouth and willed herself not to overreact. Just because her assistant and friend was stepping up to her back door dressed like a street thug and holding what she assumed was an unauthorized key to her house didn't mean she was behind the robberies at the gallery.

But it didn't look good, did it?

From the corner of her eye, she watched Grey disengage the alarm completely. Judi would be able to come right in with no piercing sounds to frighten her away.

They watched her pull the screen door open just enough for her to insert the key.

"Did you give her a key to the house?" he asked.

Reina shook her head. "No, Zane has the only spare."

"She had access to your purse, though, right?"

This time, she nodded. Of course Judi had access to Reina's purse! They were friends, associates. She'd introduced the young woman to her mother, an actress Judi claimed to have admired for years, having once seen her perform in New York, her hometown. Having no family in New Orleans, Judi had come to Pilar's house for Thanksgiving, had exchanged gifts with Reina on Christmas Eve, then slept in the guest room—which she and Grey now shared with security equipment that would prove her betrayal.

"She knows about your workshop in the solarium?" he asked.

"She knows everything I know. But she didn't know the combination to the second safe. I didn't tell her, and I didn't write it down anywhere she could see."

Grey shook his head, his expression dire, as if that fact made little difference. "But she knew about the security cameras you added after the first robbery, didn't she? She could have positioned the camera at the safe and recorded you using the code."

Reina didn't want to believe this. Judi was no criminal mastermind! She'd taken nearly a month to learn how to operate the new voice-mail system. "The security guard would have seen."

"The same security guard who *claimed* to have been rendered unconscious during the second robbery?"

She stamped her foot but knew Grey's theory held more likeliness than she wanted to admit. "They both passed lie detector tests."

He frowned. "Lie detectors aren't infallible. You said that yourself."

They heard a scrape downstairs and a pinched scream, as if Judi had collided with some piece of furniture, probably the wicker chaise they'd moved to the other side of the solarium after Grey had dismantled Reina's worktable and brought it upstairs.

Reina couldn't deny that things didn't look good for her assistant. She had more opportunity than anyone else to take the jewels from the safe in her office, and if she'd somehow enticed the security guard to help her, they could have taken the second stash. But why? What motive? Money? If that had been the reason, neither Reina nor the police had noticed any change in Judi's spending habits. She still drove the same battered car, used the same secondhand Prada purse.

"I'd never figure Judi for such a cool liar," she admitted. "And I've met some of the best in the Western hemisphere."

Grey shrugged. "We don't know what Judi's up to yet. Maybe we should find out before we start accusing her of crimes."

"We can start with breaking and entering. We can prove that much, can't we?"

Incensed and betrayed, Reina pushed past him, stopping with a jerk when he grabbed her by the wrist. Her mind flashed to the last time he'd held her arm so tightly. When he'd been inside her, manipulating her body into an exquisite shape, joining with her for the most awesome lovemaking she'd ever known.

"What do you plan to do?" he asked.

Reina arched one eyebrow. Her stomach burned with the need to knock the two-faced twit on her ass, but Reina hadn't been raised for actions so coarse. "I honestly don't know. Let's head downstairs and just play it by ear, shall we?"

12

REINA LEANED AGAINST the doorway for a moment, taking quiet, deep breaths, harnessing her anger into a manageable ball clutched in the pit of her stomach. A shadow in the darkness just outside the solarium, she watched Judi toss the pillows off the wicker couch in frustration. Grey pressed close behind her, the muscles in his chest and his soothing, spicy scent fortifying her resolve.

She flipped the light switch, bathing the room in a deceptively warm glow.

Judi spun and lost her footing, stumbling back onto the couch. "Reina!"

Reina smirked. Seasoned criminal? Not in this universe. "Judi."

Her assistant sputtered, then swallowed, scrambling to her feet with the grace of a pregnant elephant. "Zane! Oh, wow. I didn't think you were home. I rang the doorbell…"

"That's lie number one." Grey whispered into Reina's ear, apparently content to let her handle the situation. Judi could hardly be considered capable of inflicting any real harm, unless Reina acknowledged the true depth of her betrayal. In that case, Judi could indeed cause serious emotional damage. Judi had been her friend, not just an employee. Reina had taken her into her home, had her accepted into her family. Judi had attacked more than

Reina's valued business and reputation. She'd raided the very foundation of her trust.

Trust she'd only now begun to share with Grey. Trust that could have, perhaps even tonight, started her on a path toward love. Despite the strength his presence gave her, Reina stepped away from his rock-hard body.

"Funny, you'd think I would have heard it, since the bell is at the top of the stairs."

Judi's eyes darted back and forth between her and Grey. Reina doubted her assistant would turn to the man she knew as Zane to corroborate her story or provide any type of support. The two shared a mutual hate-hate relationship since the first time Judi came on to him and Zane turned her down flat.

"Maybe you were too busy." Her sneer rang loud and clear.

Reina ignored it. "Why are you here, Judi?"

She dug frantically into the pocket of her oversize jacket, which Reina recognized as identical to the one her security guard wore on a rare cold New Orleans night, but with the insignia removed. "I was bringing this to you." She shot forward, handed Reina a bill of sale, then slunk back to what she assumed was a safe distance.

She read the information on the yellow carbon copy. "Mrs. Davis bought Razi's sculpture. It's about time. She's been pawing the thing for over six months."

Judi grabbed Reina's easy tone as a sign that she was safe. Her relieved sigh could have been heard on the next block. "Yeah, I know. And the commission on that piece is huge, so I thought you'd want to know right away. Now maybe you don't have to find an investor. You can afford new insurance."

Reina narrowed her eyes. In all fairness, she *had* told her gallery employees and the artists about her canceled insurance, and the Davis commission *was* significant, nearly ten thousand dollars.

But none of that explained how or why Judi had entered her house without her invitation. "You could have called."

"I did! No one answered."

Reina zapped the next question quickly, pulling out the one truth she was one hundred percent certain about. "Where did you get the key to my house? I didn't give it to you."

Judi's eyes darted to the door, to Zane, back to Reina, brimming with confusion. After a long, silent minute, they widened with realization. "What are accusing me of, Reina?"

Reina met her stare without blinking. "I'm accusing you of coming into my house with a key I didn't give you."

Judi straightened her shaking shoulders. "Your mother gave me the key. She was at the gallery when Mrs. Davis bought Razi's sculpture. She thought you'd want to know, under the circumstances."

Reina crossed her arms casually, hiding her clenched fists from view. Why couldn't she accept Judi's story as the truth? What was it about Judi's pale expression and darting eyes that made her believe some part of the story was a lie?

Without a word, she turned and went into the kitchen, snagging a glass from the cupboard and filling it with water from the dispenser on the refrigerator. Grey stepped toward her, but she held up her hand to keep him from coming closer. She needed a minute to regroup, reharness her famous cool exterior, the facade she'd dropped around Judi on more than one occasion. She hoped he understood.

He winked at her, then turned back to Judi.

"Why was Pilar at the gallery?"

Grey took over the interview, figuring this was his strongest talent anyway. Though to any casual observer, Reina appeared to be nothing more than a little thirsty, he could see she was rattled to the core. She needed space and time to digest Judi's seemingly innocent story after suspecting her of something much more sinister.

He'd already learned that Reina didn't make friends easily, but those she took into her life, she believed in completely. If Judi was somehow involved in the robberies, it would cost Reina more than the jewels, more than the insurance policy or even the solvency of her business.

"She came with Mrs. Davis."

Grey glanced over his shoulder. Reina didn't react, so Grey assumed the connection between Reina's mother and the art patron with the fat wallet came as no surprise. He did wonder, though, why Pilar hadn't mentioned the purchase when she'd called earlier to speak to her daughter. Or why Judi's hadn't phoned her boss earlier in the afternoon, immediately after the sale.

That was it. The timeline was off, which could explain why Judi remained so quiet, why her hands shook so violently that she finally slipped them beneath her thighs. She looked everywhere around the room but at them, yet when she finally met Grey's gaze, a tear spilled down her cheek.

If Judi was faking, the woman had more talent than Lane Morrow, who'd already won a Golden Globe for her ability to turn on convincing waterworks. Judi was either hurt by Reina's suspicion or, as Grey suspected, she was trying to hide something—like a guilty conscience.

Though Reina remained in the kitchen, her face expressionless, her eyes had darkened with speculation. Like that night in the parlor with Claudio, she'd removed her-

self from the situation and had become an outwardly passive observer. Grey now knew her well enough to know
there was little that was passive about Reina Price. She
was listening, watching, assessing the situation from a distance.

So smart. So beautiful.

Reina finally entered the room again, this time with a
glass of wine, which she held out toward Judi.

"Drink this."

Grey stepped aside, questioning her with a perplexed
look she didn't acknowledge. Hospitality?

She followed the goblet with a tissue. Judi used both.
"I'm sorry, Reina. I shouldn't have listened to your
mother. I shouldn't have come here tonight."

Reina sat beside her. "Following Pilar's advice is usually not a wise choice."

Judi sipped her wine and didn't reply. This must have
been significant to Reina, because she glanced at him tri-
umphantly before laying her hand over Judi's knee.

"Judi, I need to ask you something important. How
much does Pilar know about the robberies at the gallery?"

Eyes flashing, Judi drank more wine, jerking her glass
and sloshing a few drops over the side. "I don't know.
Whatever you told her."

"I haven't told her anything since the first robbery."

"You haven't?"

Reina shook her head. "She doesn't know about the
insurance or about my need for more money. At least, she
doesn't know from me. And I'm fairly certain I asked you
to keep the information to yourself."

"I did!"

"Then why did my mother encourage you to contact
me about a ten-thousand-dollar commission? That's a
small amount of money to a woman like her."

Judi gulped the last of her wine, then shot to her feet. "I don't know, Reina. I don't. I just did what she asked." Tears rained from Judi's eyes with renewed flow. She swiped them away with what was left of her tissue. "I—"

With a graceful nod, Reina stood, cutting Judi off before she said anything more, anything that might be incriminating, Grey suspected. What was she doing?

"Why don't you go on home, Judi?"

"What?" he exclaimed.

She turned toward Grey, her look indignant. "Judi didn't mean any harm tonight." She turned back toward her assistant and patted her shoulder, but a slight stiffness in her movements clued Grey in that she didn't believe her claim one bit.

Judi set the wineglass on a table and clutched her jacket close. "I didn't. I really didn't." She stepped past Reina, then with a quick and muttered curse, turned back and threw herself into Reina's arms. "I'm so sorry, Reina."

Reina didn't answer. She didn't quite return the embrace, didn't say a word as Judi scrambled toward the back door. Grey grabbed her by the oversize coat.

"Zane, let me—"

"Keys," he demanded, hand out, palm up.

Wisely she snapped her mouth shut, gave him the keys to Reina's house and ran out.

Grey tossed them onto the kitchen table with a clank, then took a deep breath. "I can't believe you let her go. She knows more than she's saying."

The sympathetic expression Reina had cast on Judi was now replaced with stonelike determination. She snatched the keys, examined the tiny crystal key chain, nodding at first, then shaking her head. Her bottom lip quivered, but when she turned to meet his gaze, he saw nothing but steel.

Reina's smile lacked humor, but made up for it in weary irony. "This key chain does indeed belong to my mother. Dahlia gave it to her years ago when we lived in Austria."

"Then you don't think Judi came here looking for Claudio's jewels?"

"I didn't say that. Did you notice her choice of outerwear?"

He remembered the black bomber-style jacket. "A strange choice for someone so fashionable."

Reina took the wineglass to the sink and rinsed it clean. "The security guard I hired after the first robbery wears a very similar style, not to mention that it's probably eighty degrees outside tonight."

Grey watched Reina calmly and carefully towel-dry her crystal, never once letting on that her suspicion bothered her in the least. Man, if she could bottle that cool, she'd be one rich woman.

"Do you think Judi was involved in the robberies? With the guard?"

At that, Reina glanced aside. "Judi's shown no sign of new wealth. The security guard still has his job. Besides, selling jewels of that quality for a decent price requires connections. You don't exactly get full value at a pawnshop. I think the time has come for me to ask some serious questions."

"But you let Judi go."

"If she's betrayed me, I'm the last person she's going to tell. And if she's involved, I don't think any of this was her idea."

"Who would she tell?"

Reina strode back to the table and closed her fist tightly around the key chain.

"That's easy. She'd tell my mother."

DIALING THE CELL PHONE as he drove, Grey called the security company and reinstated the monitoring of the system. If anyone broke into the house while they were gone, the police would be notified, and so would he. And with the majority of the jewels from Claudio's collection tucked in a pouch Reina wore around her waist, and the original schematics concealed in the hidden room, they had left the house without much worry about the safety of il Gio's legacy.

The safety of Reina's heart was another matter entirely.

Once she'd given him Pilar's address, she hadn't said another word. He hadn't forced her to either, wondering what could possibly be running through her mind. One irrefutable fact remained—Judi had gotten the key to Reina's house from Pilar. A key Reina had never given to her mother.

Grey suspected Pilar was somehow involved in the robberies. He felt it in his journalist's gut. Though Reina insisted her mother had enough wealth to last a lifetime, she also acknowledged that her mother would know precisely how to dispose of the jewels and receive full value in return. And even though she insisted that her mother would never betray her own daughter so callously, Grey wondered.

But, for now, he'd trust her judgment and follow her lead. An intelligent woman, Reina knew her scheming mother better than anyone else. And, without proof, he decided not to speculate aloud, especially after he spied the defeated look lingering around Reina's eyes. He'd thought he'd experienced the ultimate betrayal when Lane had published her book and then traveled the talk-show circuit to make sure even the people who couldn't read knew that he was a sex maniac.

But if Pilar was involved? Her mother? If there was anyone in the world Grey knew he could count on, it was his family. Zane already proved as much by handling the newspaper and his stalker for him with his usual devil-may-care effectiveness. His parents, though they spent more time lately traveling the West than preparing family dinners, still kept in touch. They'd called him immediately after Lane's book hit the scandal sheets, claiming they didn't believe a word, insisting he not worry about them or their opinions in the coming backlash. They loved him, point-blank.

Just like he loved Reina, point-blank.

The emotion punched him like a fist to the gut. Love? Really? Now?

He clenched his jaw together. He was no idiot. He'd never told a woman he'd loved her before, but he certainly wasn't going to make his debut with someone who now faced the kind of betrayal that would send most people over the proverbial edge. Reina was too cool for hysterics, but as he maneuvered the car toward her mother's house, he could feel her retreating from the world, wrapping herself in protective layers from head to toe.

They found Judi's coupe parked in front.

"She ran straight to her," he said.

Reina's lips pursed slightly. "That's not entirely surprising. Judi and my mother have become quite close. She even stays in the guest room sometimes, when she fights with her roommate. If she's upset about being caught in my house, she'd run right here."

Grey turned the corner, spying the driveway around the other side of the house. He stopped to allow a dark sedan to finish backing out. The midsize limousine quickly pulled away. When Grey started up the driveway, Reina stopped him.

"Wait, there's someone at the back door. There. Going inside."

He doused the headlights. "It's a man."

Reina leaned across him to see more clearly, her perfume teasing him with its sultry scent. Unable to resist, he bent forward to kiss her, then swallowed a silent curse when she made a huffing sound and sat back in her seat.

"No use confronting her now," Reina said, clearly exasperated.

Grey hesitated, not willing to give up so easily. He understood that she'd be reluctant to challenge her mother with only vague suspicions and an unaccounted-for key, but he didn't expect Reina to be waylaid by yet another late-night guest. "You don't want to find out what this is all about?"

Reina waved her hand impatiently at the house, not completely successful at hiding her frustration. "No use. My mother obviously has a paramour tonight. If I know Pilar, she's banished Judi to Dahlia's care and is concentrating on her newest lover."

"She won't make him wait to talk to her own daughter?"

Reina skewered him with a look that bespoke her years of experience with Pilar. "I suppose if I barged in and demanded an explanation, she'd put him off long enough for me to make a fool of myself. No, when I speak with my mother, I can't come across as accusatory. Not without more proof than a key and Judi's odd behavior. Not if I want her to tell me the truth."

This time, it was Grey's turn to trust. It was *her* problem and *her* mother. And besides, why was he in such a hurry to figure out who had orchestrated the robberies at the gallery? Once the mystery was solved, he'd have no other reason to stay at her house, no other reason to remain in her life.

"Your mother may be just an innocent pawn. Judi could have used her to find out things about you, to ingratiate herself into your family."

Reina nodded, but the gesture was noncommittal.

"But," he surmised, "you don't think that's the case."

Reina pressed her lips together, then speared him with a look at once icy and desperate. "My mother hasn't been anyone's pawn since she was a child. My head tells me there are a thousand possibilities to explain this away."

"But your heart?"

She didn't answer, and Grey felt a stone form in his stomach, hard and cold. More than likely, her heart wasn't speaking to her at all. She'd closed out the sounds, muted the sadness, protecting herself from a backlash of painful realizations. He knew how that worked, firsthand.

He also knew that as long as her heart remained blocked off, she couldn't acknowledge her own feelings for him or accept how much he cared for her.

"Let's go home then," he said, shifting the car into first gear.

She stopped him by laying her hand over his fist. "No. Please. Let's just drive awhile?"

The small sound of her voice nearly broke him in two. He nodded, and turned the Jaguar around, heading out of the French Quarter with all the speed British engineering allowed. Pilar wasn't going anywhere. Reina had all the time in the world to confront her mother and discover the truth.

But if he didn't find a way to put a crack in her heart, a fissure he could use to seep inside on some later date, he might as well forget ever establishing something deeper between them.

And that, he wasn't willing to do.

HE TOOK HER TO the Mississippi River, to a secluded spot on the corner of the industrial area adjacent to the newspaper's main complex. Trees and landscaping hid them from view of anyone working the night shift; the vast expanse of the raging brown waters of the river masked them from the notice of anyone on the other side. They sat on a cold stone bench, watched a barge float by, marveled how a tanker that size could look so small.

That was the river. Massive. Ageless. Loud. Loud enough to drown out the cacophony of Reina's situation.

They really couldn't speak, not with any intimacy, so, instead, Grey took her hand in his. He tugged her fully beside him on the bench, forcing her to lean her head against his shoulder, snaking his arm around her to anchor the closeness.

She resisted for an instant, but with a sigh he felt against his heart, she surrendered.

He had no idea how long they sat there. He'd totally allowed the sloshing water to wash all thoughts from his mind when Reina twined her fingers around the buttons on his shirt, releasing them. She toyed with his chest hair, threading and pulling with what he at first thought was an unconscious repetitive motion, like when he tapped his pencil on the side of his blotter.

But when she tugged his shirt out of his waistband, he knew she wanted more. She wanted to make love.

He paused, uncertain what to do or say—unsure if making love to her when she was so vulnerable was the right thing to do. That alone stopped him dead. He never would have considered that with any other woman. With any other woman, he would have counted on his prowess as a lover to distract her from whatever ailed her. But Reina was different. So different. He'd already recognized that she used sex as a weapon, as a means to keep men away from her, even when she made love to them. She allowed her lovers only so much, told them what to do, insured that they did it, then sent them away.

He wasn't about to become one of them.

When she swung onto his lap and moved to take off his shirt, he grabbed her wrists and shook his head. The look in her eyes, a mixture of confusion and hurt, instantaneously bought her release from his grasp. She pulled his shirt over his head and placed one sweet kiss just above his heart. He reached beneath the sheer jacket she wore over her cat suit and fingered the zipper, attempting to tug it down, but she leaned back, licked her lips and shook *her* head.

Then she leaned forward and kissed him softly, once over each eye, then on each cheek.

Grey knew he'd stopped breathing, felt sure his heartbeat had ceased. This wasn't about her pleasure at all. This wasn't about using sex to escape or hide or create a chasm between them.

This was about him. About her showing him how she felt, because she couldn't use words. Because of the river...and not just the mighty Mississippi. He sensed a flood of emotions raging through her right now. Conflicting, heart-wrenching conclusions she wasn't yet prepared to face. Grey remembered his own turmoil in coming to terms with his feelings for her, but realized his chaos didn't seem so daunting anymore.

He'd much rather help her with hers. And if allowing her to pleasure him was the best he could do, he could think of a thousand worse tortures. He smiled and nodded, sending her on a slow and complete exploration of his body.

First, she removed his clothes, taking her time, folding his pants into a neat square topped with his shirt, his briefs. She took off the filmy jacket she wore and undid the clasp that held her hair, but nothing more. She circled around to the back of the bench and massaged his neck deeply, showing him this was all about him—his pleasure—her need to take care of him. She rubbed his muscles with practiced precision, adding the lotion of her wet kisses across his shoulders, behind his ears.

When she tugged on his lobes with her teeth, there was nothing childish about the thrill that rang through him. A warm wind rippled the air, rustling the hair on his chest, stirring his erection. She walked around to the front of the bench again, grabbed his face with both hands and kissed him. Her tongue was hot, hard, insistent. She wanted to be in charge again, but, this time, she focused on his satisfaction only.

When she dropped to her knees and wove a path of openmouthed kisses from his nipples to his belly button, he thought he'd go insane. She wrapped her hands around him, grasping his buttocks, pulling him closer to the edge of the bench, closer to the edge of orgasm. Her chin grazed the tip of his cock, her hair dangled enticingly over his bare thighs. He couldn't stop himself from tangling his fingers in her raven locks. It was either that or break his hands from clutching the stone bench so tightly.

She didn't take him in her mouth right away, instead sat slightly back, cupping his balls, stroking his length until he was full and hard and throbbing for her touch. She kept her eyes fixed on his sex, as if his shape fascinated her. When she took a tentative taste, followed by a long lick from hilt to tip, he wondered if she'd ever done this before.

The thought flew away the minute she took him in her mouth, her hands still working magic, her tongue and teeth sending him into a tornado of spinning need, rocking desire. Damn, he wanted her. Damn, he loved her. Damn, he was going to come.

And when he did, she took what he gave, then soothed him back down to satiation with soft kisses and softer strokes. When she dropped from her knees onto the ground, cradling her head in his lap, he lost what was left of himself in the texture of her hair in his hands.

As soon as his ability to think returned, he realized she'd done more than give him pleasure. She'd showed him a part of her heart, the part she protected like some priceless limited-edition creation, more valuable than any jewel she had ever worked on, more delicate than any links of gold. She'd showed him, but hadn't given it to him. For that, they'd need words—words Grey suspected he was ready to say, but doubted Reina was prepared to hear.

First they had to solve the mystery around Judi, her mother, the possibility of their coldhearted betrayals. Then, they could turn to the issues between them. And in the meantime, Grey had to figure out just how far he was willing to go.

13
___

REINA SLEPT on the ride home. She hadn't allowed Grey to say anything after he'd dressed, silencing him with a finger over his mouth—a finger he'd wanted to make love to as a starting point for the rest of her. But he resisted. She hadn't wanted anything for herself. To force the issue would be disrespectful to the gift she'd given him. Once he'd guided the car out of the secluded spot next to the river, she'd drifted off, her shoulder propped against the door and her cheek softly pressed against the glass. The woman could even control when she fell asleep, perfect for avoiding a discussion about the significance of what they'd just shared.

And it had been significant. Grey wasn't certain about how or why, exactly, but he knew the simple act meant something significant to her. It had to him.

After he parked the car in the detached garage beside the house on First Street, he woke her with a gentle shake. Her eyes opened and the warmth in the way she looked at him, a tiny smile curling her lips, forced his hand. He wasn't letting this woman go. Not now. Not ever.

"Hi," she said.

"Hi, yourself. We're back."

She snuggled into the leather seat. "It wasn't a dream, was it?"

He couldn't contain a wide, toothy smile. "Some of it was, believe me. The best dream I've had in years."

She answered his grin with one of her own, but when she sat up, the expression faded. "But now we're home. Dream's over."

He stroked her cheek. "Doesn't have to be."

The moment his gaze locked with hers, the dome light from the Jaguar casting a revealing glow, a mechanical trill broke the heavy silence.

His cell phone.

He answered it instantly.

"Mr. Masterson? This is Dawson Security Monitoring. We have an alarm sounding at the First Street residence."

Grey shot from the car, doused the automatic light sparked when he opened the garage and leaned out the large doorway, straining to hear something from the house. But he'd disengaged the sirens earlier. The alarm was silent, meaning *he* knew someone was inside, but whoever had breached the locked doors had no idea they were about to be caught.

He motioned for Reina to get out of the vehicle. Quietly. "Have the police been called?" he asked the security representative.

"I'll dispatch them now. We have entry through the back door and tripped motion detectors. Are you sure this isn't a false alarm?"

Grey knew that most home-security systems were tripped by careless home owners or wandering pets. Most home-monitoring companies went days without catching an actual break-in. Too bad they couldn't be on the side of statistics right now. Fact was, Judi had had time to return to the scene of her crime, though he doubted that was the case. He didn't buy her story, but he did buy her fear. He also figured she wouldn't be stupid enough to try again on the same night. Someone else was inside Reina's home. Pilar, perhaps? Or someone else they didn't anticipate?

"No, this isn't a false alarm," he said, then disconnected the call.

Reina waited inside the shadows of the garage.

"Someone broke in?"

"Yes, and they are likely still inside."

She crossed her arms over her chest, rubbing her arms as if a chill assailed her, despite the warm New Orleans night. "The police are on the way?"

"They've been dispatched. They may or may not get here before whoever is inside finds something, or gives up and leaves."

She dismissed his doomsday prediction with a quick shake of her head. "I have the most valuable pieces with me. And no one will find that secret room."

"Not on purpose, maybe."

Her voice shook with surprise. "You want to go in?"

"You did ask me to help you solve your mystery. Our best shot at doing that is catching someone in the act."

Grey noticed she kept her eyes peeled on the back door. Once again, he could see no signs of forced entry—not from this distance, anyway.

"What if Judi was lying?" Reina reasoned. "What if she stole the key chain from my mother to falsely implicate her, and is only biding her time until she cashes in on what she's stolen."

"Do you normally keep valuable stones in your house?"

She frowned. "I use the safe at the gallery, and only take out the precious gems when I'm almost done with the piece. I never bring them home."

He figured she'd employ such caution. "And as far as we know, Judi doesn't know about Claudio's jewels or have any reason to believe you were working on anything valuable. But then what if she somehow found out? She did go straight to your work area.''

''There's no way Judi knew about Claudio's collection.''

''She could have eavesdropped during your initial meeting. You might not have noticed.''

She pressed her lips together, thinking. Lips that had just given him intense pleasure, lips that had yet to open with any confession of how she felt about him. But did she have to say anything? She'd shown him, hadn't she? Just as he'd show her now by solving her problem and making good on his promise to help her. Grey still wanted to be with Reina, spend time with her, make love to her. But he wanted to have a chance to do this with nothing in the way to distract them, nothing to tug her heart apart before he had a chance to sneak inside.

''I would have noticed. My office is across the gallery from her reception desk. She can't answer the phone or buzz people in from that distance without my noticing through the glass door.''

Grey conceded that, but added, ''Could she have used the phone system to listen in? An intercom feature?''

At this, Reina paused. The possibility narrowed her eyes, but when she twisted her neck to meet his gaze straight on, he saw her suspicion.

''What about the men who helped Claudio deliver the stones?'' she guessed. ''They could have decided to come back, double-cross Claudio. I don't want you going inside before the police arrive. It's too dangerous, Grey. We should just stay here and wait.''

Grey knew Reina's decision made sense. He might own a gun, one he'd tucked into the glove compartment of the car when they'd left to find Pilar, but he wasn't a cop.

Still, he had to make sure she understood the big picture of letting the police be the first to discover the identity of her intruder.

"What if your mother is inside? Do you really want the police to find her there?"

Reina's face melted into an emotionless mask. After only two days together, he now knew that her stoicism meant that she struggled bitterly with her fear, rage and betrayal. All the emotions any average person would experience in the same situation. All the emotions she'd taught herself to hide in order to keep others from ever considering her to be just like anyone else. Human. Fragile. Vulnerable.

"She'd be better off if they do. She might be able to flirt and seduce her way right out of their handcuffs. I don't think she could work the same magic on me."

Grey nodded, not doubting for a moment that Reina's anger would be formidable once she allowed the rage to show. If Pilar was indeed inside, she'd better hope the cops formed a shield to protect her from her daughter's wrath.

If the police ever arrived. Grey checked his watch, then looked for any movement inside the house. Only five minutes had passed, but he knew that a home invasion, particularly where no one was in danger, wouldn't rate as a top priority for the police. They could be waiting long after the would-be thief escaped. And the longer the trespasser remained inside, the better the chance that the secret room would be discovered.

"At least we should keep a watch on both entrances. I'm going around front. You stay here." He handed her the cell phone. "Call 911 if you see anyone, and stay out of sight."

"You're awfully bossy," she said wryly.

He nodded. "So I'm told." He touched her shoulder lightly, drawing a line up her collarbone to her cheek. "I don't want you to get hurt."

"You're sweet," she replied.

Grey grabbed the gun from the car, then brushed a kiss across her mouth before tucking the weapon out of sight. "I am, aren't I? Stay hidden."

She rolled her eyes at his final command, but as he slipped into the shadows cast by the tall hedge that surrounded her yard, he noticed she'd done as he asked by ducking into the darkness. He moved toward the front of the house, hoping it was the mob or even a stranger inside Reina's house, rather than her mother or anyone else close to her heart. She didn't deserve another dose of betrayal tonight.

Or ever. And it was up to him to make sure he kept her safe.

REINA FOUGHT to keep her eyes peeled on the back door. She was so sleepy. Yet every time her lids fluttered closed, even for an instant, the image of what she'd done with Grey—to Grey—on the bank of the Mississippi flashed in her mind.

So what? She'd performed the sex act before, though, at the moment, she couldn't remember where or with whom. There was an intimacy about what she'd done, a selflessness that had her reeling. For the first time in her love life, she'd allowed only her lover's pleasure to be sated…she hadn't wanted anything for herself. At the time, the significance hadn't even occurred to her. She'd simply wanted to bring the man she loved to orgasm, watch the play of pleasure on his face, feel the reflexes of his body's response.

The man she loved?

Reina laughed and shook her head. Utterly ridiculous. She'd known Grey Masterson for less than three days, two if she counted the time it took for her to discover he wasn't his brother.

And yet, she knew his twin, didn't she? She loved Zane on a level she'd never shared with any other man—like a brother, really. And despite the differences the public saw between the Masterson men, Reina knew they shared more in common than either would admit. They were both loyal, caring. Zane's dedication to his hedonistic lifestyle hid a heart she knew to be protective of his family. He'd switched places with his brother, hadn't he? He'd taken on a business he'd avoided all his life. Thanks to his maverick ideas, like the column detailing his love affair with Toni Maxwell, he had probably breathed new life into the struggling venture. She'd never doubted Zane's intelligence or his ingenuity, and she'd learned Grey matched both of those qualities point for point.

So how could she not love Grey? How could she not love a man who was a carbon copy of Zane and yet, as her lover, had touched her deeply, intimately, in ways she had never thought possible? Not since Martine had she allowed a man such mastery over her body, such control over exploring her sexual needs and responses. After that first affair, she'd realized what she'd liked and had taken control. She'd told her lovers what to do and when to do it. And they'd all complied.

But Grey took her experience one step further, outside the realm of the physical. He'd turned the tables, usurping her control with a passion that broke through the walls she'd erected to keep her from ever falling in love.

So how did she know she loved him now? How could she possibly be so involved with him so soon? And if she was, what would she do about it?

Her eyes darted to Zane's Jaguar, the keys dangling in the ignition, catching the faint light from the back porch.

"Oh, God," she said with a sigh, her voice a hoarse whisper.

She wanted to run. Escape. But cowardly flight wasn't her way. She'd simply have to find a way to take control of the situation. Soon. Before it was too late. Before she'd lost her heart entirely.

Because that would be tragic.

Submissive.

Weak.

Wouldn't it?

Movement on the back porch snapped her attention to the present. She slipped farther into the shadows, her gaze fixed on the house. The inner door swung open, leaving only the screened door between the intruder and the porch.

A male figure stepped out just as blue-and-red flashing lights twirled around the yard with dizzying, sickening spin.

She breathed his name before collapsing against the wall.

"Claudio!"

THE NEXT FEW MINUTES EXPLODED with frantic activity. Police swarmed the yard and house. At first, Grey thought they'd been besieged by the entire New Orleans Police Department, but once his nerves calmed, he realized only four patrolmen had responded to the alarm, two in each cruiser now parked out front. Reina walked toward the house with an officer beside her, apparently having identified herself as the resident. Grey had done the same, and now waited near a hedge halfway between the front yard and the back gate while the officer ran his ID and his permit to carry arms through for verification.

Claudio, shocked and sweating, stood on the porch with his hands cuffed behind his back, his face pressed against the wall, his voice breaking the silence with outraged curses, all luckily in Italian so the police didn't understand how thoroughly he insulted them. Yet, the minute Claudio spied Reina walking toward the house, he turned his attention to her.

"Reina, *bella,* you are all right? Please, tell these men who I am. This is all a—" he paused, searching for the right word in English "—a misunderstanding."

Reina crossed her arms over her chest, her eyes livid, her mouth firmly set in a thin line. Grey's mind flashed with countless scenarios, the strongest one involving Claudio stealing his own collection to receive payment on an insurance policy he had claimed not to have. Why else would he break into Reina's house in the middle of the night?

"Then you should start explaining, *signore,*" she answered, her signature coolness quavering so slightly Grey was certain only he had heard it.

The policeman who'd taken Grey's driver's license and carry permit to verify his identification returned the laminated cards.

"You don't have to speak to him, ma'am," the officer beside Reina said. "We can handle the questioning."

Grey jogged across the yard, shoving his wallet back into his pocket.

"I'm sure you can, Officer," he interrupted, "but first, I'm curious as to why so many policemen responded to a tripped alarm."

"We had a call from a concerned citizen just before the alarm came in. Two cars were dispatched separately." The cop, speaking with more authority in his voice than matched his young face, turned to Reina. "Do you know this man, ma'am?"

Claudio released another long string of Italian curses. "I called the police!"

"You what?" Grey asked.

"*Sì.* I tried to call you earlier," he said to Reina, "to check on your progress with the collection, but you didn't answer the phone. I even came by the house and knocked. Lights were on upstairs, but you didn't answer."

Grey thought back, realizing Claudio could have arrived when he and Reina had been upstairs making love. "I went to look for you, and when I couldn't find you, I returned. Again, I knocked. Again, no answer. This time, no light. I was worried, so I called the police, then came inside to make sure you were all right."

Reina eyed him with pure skepticism. "Why would you be worried? You knew I was with…"

Her voice trailed off, and Grey piped up. He'd already shown his correct identification to the police, figuring he'd have more clout with the cops as himself than as Zane, who tended to annoy law enforcement officers whenever he had the chance. But Reina didn't know that. Neither did Claudio. And with his brother living it up with Toni Maxwell while pretending to be him, he figured the less people aware of the switch, the better.

"Me," he supplied. "I've been with Reina since you left the other night. You had no reason for concern."

Claudio looked at the ground, and the skin along Grey's neck prickled with electricity. Just as he sensed Judi had been earlier, this man was hiding something—something important—perhaps something even more shocking than an attempt to steal his own collection. He hoped his friend at Interpol sent his files soon. He'd check his e-mail just as soon as he could.

"I had my reasons," he said, his voice soft.

Reina turned to the policeman beside her. "Officer, it's quite clear that all of these patrolmen searching the grounds of my home is an unnecessary disruption to the neighborhood. If you'll give me a moment to check inside, I can let you know if my valuables are undisturbed."

"Sounds reasonable, but I should check out the house myself first. Make sure there isn't anyone else inside. Then I'll take you in."

Reina glanced at Grey, obviously reluctant to reveal the hiding place of the collection even to the police. He couldn't blame her. The department had yet to solve her robberies and she had no reason to trust these strangers, not when the people she knew—Judi, Claudio and possibly Pilar—had already proved themselves untrustworthy.

The police made a quick sweep of the house, after which two officers returned to their beat while the other two, at Reina's request, remained outside on the porch with Claudio and Grey while she went upstairs to check on the collection. When she returned, she nodded at Grey, indicating that all was well.

"Officer," Grey said, "this man is Ms. Price's client and, while his story sounds outlandish, I think he's telling the truth."

Reina rewarded Grey with a gentle smile. "Nothing is missing from the house."

The police officer didn't look the least bit happy about admitting that there was no sign of forcible entry, but he did, and after both Grey and Reina vouched for Claudio one more time, the officers left, with a warning to the Italian that if he got in any more trouble, they'd be calling Immigration.

"How did you get inside?" Reina asked immediately

after the officers drove away. "The door was locked when we left."

"I'm handy with...tools," Claudio admitted, then dipped his hand into a flower box and retrieved a small case that must have held the paraphernalia he'd used to bypass Reina's lock without leaving so much as a scratch on the door.

"So you're a thief by trade?"

"No, no. In Italy, I work as a private investigator."

She pressed her lips together. "Why did you break in?"

"I was worried for you," he insisted. "That is the truth."

"Why? There's something you aren't telling me, Claudio. If I'm in danger, I want to know why and from whom. And I insist you tell me now."

Grey sat back and watched Reina work Claudio over—though this time she didn't use any of her latent sensuality on the man. Not a single flirtatious glance or provocative pout. Just plain, deep-set onyx eyes and flaring nostrils, enhanced by rigid hands on her luscious hips. Grey shook his head, knowing the Italian didn't have a chance.

"Please, let's go inside," Claudio implored, suddenly looking a tad older than he had a moment before. "I mean you no harm, Reina. I could never hurt you. Never."

"Why not? I'm nothing to you. A stranger. An artist you hired to help make you rich."

Claudio's gaze darted toward Grey and again Grey felt adrenaline pump through his veins the way it did whenever he discovered a lead to a great story. Whatever Claudio knew, whatever Reina had him just on the edge of confessing, was going to rock her world.

Claudio turned back to Reina, his hand outstretched as if he meant to stroke her cheek. "But, you see, none of that is true. You're not a stranger to me, not really. We met once. A long time ago."

14

REINA DIDN'T OFFER wine or brandy, didn't even present Claudio a chair in her living room as her breeding shouted at her to do. She couldn't speak. Words flew through her brain like a flock of ravenous vultures that had found a carcass to feast on. She forced herself to remain quiet rather than look like some babbling idiot. Luckily, Claudio didn't seem to expect anything more.

At Reina's insistence, Grey had taken the jewels back upstairs. She hated how she missed his presence, the way his magnetism added balance to her equilibrium, but she wondered if Claudio would be completely honest with her with Grey in the room. So she took a chance. So far, Claudio hadn't been honest with her, but she didn't think he was dangerous. Of course, only a day ago, she would have had a great deal more confidence in her instincts than she did tonight.

"*Per favore, bella.* Sit down. You've had a shock tonight, I know."

She chose to remain standing, even if her action was a blatant attempt to gain some sort of control over a downwardly spiraling situation. "Shock, Claudio? No, just a lot of confusion."

She snorted, amused by her own understatement. Confusion didn't begin to describe the ricochet of conflicting feelings rocketing through her, starting with her deepening emotions for Grey. That had thrown her most of all. Judi's strange behavior and possible involvement in the thefts? Surprising? Sure. She'd counted the younger woman as a friend. But Judi wasn't the brightest diamond in the showcase. Never had been, never would be. Leading her astray wouldn't be much of a challenge for anyone with strong enough motivation.

Her mother's possible involvement? Reina didn't quite know what to think about that scenario. The only emotion she could identify with regards to Pilar somehow using her for money she didn't need was anger, the kind of blind rage she'd fought all her life, the kind she'd learned to wrap in a tight ball she could hide and deny at will. She tried not to remember all the times Pilar chose to celebrate Reina's birthday by pawning her off on Dahlia, who'd take her to a zoo or amusement park while Pilar attended some vapid party or lounged in bed with her latest paramour. She tried not to think about the boarding schools, the trips to foreign places for mother-daughter bonding weekends that ended up with Reina touring the sites alone while her mother flirted and fawned over some handsome man with a thick wallet. And last, there was Pilar's hardheaded refusal to tell Reina anything about her father. She had so many questions, but she'd stopped asking them a long, long time ago, weary of the futility.

Finally she dropped into a chair and cradled her head in her hands. She couldn't deal with all this, and her feelings for Grey as well. She had to find her control. Her center.

But where?

Claudio leaned forward. "I know about your assistant."

Good. Conversation about Judi seemed the least explosive topic at the moment. *A fine place to start.*

"How?"

Claudio hesitated. The strained look on his face made

Reina yearn to call the question back. Maybe the answer was more than she wanted to know. "When I couldn't find you, I went to see your mother."

Definitely more than she wanted to know, but at least he explained the man entering her mother's house through the back door. "You know my mother?"

She'd asked this question before, back when Claudio first came to her with the offer to restore the collection. He'd denied knowing anything about Pilar except by her reputation as an actress. But all of a sudden he knew how to find Pilar in New Orleans? And felt comfortable going to Pilar's house in the middle of the night?

"We knew each other a long time ago," he admitted quietly.

Reina narrowed her eyes, but was too tired to confront him about his initial lie. Didn't really matter now, did it? "She must have been very surprised to see you."

"She didn't see me. I arrived shortly after your assistant. And after what I heard, I thought it best to check on you."

"What did you do? Hide in a closet?"

He shook his head, but weakly, as if whatever he'd done wasn't much above her guess. "No, no. Dahlia let me inside. As I waited in the hallway, I overheard their conversation, then slipped out before Pilar realized I was there. *Bella,* I think Judi was behind the robberies at your gallery. She kept talking about hurting you tonight and said something about breaking into your house. She was angry with Pilar, though I'm not certain the reason. I returned to make sure you were all right."

Reina fought to control her breathing. So Pilar was involved, though she still didn't know how or why. But for the moment, she had to deal with Claudio. With *his* lies. "You said you knew me. That we'd met once."

Claudio's smile was bittersweet.

"You were a child. Precocious, bright. No more than four, exploring the village around your mother's summer home in Venice. I don't expect you to remember."

Her chest constricted. "Then why have you remembered me?"

At that moment, Grey stepped into the doorway. His face seemed sterner, rougher than normal—his stance stiff, unyielding. And still, Reina's insides quivered at the sight of him. When he threw her a quick, loving glance, she thought she'd melt onto the floor right in front of Claudio.

"Reina has had a lot to deal with tonight, Claudio. More than she should have to all at once. I think now that we've determined that you had only her best interests in mind, you should go. Let her get some rest."

Grey stalked to the chair and cupped his hand over her shoulder, draining the last of her energy from her body. She did want more details, but Claudio wasn't going anywhere. Not as long as she still had his legacy in her possession. Whatever story he had to tell could wait until tomorrow. She nodded her agreement with Grey.

"The collection is safe. I'm safe." She reached up and laid her palm over Grey's strong knuckles. "I'll call you in the morning and we can set a time for you to look over what I've done so far."

Claudio waved his hand at her and rose. "Don't worry about that. Take a few days off, if you must. The collection is valuable, but not more than you, *bella*."

Again Claudio reached out to her, apparently wanting to touch her cheek, but he didn't breach the last few inches he needed to press his flesh to hers. She knew Italians to be an affectionate, demonstrative culture and didn't pull away from him, wanting somehow to experience a tactile representation of the deep emotion she spied in his eyes.

But one glance at Grey sent Claudio out the door with only a quick good-night.

"What was that?" she asked.

"What?"

"You seem angry with Claudio. Why?"

Grey helped her stand, slipping his arm around her waist to lead her toward the staircase. "He caused quite a lot of unneeded stress for you tonight."

Though exhausted, Reina wasn't a fool. Grey knew something. He had discovered some information, some clue, perhaps, that negated Claudio's claim to have broken in tonight solely to check on her safety. "That's not it."

They took the stairs together, slowly, his body supporting hers in a way she found highly erotic. She wanted him again. Tired as she was, she wanted to feel him inside her once more before she surrendered to sleep. She wanted him to wash away the feelings of betrayal, confusion and anxiety that threatened to rock the foundation of her world. Even if he was the cause of her ultimate unsteadiness, she knew he could anchor her with the kind of lovemaking only the two of them shared.

At the stop of the landing, he turned her to face him. Through the doorway to his guest room, she spied the glow of his laptop computer. A portable printer hummed in the creaking silence of the house.

"You're working?"

He nodded. "Get some sleep, Reina. I don't have anything definitive to tell you, but I should by morning."

"I need to see my mother in the morning," she noted, knowing that if she didn't confront Pilar soon, she might not ever discover the truth. "She has some questions to answer."

"Yes, she does. And if things go well—" he tilted his head toward his room "—I'll have ammunition for you."

Reina shivered at the thought. "I don't need ammunition against the woman who gave birth to me, Grey. I'll handle Pilar. My mother is a fantastic actress, but she's not so good at lying as she is at skillfully avoiding the truth. I won't let her do that."

"Do you want me to go with you?"

"To bed?" she asked, a smile tugging her lips despite her exhaustion.

"To your mother's," he clarified, his eyes dancing with mischievous possibilities she felt certain he wouldn't act on tonight.

"No. If Pilar has a handsome man in the room, she'll throw all her concentration on charming you and she won't pay the least attention to me. I'll be fine."

She turned toward the bedroom, knowing she really should sleep alone tonight...and wondering why, all of a sudden, the concept seemed so foreign to her.

She knew, of course. She loved Grey. She wanted his arms around her, wanted to wrap herself in the unique heat of his body and experience the warm breeze of his breath across her bare skin while her eyes slowly closed and her mind shut down. She accepted this reality without question or doubt, having no more energy to deny what was simply the truth.

He brushed a soft kiss on her cheek, then clearly struggling to pull back, placed another on her lips before taking a full step away from her. "Sleep well, Reina."

GREY WOKE TO THE SOUND of a car honking, followed by quick footsteps across the foyer downstairs, then the opening and shutting of a door. Reina had left?

He dashed down the stairs in time to see a taxi pull

away. He cursed, slamming his hand on the front door and discovering a handwritten note taped just above the peephole.

Grey, didn't want to wake you. I'm going to find my mother. If you need me, call me on the cell phone. When I return, we'll compare notes.
With love,
Reina.

With love? How he wished.

But now wasn't the time to deal with that. Better to save the emotional exploration for when he had cleared the other questions from this increasingly confusing and disturbing situation. He'd received the reports from his friend at Interpol last night, had read through them as Reina slept, and he wondered if he shouldn't call Reina right now and let him know what he'd discovered about Pilar.

Or more distressing, what he suspected about Claudio di Amante.

He decided he needed a few more facts first, and after setting a pot of coffee to brew, he showered, shaved and dressed. A quick call to Zane let him know he'd be out of the office all day, leaving Grey the freedom to go to the paper and access some of his best resources.

Before he left, he double-checked the secret room and discovered that Reina has once again taken the most valuable stones with her. He reset all the alarms—bells and whistles and monitoring. He doubted anyone would be so stupid as to try and break into the house again, particularly during daylight, but trusted the alarm company to do their job as they had the night before. He had more serious concerns. While he thought he had all the pieces to construct the puzzle surrounding the thefts at Reina's gallery and Claudio's oddly timed business proposal, he had a few more facts to check before he could make any definitive accusations.

After a quick stop at his apartment to grab some "Grey" clothes—a conservative pair of slate slacks to replace Zane's trendy khakis and a button-down dress shirt with requisite patterned tie, instead of Zane's chest-hugging silk T-shirt—he drove to the office, parking Zane's candy-apple-red Jaguar down the street and used a side entrance into the main building. He noticed security had been beefed up considerably. More guards, more closed-circuit cameras, fewer visitors roaming the halls. Luckily no one challenged him and he was able to make it to his office without even his secretary noticing.

The minute he closed the door behind him, he felt a surge of something powerful seep into his veins. Damn, he missed this place. More than he would have guessed. More than he thought possible. He breathed in deeply, certain the odor of ink really scented the air, even if the presses were several floors down. He listened to the sounds of activity in the city room just on the other side of his wall. Phones ringing constantly, the whistle of faxes, the tapping of keyboards. Voices carried even through his well-built office. Some story was breaking. On any other day, he'd have dived right into the fray, anxious to swim into the strongest current to pull the facts to the *Herald*'s shore.

Or would he? It had been so easy to walk away, to leave the hustle and bustle of the newspaper game to play recluse with Reina. He'd left the paper at a time the business had needed him the most—with circulation on a downward slide and a saboteur wreaking havoc in production. He'd valued his own personal healing over the health of the family legacy. Not that he'd left the newspaper high and dry. He had left his twin in his place.

And judging from the memo he found on the center of his desk detailing the upswing in sales for Sunday's edition, thanks to Zane's column about his affair with Toni Maxwell, Grey knew he'd made the right decision. But it hadn't been becoming Zane or living Zane's lifestyle that spurred his nearly instantaneous rebirth.

It had been Reina.

Sunlight streamed through the windows. He walked to the long bank of windows and watched the Mississippi River churn by. He scanned the corner of the property, just beyond the parking lot, for the private spot he'd taken her to last night, but the trees shielded his view as he knew they would. He felt a quick flash of desire burn through him, but he tamped down the reaction. The next time he made love to Reina, the next time they shared any sexual pleasure, it would be to celebrate their new relationship—one based on love, not just sex.

But before he could force Reina to work past her demons to reach into her heart, he had to help her identify those demons, even the ones she loved.

He sat in his chair, taking a moment to allow the soft leather to mold to his body. He missed his desk. He'd only been gone four days, but the minute he typed his password into his computer and snapped on the headset for his phone, he knew he'd never be able to do anything else. In the aftermath of Lane's book and the saboteur and the stalker and the falling circulation, he'd considered trying something new, something he hadn't been groomed for his entire life.

But now that Zane seemed to have things in control, Grey knew a complete career switch wasn't the answer. As an idea brewed, he connected to the Internet and found his favorite search engine for online newspaper articles. He typed in the name Claudio di Amante and waited. After several seconds, a surprisingly large collection came up, most from Italian newspapers.

He activated the translation software and tried again. There, in an article from a Venice daily, he found what he needed. He sent a print command, then flipped open his cell phone, where he'd programmed the number to Claudio's hotel.

"Di Amante," the older man answered.

"Claudio, this is—"

He hesitated, but realized that if he expected the Italian to tell him the truth, he'd have to employ at least an equal amount of honesty himself.

"This is Grey Masterson. Zane is my brother, my twin."

"Is Reina all right? Has something happened?"

The worry in the man's voice shot straight into Grey's gut. He'd had suspicions about the man. Now he knew he was right.

"Reina is fine, so far as I know. She went to find her mother, ask her some questions."

After a silent pause, Claudio responded. "She deserves as much."

Grey grinned. "That's what I figured. So I was wondering if we could meet. You see, I'm a newspaper editor, *signore,* but what you say to me will be off the record. I'm not sure Pilar Price will tell her daughter the whole truth. Reina deserves that after all these years, don't you agree?"

Claudio did agree and, after giving him directions to the coffee shop across the street, Grey hung up the phone. He drummed his fingers on the desk, wondering. The idea he'd left to simmer in his brain a few minutes ago started to thicken. He took a chance. He dialed the extension of the newspaper's art director, a young woman he'd hired fresh out of college about three years ago. While she'd done well in insuring that the *Herald* looked crisp and neat in black ink and newsprint, Grey had always wondered what the talented Gen Xer could cook up if given an innovative idea.

He was about to find out.

REINA SLIPPED BACK inside her house, exhausted yet again. She'd spent the entire day trying to find her mother, but Pilar had proved an evasive quarry. Her mother had turned off her cell phone, as had Dahlia. With no answer at the house, Reina had hired a taxi and set out to track her down. She'd just missed them at the spa where they had standing Tuesday morning appointments, then waited outside the restaurant where they normally lunched, only to watch their car speed away the minute Reina spotted them. Reina had hailed another cab again, then parked herself inside her mother's house until she'd tired of playing cat and mouse and returned home.

She changed into work clothes, and after grabbing a plate of fruits and cheese to nibble, knocked on the wall of her bedroom to gain entrance to the secret room. She closed the door behind her, allowing herself a moment's disappointment that Grey hadn't come back, hadn't called. Her body ached for him. Her shoulders possessed a tightness only his hands could work away. Her chest constricted with the need for—a hug?

So simple, elemental. Vulnerable. And still, Reina wanted his touch more than she wanted to find out the truth. It was just a matter of time before she caught up to her mother and worked out the undoubtedly complicated reasons and excuses for whatever she'd done. Reina had desperately wanted to confront Pilar and learn the who's and whys to put this entire fiasco behind her before Grey returned.

Behind her? And how long would that take? An hour? Maybe two? Even she wasn't that cool and in control. Reina, alone in the privacy of her workshop, laughed until she cried...then cried until she ran out of tears. She cried for her mother, a woman so selfish she'd likely manipulated her own daughter and risked Reina's business reputation for some unknown but inevitably shallow pursuit. She cried for Judi and Dahlia, probably drawn into the web before they knew what they'd done. But, mostly, she cried for the woman she'd allowed herself to become—aloof, detached. Sensual, but starved. Able to feel the physical pleasures of lovemaking, but scared to experience real love. How could she truly love someone when she lacked the ability to open her heart without fear? To trust? And how could she trust anyone completely when the one person she should have been able to count on in any and all situations—her mother—had taught her that trust was a weakness that someone, somewhere, would exploit?

And if Reina's suspicions were on target, Pilar had just done exactly that. And though Reina thought that she loved Grey, how could she...really? She had so many walls erected, so many locks and gates, even a talented and resourceful man like him would probably wear out before he breached them all.

And why should he have to work so hard? His burns from his love affair with Lane Morrow had to be fresh. Yet, he didn't talk about her much, and claimed to have put his anger behind him. He hadn't once used Lane's mendacious nature as an excuse to hold back from caring about Reina.

The irony slapped her in the face. Grey, a man on the run in disguise as his twin, was more honest than she was.

A sob choked her, but she forced the thick pressure down her throat with a large sip of wine. With a defiant sniff, Reina grabbed a tissue from her worktable and swiped her tears away. Enough of that. She had a job to do. Regrets, she'd save for later. She checked her watch, then shuffled through Claudio's schematics and chose a brooch and a hair comb to work on next. They were both simple designs, with no sensual use according to both diaries, only evocative shapes. She worked until the sunlight outside died and the lamp no longer aided her tired eyes. She'd polished all the stones for the brooch and had cut some of the prongs, and still had to solder the smaller pieces on the comb, constructed of silver and ebony. She laid a soft cloth over the unfinished pieces. She'd finish one of them in the morning. If nothing else intruded. Like her family, sorry as it was.

While at Pilar's house, Reina had done some snooping, and after numbing her emotions with hard work for a few hours, she felt at ease to think about what she'd found. Hidden in Pilar's antique secretary, she'd found an old stack of letters from her mother's mortgage company, a mortgage Reina didn't even know her mother had. So far as Reina knew, Pilar had never bought anything on credit in her life. She couldn't be bothered with remembering to make monthly payments and rarely stayed in any one place long enough to receive timely bills. And, besides, the rich and famous paid cash for everything, according to her. But her rich and famous mother hadn't paid what she owed the bank on her house for at least six months, then had made a large payment that had brought her up-to-date.

So maybe Judi hadn't been the one to need money. But

Reina didn't know the details and had no way to figure them out until Pilar decided she wanted to be found. After penning a note to her mother demanding a phone call, she'd come home. Now she'd worked until she couldn't see straight. She left the secret room, listened for Grey, who still hadn't returned, then undressed, filled her tub with hot water and essential oils and eased her tired body into the slick, wet heat.

When all else failed, she turned to her bathtub to provide her some relaxation. And while working off a little sexual energy at this point seemed like a great idea, the contents of the pink box under her bed wouldn't do the trick. She wanted Grey. She needed him. And for once in her life, she decided not to be too cool to admit it.

So when he knocked on the door, the temperature of the bathroom shot up as if she'd just run another long blast of piping hot water.

"Reina, you okay?"

"Absolutely not."

His chuckle rumbled through her like a sexual thrill.

"Anything I can help you with?"

"Mmm," she answered, noncommittal, silently amused by her desperate attempt to being standoffish when all she wanted to do was shout at him to hurry the hell up and come in and join her.

He didn't hesitate, turning the knob and flinging the door open, his shoulder leaning cockily against the jamb. "I'm sorry. I wasn't sure if that was a yes or a no."

"You're the newspaperman." She lifted her sponge and drizzled steaming water over her breasts. With no bubbles to cover her, her hair lazily knotted at the top of her head, she knew he had only the slight fog from the heat to hamper his view. "What do you think?"

15

GREY LICKED HIS LIPS, then watched in the hazy distance as Reina's nipples tightened in instantaneous response. Lord, he wanted her. His erection pressed against the zipper of his slacks. The knot of his tie, already loosened sometime during his sequestering in his office, seemed to tighten like a noose. He tore the silk away but left the length dangling in his pocket. Never know when something like that could prove useful.

"I brought you something," he said, reminded by the crinkle of newsprint that he still had the mock-up in his hand.

She leaned over the edge of the tub and spotted the glossy papers. "Did Zane write another interesting article about you and Toni Maxwell?"

"Yes, but that's not what I have for you." Grey had gone to the newspaper for two reasons—one, to find out if he missed his job as much as he wanted to deny he did, and, second, to pull together facts that would set Reina free of her troubles with her gallery and family. Unfortunately, what he'd learned on the second count might do more harm than good.

He tucked the newspaper behind him. "Maybe this can wait for later."

What harm would it do to spend a few hours loving Reina before he rocked the very foundation of her world? For the first time in his life, he'd cursed his natural investigative skills. For an hour this afternoon, he'd sat at his desk, scanning the facts, chewing two pencils to splintering nubs before Zane's latest column about Toni Maxwell caught his eye and spawned an idea. He'd called his art director and his best mock-up guy into his office, ordered in dinner and started typing. Now, at half past ten o'clock, he held the fruits of their labor. Half of him swelled with pride at creating what he considered a revolutionary piece of journalism.

The other half of him just swelled with desire. But a noise from downstairs reminded him that now wasn't the time to play.

"On second thought, this shouldn't wait. You might want to get dressed."

She chuckled and poured more water over her enticingly bare, sensually curved shoulders. "I most definitely don't want to get dressed, Grey."

Good Lord, but he could easily spend an entire lifetime with a woman so focused on what she wanted. He only wondered if she would let him stick around that long.

Only, in a minute, she wouldn't have a choice, would she? He'd gotten in, forced his way. Would she forgive him for invading her personal life so thoroughly?

"You may change your mind when you read this."

He handed her a towel to dry her hands, then turned on the light, doused the candles rimming the tub and traded the towel for the mock-up magazine. She scanned the masthead, raising her eyebrows before reading the name aloud.

"The Weekly Confessional?" she questioned.

"I'm not married to the name, just the concept. It's edgy, if I do say so myself. A collection of first-person, epistle-style reports. News from the point of view of the people in the news, told with the help of a seasoned reporter—in this case, me. This is just a mock-up. For your eyes only.''

She scanned the headline, Centuries of Secrets, then spied the byline underneath.

''Claudio?''

''I interviewed him for two hours today. What's written there, I believe with all my soul, is the truth. Reina,'' he said, snagging her bathrobe off the hook beside the door and extending his other hand to help her out of the water, ''I think you'll want to be on dry land when you read this.''

She must have understood the seriousness in his eyes, because she instantly complied, silently toweling off and covering herself before joining him in the bedroom.

He handed her the magazine again, then wondered if she would want him to leave the room. Deciding he'd rather stay, he parked himself in the chair she kept in the corner of her room. She reclined on the bed, the pages spread open, her eyes darting across the page so rapidly he wondered if anyone truly read that fast.

Then he realized she was reading the same passage over and over.

She sat up, crossed her legs like a child reading a storybook, trailing her index finger underneath the words to make sure she didn't miss a single letter, a single implication.

He'd almost decided to get up and pour her a brandy when he watched her bottom lip quiver.

She speared him with a look of complete desperation. ''Where is he?''

''You haven't finished. Read it all, sweetheart. Learn all the facts before you confront him.''

She slammed the magazine shut and jumped off the bed, desperate, as close to enraged as he'd yet seen her.

"Where is he?" she demanded.

Grey stood up and placed both hands on her shoulders, lightly. He breathed easier when she didn't yank away.

"Downstairs."

She dashed out, nearly forgetting to open the door first, nearly tripping over the stairs that she took two at a time. When she reached the front parlor where he'd left Claudio, she grabbed on to the threshold, panting.

He caught up behind her, but remained a few inches away. As much as he wanted to put his arms around her, anchor her, allow her to falter within the safety net of his presence, he had no idea how she'd react. The last thing he wanted to do was make this harder.

When he saw the reflection of her expression in Claudio's broken spirit, Grey knew he couldn't help. He couldn't edit this scenario. This had to play out and all he could do was watch. He'd done his part today. And like any decent reporter, the fallout of his words were completely beyond his control.

"How long have you known?" she asked.

The menagerie of emotions clinging to the desperate tones of Reina's voice clutched at Grey's heart like talons. Anger. Sadness. Fear. As if the answer had the power to shatter her heart like the delicate glass figurines displayed in the curio beside her. She clutched the top, rattling the contents, steadying herself as she stepped farther into the room.

Claudio nearly faltered over the coffee table. "Only for a few months, I swear. After the first robbery, Dahlia contacted me. She told me the truth—who had stolen the diaries from me all those years ago, who had arranged for the robberies at your gallery. She told me I was your father and that just as Pilar had never told me, she'd never told you. Dahlia thought I could help. The restoration of the collection was my way.''

Grey watched Reina's hands quivering at her sides and he ached to yank her away from Claudio and protect her from the aftermath of her father's full confession. Grey never realized he had a knight-in-shining-armor complex, so he tamped down the instincts. Reina wasn't the type to appreciate his rescue. He firmly planted his feet on the fringe of her Turkish carpet, and willed himself to keep from planting his fist on Claudio's face.

Even if Claudio wasn't responsible for the string of lies now threatening Reina's world, his honesty hurt her. Now that Grey had the whole story, thanks to his afternoon interview, he couldn't help admiring the man any more than he could curb his anger. Yes, Grey resented the complicated web of mistruths and misrepresentations that Claudio had initiated when he'd showed up in Reina's gallery with his lucrative offer. He should have told her the truth then.

But Grey also knew the man's reasons were valid. Why would Reina believe a stranger over her own mother? Dahlia had refused to corroborate his story, fearing for her own status and job. So Claudio had found a way to gain his daughter's trust, and Grey hoped that Reina could fight past the lies and see the strength in Claudio's character for herself.

''Why did you care? You never knew about me, never even knew you had a child somewhere.'' Her voice trembled against the silence.

''Because your mother once loved me.''

''Did you love her?''

''No, but that doesn't mean I can't love you. And it doesn't mean she had a right to keep you from me. *My daughter*. I never knew.''

This time, Claudio bridged whatever barrier had kept him from grabbing Reina and pulling her into his arms. Grey watched the older man curl his head over her shoulder, witnessed the quiet desperation of his embrace, as if by holding her so tightly, he could squeeze out all of the pain and shock and make it seep away like water pressed out of paper pulp.

But Reina's response didn't match his warmth. Her back stiffened. Her neck elongated regally and her shoulders squared. When Claudio could no longer ignore her wooden stance, he released her and let her go, taking only her hand as he led her to the couch.

Grey considered leaving them to their privacy, but his decision to stay solidified the moment Reina's front door burst open and Pilar barged in like a well-dressed tornado.

"Take your hands off my daughter!"

She flung her purse at Claudio's head, but he had the alacrity to duck at the right moment.

Reina stomped to her feet. "How dare you! Mother, this is my home. You will not throw a tantrum here to avert the fallout of what you've done."

"I've done nothing," Pilar claimed, but even this seasoned actress couldn't pull off such a blatant lie. She stepped back, nearly knocking into Grey, who steadied her with a hand to her elbow.

Reina's gaze darted between her father, whose stare remained fixed on the floor, and her mother, who seethed with more righteous indignation than any guilty woman had a right to show. Grey could see that Reina didn't know where to start, whom to speak with first. Did she want to confront the lies of the past or the ones of the present? Did she want to spend a moment with the father she'd never met, or face the betrayal of the mother she'd apparently never truly known?

How she made a choice, Grey didn't know, but the minute her onyx eyes fixed on his, he knew precisely what she wanted him to do.

With his palm cupping Pilar's elbow firmly, he guided her in the direction of the kitchen. "Ms. Price, perhaps we should wait in the other room."

"I will n—"

Reina cut her mother's protest off with a glare as hard and black as petrified coal. A battle of stares ensued, with no words, no gestures—just the cold, heartbreaking eyes of two women who'd once possessed a bond that now lay tattered on the floor. With no guilt or fault to weaken her resolve, Reina easily won.

Yanking her arm away from Grey's touch, Pilar stomped off toward the back of the house, her heels knocking an unsteady stiletto rhythm on the hardwood floors.

"I'll just be in the other room," Grey said, "if you need me."

Reina pulled the magazine close to her chest, as if she meant to embrace the paper and ink for all the truth it had provided. Her eyes were glossy, but her lips no longer quivered so visibly.

"I will need you, Grey. Soon. But first I need to speak with Claudio alone."

He nodded, then turned to follow Pilar before she could stir up more trouble or slip out of the back door, which he suspected she would attempt to do now that she realized she couldn't manipulate her way out of this fiasco. Reina crossed the room and snagged his hand with hers before he had moved more than a few steps away.

With her small fingers, she raised his knuckles to her lips and pressed a soft kiss on his skin.

"Thank you, Grey." A wave of moisture, dammed by

her lashes, turned her eyes to pools of emotion. "You are very good at what you do, aren't you?"

He bit the inside of his mouth, willing himself to not take her into his arms and kiss away the tears she so valiantly kept at bay. "I've been told."

His wink produced a smile, however small, on her bow-shaped lips. He forced himself to leave before he changed his mind, knowing she had to find closure in this part of her life before she could make any decisions about him.

Pilar had stalked through the kitchen and now reclined on the wicker chaise in the solarium, her arm draped dramatically over her eyes, her long, flowing skirt hiked to show what he supposed was meant to be an alluring view of her shapely legs. Grey shook his head and set about making a pot of coffee. His shoulders ached from his long day hunched over his computer, putting his interview with Claudio into words that were worthy of his talent and the Masterson name.

The Weekly Confessional had been a brainstorm. A good one. Zane's column had given him the idea for something new. Something his. And for the first time in years, he was excited about a project—truly, totally invigorated by a business venture that wasn't weighed down by a century of tradition and family responsibility. No, the building blocks of *The Weekly Confessional* came from his twin's inventiveness and Grey's need to find a way to tell Reina the truth she desperately needed to hear.

He knew he could have just told her. He could have simply encouraged Claudio to meet with the daughter he hadn't known existed until a few months ago and tell her the story of Claudio's affair with her mother. He didn't know why he'd been compelled to put the complicated tale into words first, but figured he'd resorted to his comfort zone

Grey knew words. But, until today, he'd honestly forgotten how to use them for anything other than reporting some facts and making a buck. *The Weekly Confessional* would change that, make his work interesting and unpredictable for the first time in his career. He had his best team of marketing gurus and accountants working out a business plan. Grey had no intention of letting the newspaper go, but he hoped *The Weekly Confessional* would become a regular Friday supplement, another asset to add to the burgeoning Masterson empire. One that could be his from the inception. One that would complement and enhance the legacy left by the Masterson men before him.

And if Zane wanted, he could be involved however he desired. In fact, Grey hoped his brother would jump at something along the lines of creative director. He and his twin had never worked on anything together except switching places. They'd always been intent on proving that their differences somehow canceled out the fact that they looked exactly alike. Grey prayed that would change, the way his whole life had changed since he'd slipped into his brother's life and discovered the woman of his dreams.

How Reina fit into the entire scheme of things, he didn't know. He had no idea how tonight would change who she was. For all he knew, she'd leave New Orleans. Leave him.

He held the coffee carafe under the faucet, filled it, then emptied the water into the machine and shoved the pot back in place beneath the brew basket. He concentrated on the task, knowing if Reina would read what he'd written, she might—just might—come out of this mess without her heart broken in a million pieces.

As he set the coffee to brew, he leaned against the counter, ignoring Pilar's pathetic groan, just as certain that she wanted him to talk to her as he was that he wasn't about to say one word.

"YOU WERE THE FIRST IMPRESARIO, weren't you?"

Reina clutched Grey's article in her hand, wanting desperately to read what he'd written in her attempt to understand, but somehow knowing that she wanted the details from Claudio first. In his own words. While she watched his eyes for signs of honesty. Regret.

"Impresario is a big word. I was a child like she was, a boy with big dreams. Pilar was the most beautiful girl I'd ever met, and her talent for acting was unbelievable. I wanted a life in the theater and she could have helped me as I wanted to help her. If she'd given me the chance."

"How old were you? She told me she was fifteen when she met the man who discovered her."

The memory cast a sweet nostalgic glow in Claudio's dark eyes. Eyes the same hue and glossiness as polished ebony. Eyes exactly like hers.

"Seventeen, maybe? I'd been traveling through Spain as the assistant to a man who produced plays all over Europe. We were in her village on vacation when I met her, and I promised to introduce her to my employer. I don't remember why, but he left suddenly. Before I could fulfill my promise. So I stayed behind with Pilar."

"But you didn't love her?"

Claudio shook his head, then met her gaze directly. "I was seventeen, Reina. What did I know of love? No more than Pilar knew, I promise. She didn't want me to love her, anyway, at least, not in the beginning. She wanted me to make her a star."

"And you tried."

"I took her to Rome, I introduced her to everyone I knew. We were young, enamored of each other. It was an adventure. Then she left me for Salvatore Balducci, an older man with real connections. He arranged her first roles in the theater. Started her career.''

"And she never told you about me?"

"Not exactly."

"What does that mean?"

"We'd been together for three years before Balducci finally took her seriously. She came to me with a choice. If I married her, if I loved her, she would stay—go back to Venice with me and be my wife. If I wouldn't marry her, she would go with Balducci and be a star."

"Was she pregnant with me at the time?"

He shook his head. "No, no. You'd be much older if that were the case. But I didn't love her, not enough to make her my wife, but enough to know she had to follow her dream. So I told her to go and she did."

Reina mulled over his words, superimposing them onto the stories she'd heard from Pilar all her life, stories that never once hinted that the man who'd toyed with her mother's love had been the one who'd fathered her child. "You broke her heart. If my mother ever had the capability to love, you destroyed it. Didn't you?"

He pursed his lips, considering her words with the seriousness only his age and personal hindsight could provide. "Perhaps. Perhaps, ultimately, this is all my doing."

His voice faded with each word to a long silence. Reina glanced down at the newspaper, scanning the words, understanding how they matched what he'd already told her, then realizing if she wanted to know more, she'd either have to turn the page or ask him. Grey's instinct to put all of Claudio's claims in black and white struck her as brilliant for a thousand different reasons, not the least of which was that under the pressure of facing the daughter he'd never known he had, he might be tempted to lie. But, with the story in print, he would be unable to alter his original story and get away with it. And Reina trusted Grey's ability as a reporter enough to believe every word he'd set to type.

So she kept reading. She scanned every word, searching for her answers, trying to ignore the arms of emotion reaching out to her from the pages.

"She came back to you..." Reina said, "later, when she was a star."

Claudio chuckled softly. "The ultimate revenge, no? She wanted to show me all she'd become without me, how she could resist me now that she'd made a name for herself. But she didn't count on my secret weapon—il Gio's diaries. Our second affair became a conquest, a battle of wills. In the end, she still wanted me to marry her, but I still didn't love her. She left. I never heard from her again. I didn't even realize she'd stolen the diaries until months later and, by then, she'd gone to the United States."

"Why would my mother take the diaries?"

"Revenge," he answered stiffly. "She knew I planned to somehow use them to make my fortune. When I wouldn't marry her—because I didn't truly love her any more than she knew how to love me—she wanted to hurt me."

"But she didn't do anything with them."

"She didn't need to. Taking them destroyed my dreams for a long while."

"But you lived in Venice?"

He nodded.

"We vacationed in Venice. My mother had a home there. You said you saw me once. Didn't you ever wonder?"

Claudio took the paper from her, scanned the page, then

pointed to a paragraph near the bottom of the second column. "Pilar took lovers like a pickpocket takes wallets. I didn't love her, but what man could help but desire her? Whenever she came to town, I found some reason to go away."

"You saw me! You said so last night."

"*Sì, sì.* But everyone who knew Pilar, who knew you, believed you to be the child of some foreign prince or Hollywood celebrity. The rumors were endless, but they never once pointed their fingers at me. Believe me, had anyone suspected, I would have found out. Pilar made sure no one ever knew."

Claudio slipped his hands in hers again and when his eyes captured her gaze, she knew whatever he said next would be the truth.

"I was a fool, Reina. A young, reckless fool who never considered that Pilar would give me the rare and treasured gift of a child. I'm sorry. I should have known."

Reina shook her head. How could he have known? And what was the point of belaboring the point now? The minute he'd found out he had a daughter, he'd left his country, traveled to the States and tried to help her out of the mess her mother had created. If he'd shown any hesitation to come to her aid, Reina had no proof of it. Dahlia called; he came. End of story.

"Why did Pilar finally publish the diaries?"

"You'll have to ask her, but Dahlia talked about money."

"And she arranged the robberies at my gallery?"

Claudio folded his lips inside his mouth as though unwilling to speak, but he nodded.

"Why didn't Dahlia just tell me? I would have believed her."

He shook his head sadly. "She didn't know that. Your

mother is a formidable woman. But I can't tell you why Pilar did what she did. I've never understood her. I just know that with the diaries published, the only way I could help you was to have you rebuild the collection, try to protect you and the jewels with my limited resources. After the diaries disappeared, I became a private investigator. But I had no connections here. Luckily, you found Mr. Masterson to help you."

"Lucky is right."

Claudio snapped the newsmagazine straight, then folded it back with the cover on the outside. "He's a good man, Reina. Very patient. Smart, too."

"Sounds like he's got an admirer," she quipped, then smiled when Claudio responded to her humor with a hearty chuckle.

"Maybe he does. I think it's you. I saw your eyes when you looked at him a moment ago. You've fallen in love with him."

"I can't think about that now. I finally found my father and I really don't know you. I have the collection to finish and..."

"Stop," he ordered, insistent.

"Excuse me?"

Claudio grabbed her by both shoulders, gently but with firm resolve. "You're no coward, *bella*. All those things you mentioned can wait. Haven't you learned anything from il Gio and Viviana? Didn't you feel their regret when you read their words? They both would have traded their souls to be together for always, instead of just for brief moments of time. They lived in a different century, when such limitations existed, but you, you have the freedom to do whatever you want, take whatever you want from life. Don't make excuses just to guard your heart."

"I've never been in love before," she admitted.

He smiled. ''Neither have I, and it's been my greatest regret, next to not knowing you. You have a chance, Reina. Take it. Find what neither your mother nor I ever did.''

Reina stood, cupped her father's face in her palm and choked back another wave of tears. No wonder her mother had thought herself to be in love with him.

''We have so much to talk about,'' she said.

Claudio patted his chest with confidence. ''I'm a fine specimen of an older man, *bella*. Healthy and, soon, thanks to your collection, very rich. We have all the time in the world to know each other.''

She rolled her eyes and huffed. ''Even you aren't that naive.''

''No, but I am…what is the word? An optimist. Go to your mother now. Find out the rest of the truth so you can put it behind you.''

She laughed. ''You make it seem so simple!''

''Why can't it be?''

Reina moaned, fighting the urge to bury her throbbing head in her hands. She combed her hair with her fingers instead, tugging at the strands to counteract the pressure building inside her skull. ''Because I have to deal with Pilar.''

''Deal then, darling,'' Pilar said, standing in the doorway as if it was a gilded picture frame and she was the subject of some priceless masterpiece, ''because I'm tired of waiting.''

16

WITH ONE HAND ON HER HIP and the other draped languidly down her side, Pilar issued a challenge Reina couldn't ignore. *Accuse me now or leave me alone.* Reina stood and tugged at the sash on her robe. Better than anyone, she knew how her mother operated, playing on emotions to wrangle her way out of trouble. If Reina showed any sign of regret for calling her mother to the carpet, she'd never get the whole truth.

Claudio stood and sidled in close, his hand on her shoulder.

"Sit down, Claudio," Pilar sniped, her tone dismissive. "My daughter hasn't needed you for thirty years. She doesn't need you now."

Reina cleared her throat. "As if my needs ever mattered to you."

"Don't be ungrateful. You know the sacrifices I've made for you."

Reina paused, certain her mother had the capacity to act out of love—when it suited her. She couldn't pretend that Pilar hadn't been generous and affectionate as a parent any more than she could ignore the times she was self-serving and remote. With Pilar, you either accepted the good with the bad, or you sought therapy. Reina had never spoken to a psychiatrist in her life.

"Well, Mother, let's hear it." She motioned for Claudio to sit and then relaxed into the cushions on her couch, crossing one leg over the other. "I'm sure you have a wonderful performance planned. How should we start? I know—" she held out her hands, creating a rectangular frame around her mother "—action."

Pilar narrowed her eyes, but didn't respond to either Reina's venomous tone or her condescending attitude. Right then, Reina knew her mother was as guilty as she believed. When all else failed, Pilar would resort not to lies, but to putting a positive spin on the truth.

"Don't be disrespectful."

"Don't lie," Reina said.

"I didn't mean to hurt you."

"When? All my life when you wouldn't tell me who my father was, or before that when you didn't tell him, or more recently when you arranged for Judi to steal jewels from my gallery?"

Pilar didn't falter, at least not physically. Her eyes betrayed the sting of Reina's words with a gloss of moisture, but Reina couldn't believe even that. The woman could cry on demand and win awards for her emoting. Nothing would keep her from utilizing that talent now.

"Claudio didn't love me. I had too much pride to tell him I'd gone and gotten myself pregnant. Instead, I concentrated on doing what I had to do, making myself a wealthy woman. You never wanted for anything, did you? Not even love. I may be shallow and self-centered, but you've always known love."

Reina couldn't contradict this. She knew her mother loved her as much as she could. And she had enjoyed a wonderful life of travel, adventure and education. Past sins were moot. She was more interested in why her mother had decided to destroy her business.

"Let's focus on the gallery, then. How did you get the combination to the second safe?"

"With my instruction, Judi seduced the guard. They used the cameras to watch you enter your code."

She nodded, since Grey had mentioned that scenario. "Okay, now the big question. Why?"

Pilar waved her free hand, as if the query was inconsequential and painfully simple. "I needed the money."

She knew that much, but even the letters she had found didn't explain where her mother's millions had gone. "Where's all the booty from your love affairs? From your endorsement deals and long-running plays?"

Pilar glided into a chair and poured herself a brandy from the decanter nearby.

"I sank a great deal of my personal capital into my theater project and it seems that while amassing money is a talent of mine, investing it isn't."

"Why didn't you just ask me for help?"

"You didn't have it, either. You put every dime into your gallery, I knew that. Your cash flow was tight, even before Judi took the first set of jewels."

"Did you ask her to steal from me?"

"I was desperate. She's young and begging for approval. You had insurance. You were protected."

Claudio asked his own question before Reina could protest her mother's warped justification. "What about the diaries? You sold them to a publisher and the sales have been phenomenal. Why didn't you use that money to pay your debts?"

Pilar sipped her drink. "The advance money was pitiful, there was no guarantee an obscure jeweler's erotic diaries would sell. And I won't see royalties for another three months, at least. I needed the money immediately or I would lose my home. Can you imagine how mortifying that would be? Me? Pilar Price? The tabloids would have had a field day."

"That doesn't justify stealing from your own daughter," Grey said. Until that moment, Reina hadn't noticed that he'd entered the room. Warmth washed over her. Relief, not because he'd arrived to intervene on her behalf, but because she knew that as long as he was nearby, she could triumph over the betrayal she now faced. He'd done it. So could she.

"Stealing is a misnomer," Pilar emphasized. "I was borrowing. I would have told you, Reina, but if my scheme came to the attention of the authorities, I didn't want you blamed as an accessory. When the royalties arrived, I had every intention of repaying you three times over. But then you came into her life," she said, staring daggers at Grey, "and decided to play Hercule Poirot. And you!" She sneered at Claudio. "Eavesdropping like the commoner I always knew you to be."

Reina stood, ending her mother's tirade before she went too far. She now knew the truth—at least, she knew all she needed to know. Claudio di Amante was her father. He'd chosen her to restore his collection as a means to make up for the years he'd missed and to counteract her mother's terrible scheme. Pilar had orchestrated the robberies to fill her own coffers and had been caught because Dahlia had a wave of conscience and had contacted Claudio and because Grey had a talent for finding out the truth.

What more did she need to know?

"I'm tired," Reina admitted. "I'd appreciate if you'd both leave now."

Claudio had come to his feet the minute Reina had. He leaned across and placed a soft kiss on her cheek, then headed toward the door. "May I call you tomorrow?"

Reina smiled. The man may have only known her for a few days, but he knew how to ingratiate himself, didn't he?

"Yes."

Pilar wouldn't be dismissed so easily, stamping her foot the minute Claudio closed the door behind him. "That's all you have to say?"

"Actually, I have nothing to say to you, Mother. I'm too angry. I need time to decide what to do."

"What to do?" Pilar stalked toward her, incredulous. "Do you plan to call the police?"

Reina didn't move or react. She wondered if she should reassure her mother that she could never betray her as coldly as her own mother had betrayed her, but figured a night's worth of worrying would do Pilar some good.

"I don't know what I plan, Mother. But if you ever want to repair all the damage you've done, you'll stick around and find out. Find Judi a new job and leave Dahlia alone. She tried to do the right thing, which is amazing when you take into account all the years she's spent under your influence."

Pilar didn't respond, but a quick flash of regret darkened her eyes, making Reina believe, if only for now, that she'd made her point. She'd forgive her mother, of course. She'd make sure those royalties went straight toward restitution to both the insurance company and the clients who'd lost their valuables. She's also do whatever she could to find the originals and return them to the rightful owners. If she could keep things quiet, she could set everything right without ruining any more lives or careers.

With nothing left to say, Pilar left the house in the same manner in which she came—like a storm. As the door closed behind her, Reina was certain the pressure in the air hissed out like a punctured balloon.

Only she and Grey remained. He stood near the doorway, looking as wiped out as she felt. She ached to fling herself into his arms, experience skin to skin the warmth he radiated from his tired half smile.

"Thank you," she said.

He slung his hands into his pockets with a humble shrug. "For what? Turning your life inside out? Exposing your mother? Outing your father before he was ready? You need to be more specific. The choices are endless."

Reina couldn't contain a grin, or the instinct to slip her arms into his and listen to his heartbeat with her ear pressed to his chest. His heat instantly ensnared her. His scent acted like an aphrodisiac, injecting her body with just enough energy to become aroused.

"I think I'm most grateful for you causing me to lose my cool. Disaffected ennui may be very fashionable and sexy—" she glanced up at his face in time to catch his burgeoning grin "—but it does a hell of a number on your insides."

"Tell me about it. I think that's the best lesson I learned about being Zane. There's an incredible freedom that comes with not putting boundaries on your life."

She nuzzled her nose just a little closer to his chest. "Don't kid yourself. Zane has boundaries and walls just like you and I do. His might even be tougher to break through. I hope this Toni Maxwell woman is up to the task."

Grey bent down and kissed the top of her head. "Why are we talking about my brother and his lover?"

"Because if we do, we don't have to talk about us."

"What's so bad about that?"

She stared at him, surprised he didn't know. "We're not exactly good at it."

"We don't suck," he quipped.

"Speak for yourself." She licked her lips and pressed

her body against his, instantly aroused by the hardening length of him.

"You're trying to distract me," he said with a groan.

"Am I succeeding?"

"*Chère,* you know you are."

"Make love to me, Grey?" she asked, wondering if she'd ever spoken those words aloud to any other man. In her lifetime of lovers, she'd never had to ask. But in that same lifetime, she'd never wanted a man for anything other than what he could do to her body. With Grey, she craved what he did to her soul, what he'd done to her heart—showing her the emptiness and then offering her a way to fill it up. She took his hands and led him toward the staircase.

He hesitated at the bottom step.

"Wait," he said.

She turned. "Why?"

"Because I love you."

Reina shouldn't have been surprised to hear his confession. He'd showed her the depth of his feelings in so many ways. Now she had to show him. The minute she coaxed her lungs into cooperating again, she reached out and touched his cheek. "All the more reason to come upstairs."

His eyes narrowed, his lips turned down at the corners. She thought a moment, realizing returning the words might have been a better choice of things to say. Funny, but it never occurred to her to say her feelings out loud. She'd rather show him.

"No more hiding, Reina," he challenged. "No more pretending to be someone you're not."

She raised an eyebrow. "This coming from you? It wasn't so long ago that you pretended to be your brother."

"I'm not pretending now. I'm Grey Masterson, and I'm in love with you, Reina Price. I don't know how it happened, since only a few days ago, I was completely certain that most women couldn't be trusted, and the few who could were related to me. Sexy, alluring women like you were the least trustworthy of all. But you've been clear about what you wanted and what you didn't want. I even managed to break several of your rules, and still, I'm here. Care to explain?"

She pressed her lips together, her body quivering, her head spinning. She felt, almost...could it be...shy?

"You want to hear me say it, don't you?"

His grin, triumphant and irresistible, bordered on smug. "Yeah, I do."

She glanced up at the bedroom. "I'm so much better at expressing my emotions through my art."

"I'm not a piece of jewelry."

Why couldn't she say it? Because she never had? Hell, she'd done countless things with Grey in the past three days that she'd never done in her lifetime and she hadn't hesitated then. What kept her from being honest now?

She danced from foot to foot, tugged at her sash, felt hot and confined. Suddenly inspired, she jogged down the stairs, grabbed his hand as she passed and pulled him out into the garden.

Sharp cricket song filled the thick humid air with music. The night-blooming jasmine kicked in the sweet perfume. A crescent moon bathed a silver glow over the wild foliage that crept across old stone walkways, tickling her bare feet as she led him toward the center, where a small stone bench sat beside a fountain she'd planned to restore when she'd first moved in, but had never found the time.

She undid the sash and dropped her robe to the ground.

She combed her fingers through her wild, tangled hair then spread her arms to the side and inhaled deeply.

"What are you doing?"

"I've never made love outside before. Have you?"

"You know I have," he said with a grumble.

"No, I don't. I never read Lane's book. I promise I never will if you'll promise to let me do this my way."

"Do what?"

She answered by sashaying toward him and unbuttoning his shirt. First, the cuffs. Then she tugged the material out of his waistband and worked the buttons from the bottom up. She placed her hands against his hot skin, then kissed a languid path from his nipple to his shoulder, loosening one sleeve, then the other. Her mouth then blazed a trail down the center of his belly, over his washboard pecs and silky navel. She undid his belt, removed his pants and shorts, then his shoes, which, surprisingly, he wore with no socks.

Seeing him in his "Grey" attire hadn't sunk in when he'd first appeared in her bathroom. She had other things to think about. But now? She glanced up at him, surprised at the casual touch.

"Some of Zane wore off on me," he explained.

She smiled, knowing that the more the brothers "wore off" on each other, the better they'd both become. They'd been living in the extremes, playing their "good twin, bad twin" roles for way too long. She wanted to make love to the real Grey Masterson as much as he wanted her to be honest about her feelings for him. And tonight would be her first chance to make both their wishes come true.

"Some of you, I think, wore off on me." She kissed his palm, then led him to the stone bench, which she cushioned with her fluffy bathrobe.

"How so?" he asked, sitting back and patting his lap.

She climbed over his thighs, invigorated by the way her breasts brushed against his hard chest, by the special fit of his sex against hers. A wet warmth connected them, a conduit for the electricity simmering beneath the surface of their skin.

But confessions first, sex later. Not much later, Reina thought wryly, but she needed at least a few minutes to tell him what he wanted to hear, what she so desperately wanted to say.

"I love you, Grey Masterson."

"You had to get naked outside in your garden in order to admit that?" he asked with a laugh.

The sound rumbled from his chest to hers, but she was ready to laugh at herself, ready to see the image she projected to the world. Grey had discovered the real woman within, the one who wanted to find love, but who hid behind her sensuality in fear she'd actually encounter the real emotion and then wouldn't know what to do. She'd be out of control, uncertain, as she was now. Yet in Grey's arms, the lost feeling wasn't so difficult to face.

Grey had worked beyond her persona, sneaked past the sentries she'd posted to keep anyone out. Luckily his craftiness could be easily forgiven. He was, after all, one fine specimen of a man, from the inside to the outside and everywhere in between.

"Are you complaining about our attire? Our location? Or both?"

"*Chère,* I'm not complaining."

"You're a man of words. An artist, in a way. Don't you see the symbolism?"

"All I see is a beautiful, amazing woman. You've been through so much tonight."

She wanted to shrug off the sound of his concern, but she couldn't deny that she'd been twisted and tugged in one hundred emotional directions over the past few days. Maybe she shouldn't be making life-altering decisions without taking some time, but she had to go with her instincts this time. For once.

"Enough to know that I'd be a fool not to treasure love once I've finally found it. I won't be like Viviana, willing to share my one true love. I'm in this for the long haul, Grey. If that's not what you want, let me know right now."

She grasped his cheeks in her hands and ended her confession with a long kiss. He allowed her to set the tempo, but he quickly took control of the melody. His tongue to her tongue, his taste to hers. Sensations ripped through her body like a torrent, washing away the last of her fears, cleansing a path to her heart that Grey could take if he chose to. And if he didn't, she'd survive. She knew her heart well enough to have that courage now. All thanks to him.

Grey couldn't believe the irony, couldn't grasp all that had happened over the past few days with Reina. He'd discovered his true self, his truest desires, by stepping into his brother's life. He'd walked away from the business he'd always seen as a birthright more than an ambition, but found a way to make the newspaper his—with the news supplement he'd created in his quest to bring Reina the truth about her father.

And best of all, he'd found Reina. A woman as sexually exciting as any of his secret conquests, a woman he wouldn't want to hide from the world any more than il Gioielliere had wanted to sequester Viviana away. If CNN came into this garden right here and now and caught them making love then broadcasted the news to the four corners of the universe, Grey wouldn't give a damn. He wanted her, he desired her, he loved her, and he didn't care who knew.

"I want to be with you, Reina. For always."

She tried not to look smug, he could tell. He also determined that smug was a look she wore incredibly well.

"*I* want to be with *you*. Amazing, huh?"

"Not quite yet."

He shifted their position, easing inside her body with tender slowness, closing his eyes as their bodies merged, wanting to memorize each and every sensation, though he knew this wouldn't be the last time he'd experience such heaven.

"This. This is amazing. Making love to a woman you love and who loves you back."

She shifted her feet on the bench, lifting her soft bottom, testing her balance, driving him wild. "Hmm…could be very, very amazing. And we don't need any jewelry or toys to double the pleasure."

"Not that I'd ever complain if you wanted to experiment. We can't forget our beginnings."

Reina moved until Grey's body and hers were joined center to center. She'd never felt so complete, so matched, like a precious gem placed in a perfect setting. "I won't forget if you won't."

And from the climaxes that soon followed, both knew they never would.

Don't miss Zane Masterson's story
DOUBLE THE THRILL
by Susan Kearney

IN STORES NOW!
For a sneak peek, turn the page…

———————

HIS STALKER HAD ARRIVED.

The exhausting day of pretending to be Grey dealing with one difficulty after another suddenly disappeared as Zane found himself getting his second wind. The thought of leaving and missing whatever his stalker had planned for him seemed intolerable. Totally unacceptable. All day, he'd waited for her to show. Now she'd arrived with a cryptic Mona Lisa smile on her lips, and he yearned to know what it meant.

Toni Maxwell carried herself with the posture of a queen. Straight back, head high, she nevertheless had a friendly look in her eyes—and enough curves to make any man happy. With the slick soap bubbles causing her skin to glisten, he had the strangest and most compelling urge to take her into his arms and dance close enough to feel her slick skin against him.

Perhaps it was the aura of mystery around her, but he couldn't account for the almost overwhelming lust that struck him with the force of heat lightning.

What did she want?

From the report Grey had on file, Zane had immediately recognized Toni Maxwell standing by the wall, almost as if she'd been waiting for him. However, the picture he'd seen didn't have the same impact as a personal view. Toni's expression sparkled with an appealing mix of mischievous minx and coy tiger on the prowl. Her short dress revealed every inch of her toned and shapely legs and hugged every seductive curve. Her breasts were perfect, designed to entice. She'd certainly arrived ready for seduction. When she'd scooped up a handful of bubbles and blew them in his direction, he had a pretty good idea who was her target.

And he was more than ready to let her seduce him. For the first time today, he thought he'd gotten the better end of his deal with his brother.

Zane held his breath, willing this stalker to stalk, hoping with every beat of his heart that she wouldn't change her mind now. She didn't disappoint him. Holding her drink above the waist-high bubbles, she swayed across the dance floor, the entire time keeping her gaze locked on his. She possessed light, mesmerizing eyes, come-hither eyes, that somehow provoked and promised and piqued his interest.

While his male instincts were to meet her halfway, it took every measure of his control to remain rooted and wait for her to come to him. Grey had to be crazy to run from this mysterious woman who exuded sex with a capital *S*.

Zane knew many beautiful women, but few with such a sense of self as Toni Maxwell. She personified sexy confidence to the nth degree, as, without hesitation, she boldly closed in on him. All he could think was *yes, yes, yes*. He couldn't wait to hear her first words, hoping her voice would prove as intriguing as the rest of her.

"I've been waiting for you," she admitted in a tone flavored with spice and as smooth as honey.

The implications of her statement rocked him back on his heels and he couldn't restrain a triumphant grin. A woman who had the confidence to admit that she was waiting for him indirectly implied that she was very sure of her own worth. He liked her boldness as much as the reckless gleam in her eyes.

Curious to see what she would say next, he countered, "You've been stalking me."

"Busted." She sipped her drink, not so much to delay saying more, but, he guessed, to call attention to her mouth. Glossy red lips, perfectly full and tempting, that left a smudge on the rim of her plastic cup. Full lips that curved upward enticingly as she swallowed. Then, for emphasis, she licked her full bottom lip with the tip of her delicate pink tongue. Slowly she reached out and placed the flat of her palm against his heart.

Her tone turned teasing. "Do I frighten you?"

"What do you think?" he countered, covering her hand with his own, locking her fingers in his. Warm and eager, she didn't act coy or try to resist. And yet he had the feeling his touch had more effect on her than she wanted to admit.

Was her attempt at bold seduction an act? Zane knew women quite well and, despite her outer attempts at bold, he sensed she was holding back part of herself. And that quality made her even more intriguing.

Grey might have just dragged her over to security and had a lawyer slap a restraining order against her. But Zane knew exactly why *he* wouldn't. There was an old saying about keeping one's close friends close and one's enemies closer. If this woman was his enemy, he could find out more by talking to her than by sending her away. Besides, he enjoyed the slick feel of her skin beneath his, the sight of her white flesh enclosed in his tanned fingers, and, most of all, the mingled heat of their joined hands.

And he wanted her with a lust that he fought to control. She exuded a chemistry that would have overwhelmed a less experienced man. The impact of her arrival had intrigued him by her mysterious boldness and his curiosity about her motivations upped the stakes.

She made no attempt to pull her hand away, but leaned closer, almost, but not quite, snuggling against him. She smelled of the bubble bath swirling around them and her own fruity perfume. And when she spoke, her tone was low, almost as if she intended her words to entwine around him and draw him closer into the net of privacy she'd woven in the crowded club. "Your heartbeat is rock steady. The rate slightly elevated. You could be frightened. You could be aroused."

Hell, with her standing as close as she was, it was only normal for his pulse to shoot up. He'd wanted to take her to bed from the first moment he'd seen her across the room. Up close, she was even more delectable. When he spoke, his deep voice more than matched the huskiness of hers. "So, are you going to answer the million dollar question?" he asked into her ear, casually watching her to catch her reactions.

She chuckled and faced him squarely. "Which is?"

"Why are you stalking me?"

She raised one eyebrow. "You're a very attractive man."

He peered into eyes so full of amusement that he had difficulty believing she could be a part of a conspiracy to sabotage their newspaper. However, she *had* sneaked into Grey's office while someone else had ruined the ink. The cost of reprinting had been enormous. Had she acted as an accomplice by creating a diversion?

"You're stalking me because of Lane Morrow's damn book, aren't you?" Zane guessed, watching her closely for the tiniest exhibition of guilt.

"Absolutely," she baldly admitted with no hesitation, not even a flicker of indecision.

He believed she'd just told him the truth. Odd how her admission shot a charge of excitement right through him. This woman was playing a game, but only she knew which one. And only she knew the rules. What did she really want? And why had she chosen Grey?

What did the book have to do with her presence here? Did she need some stud to make her happy? Or could she be one of those women who notched their bedposts with every celebrity that they conned into it. She didn't seem the type. So confident. So together. None of his former suspicions seemed to match Toni Maxwell in the flesh.

However, although she claimed she was here because of the book, that didn't mean she was telling him the truth. He needed more information, much more information. For a moment, he entertained the thought of spiriting her away to a private nook, teasing her, taunting her, keeping her on the razor's edge of sexual desire until she told him exactly what he wanted to know. She wouldn't give in easily—which would make the rewards all the more pleasant. But he didn't want to frighten her away, so instead he hid his thoughts and spoke mildly. "You shouldn't believe everything you read."

"I don't." Again she surprised him. "It's the appearances that count."

"Would you care to elaborate?"

"I'm in the fashion business, which is all about appearances. The power of fashion is that it allows people to imagine they can be completely transformed by a gown, a bag, a pair of shoes or a diamond ring."

Her insight fascinated him. "And exactly what is that little number that you're wearing supposed to tell me about you?"

"Ah, I designed my dress with an evening like this one in mind." She cocked her head, her eyes daring him, challenging him. "Red is bold and symbolizes bravery. And lust. The thin spaghetti straps suggest fun. The snug material evokes the hidden desires inside the feminine heart."

"In other words, you designed the dress not to please a man, but to make a woman feel good about herself?"

She gazed around the dance floor, her intelligent eyes taking in first one woman's attire, then another's. All the clothing, men's and women's, were now soaking wet from the endless supply of bubbles. A few of the women, those who'd worn swimsuits over toned and tanned bodies, appeared attractive. Most looked disheveled, their wet clothes sagging and wrinkling—not that the men seemed to mind.

She turned back to him. "My customers are women. I know what they like by what they buy."

"How do you know women don't buy your clothing in the hopes of snaring a man? Or to please a lover?"

"Some do," she pleasantly agreed with him, her eyes sparkling. "But the smart ones dress to please themselves. Don't you?" She didn't wait for his response. "You're wearing all black, the color of power, the color of night. It's dark, mysterious, as if you have something to hide."

Were her words simply a coincidence? Or did she know his brother well enough to speculate that the twins had switched places? Did she even know that Grey had an identical twin?

Zane had worked with Grey's employees all day long, and no one had even suggested he wasn't his twin. Supposedly, this woman was a stranger who had only met his brother once. She couldn't know him well.

But, for all Zane knew, she could have been secretly stalking Grey for years, and only recently decided to boldly come forward. According to her file, Toni Maxwell had no history of mental illness. He, a connoisseur of women, found her mentally stimulating, physically attractive. She seemed just as sane, maybe saner, than anyone Zane had met in years.

But she deftly kept turning the conversation away from herself and her purpose and back to him. He didn't particularly want to know what his choice of clothing revealed about himself. Especially since he'd had to search hard and long through Grey's closet to find anything suitable for the opening of a hot nightclub. He was much more interested in her and her reasons for stalking him.

"So women buy clothes to project a certain image—an image that may not be true?" he asked, keeping up his end of the conversation.

She lifted one delicate shoulder in a shrug. "What is true? I believe truth is what we perceive. And what I perceive and what you perceive may be very different." She gazed upward to one of the enormous erotic sculptures hanging high above the dance floor. "What do you see?"

The couple entwined in an embrace of smoked glass were naked. "I see a couple about to have sex."

"I see a man and woman in love."

"Our two thoughts aren't mutually exclusive," he mused.

"You noticed?" she teased.

More fabulous reading from
the Queen of Sizzle!

LORI
FOSTER

with

Forever and Always

Back by popular demand are the scintillating stories of
Gabe and Jordan Buckhorn. They're gorgeous, sexy
and single…at least for now!

Available wherever books are sold—September 2002.

And look for Lori's **brand-new** single title,
CASEY in early 2003

HARLEQUIN®
Makes any time special ®

PHLF-2

Attracted to strong, silent cowboys?

Then get ready to meet three of the most irresistibly
sexy heroes you've ever met in

THE SILENT *Type*

From bestselling Harlequin Temptation® author

VICKI
LEWIS
THOMPSON

These three lonesome cowboys are about to find some
very interesting company!

Coming to a store near you in August 2002.

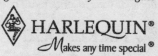

Princes...Princesses...
London Castles...New York Mansions...
To live the life of a royal!

In 2002, Harlequin Books lets you escape to a world of royalty with these royally themed titles:

Temptation:
January 2002—*A Prince of a Guy* (#861)
February 2002—*A Noble Pursuit* (#865)

American Romance:
The Carradignes: American Royalty (Editorially linked series)
March 2002—*The Improperly Pregnant Princess* (#913)
April 2002—*The Unlawfully Wedded Princess* (#917)
May 2002—*The Simply Scandalous Princess* (#921)
November 2002—*The Inconveniently Engaged Prince* (#945)

Intrigue:
The Carradignes: A Royal Mystery (Editorially linked series)
June 2002—*The Duke's Covert Mission* (#666)

Chicago Confidential
September 2002—*Prince Under Cover* (#678)

The Crown Affair
October 2002—*Royal Target* (#682)
November 2002—*Royal Ransom* (#686)
December 2002—*Royal Pursuit* (#690)

Harlequin Romance:
June 2002—*His Majesty's Marriage* (#3703)
July 2002—*The Prince's Proposal* (#3709)

Harlequin Presents:
August 2002—*Society Weddings* (#2268)
September 2002—*The Prince's Pleasure* (#2274)

Duets:
September 2002—*Once Upon a Tiara/Henry Ever After* (#83)
October 2002—*Natalia's Story/Andrea's Story* (#85)

Celebrate a year of royalty with Harlequin Books!

 Available at your favorite retail outlet.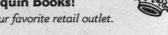

HARLEQUIN®
Makes any time special ®

Visit us at www.eHarlequin.com

HSROY02

The Trueblood, Texas
tradition continues in...

 HARLEQUIN® *Blaze*™

TRULY, MADLY, DEEPLY
by Vicki Lewis Thompson
August 2002

Ten years ago, Dustin Ramsey and Erica Mann shared their first
sexual experience. It was a disaster. Now Dustin's determined to
find—and seduce—Erica again, to prove to her, and himself, that
he can do better. Much, *much* better. Only, little does he guess
that Erica's got the same agenda....

Don't miss Blaze's next two sizzling Trueblood tales:

EVERY MOVE YOU MAKE by Tori Carrington
September 2002
&
LOVE ON THE ROCKS by Debbi Rawlins
October 2002

Available wherever Harlequin books are sold.

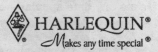

TRUEBLOOD, TEXAS

◆ HARLEQUIN®
Makes any time special ®